Aimée Thurlo
FATAL CHARM

Harlequin Books

TORONTO • NEW YORK • LONDON
AMSTERDAM • PARIS • SYDNEY • HAMBURG
STOCKHOLM • ATHENS • TOKYO • MILAN
MADRID • WARSAW • BUDAPEST • AUCKLAND

To Karen Fiss—
There are no bats in her belfry, but there are most certainly rats in her basement

ISBN 0-373-22337-4

FATAL CHARM

Copyright © 1995 by Aimée Thurlo

FLYAWAY VACATION SWEEPSTAKES!

This month's destination:

Exciting ORLANDO, FLORIDA!

Are you the lucky person who will win a free trip to Orlando? Imagine how much fun it would be to visit Walt Disney World**, Universal Studios**, Cape Canaveral and the other sights and attractions in this area! The Next page contains tow Official Entry Coupons, as does each of the other books you received this shipment. Complete and return *all* the entry coupons—the more times you enter, the better your chances of winning!

Then keep your fingers crossed, because you'll find out by October 15, 1995 if you're the winner! If you are, here's what you'll get:

- Round-trip airfare for two to Orlando!
- 4 days/3 nights at a first-class resort hotel!
- $500.00 pocket money for meals and sightseeing!

Remember: The more times you enter, the better your chances of winning!*

*NO PURCHASE OR OBLIGATION TO CONTINUE BEING A SUBSCRIBER NECESSARY TO ENTER. SEE BACK PAGE FOR ALTERNATIVE MEANS OF ENTRY AND RULES.

**THE PROPRIETORS OF THE TRADEMARKS ARE NOT ASSOCIATED WITH THIS PROMOTION.

VOR KAL

FLYAWAY VACATION
SWEEPSTAKES
OFFICIAL ENTRY COUPON

This entry must be received by: SEPTEMBER 30, 1995
This month's winner will be notified by: OCTOBER 15, 1995
Trip must be taken between: NOVEMBER 30, 1995-NOVEMBER 30, 1996

YES, I want to win the vacation for two to Orlando, Florida. I understand the prize includes round-trip airfare, first-class hotel and $500.00 spending money. Please let me know if I'm the winner!

Name_____

Address _____ Apt. _____

City   State/Prov.   Zip/Postal Code

Account #_____

Return entry with invoice in reply envelope.

© 1995 HARLEQUIN ENTERPRISES LTD.   COR KAL

FLYAWAY VACATION
SWEEPSTAKES
OFFICIAL ENTRY COUPON

This entry must be received by: SEPTEMBER 30, 1995
This month's winner will be notified by: OCTOBER 15, 1995
Trip must be taken between: NOVEMBER 30, 1995-NOVEMBER 30, 1996

YES, I want to win the vacation for two to Orlando, Florida. I understand the prize includes round-trip airfare, first-class hotel and $500.00 spending money. Please let me know if I'm the winner!

Name_____

Address _____ Apt. _____

City   State/Prov.   Zip/Postal Code

Account #_____

Return entry with invoice in reply envelope.

© 1995 HARLEQUIN ENTERPRISES LTD.   COR KAL

Tony's eyes were as dark as a summer storm

"I hope you're playing straight with me, Amanda."

The way he said her name made a shiver course up her spine. "I am." An unspoken challenge charged the air between them. Her heart raced with excitement. "I've told you all I know."

"Good, because I can be *very* unpleasant when someone crosses me." Tony turned and trapped her gaze. "Given a choice, that's not the way I'd like things to be between you and me."

Amanda forced herself to remain very still. "Tell me, Mr. Ramos, which part of that was a threat, the first or the second?"

The corners of his mouth twitched, but he didn't crack a smile. "You don't rattle easily."

"I can't afford that luxury," she said, turning away from his hot gaze, denying the seductive suggestion she'd seen there. Despite his charm and soft voice, he was a dangerous man. She couldn't allow herself to forget that.

Dear Reader,

What is it about mysterious men that always makes our pulse race? Whether it's the feeling of risk or the excitement of the unknown, dangerous men have always been a part of our fantasies. And now they're a part of Harlequin Intrigue. Throughout the year we'll kick off each month with a DANGEROUS MAN. This month, meet Tony Ramos in *Fatal Charm* by Aimée Thurlo.

Aimée and her husband, David, live in a small New Mexico town beside the Rio Grande, with their horses, dogs and pet rodents.

With our DANGEROUS MAN promotion, Harlequin Intrigue promises to keep you on the edge of your seat...and the edge of your desire.

Regards,

Debra Matteucci
Senior Editor & Editorial Coodinator
Harlequin Books
300 East 42nd Street
New York, NY 10017

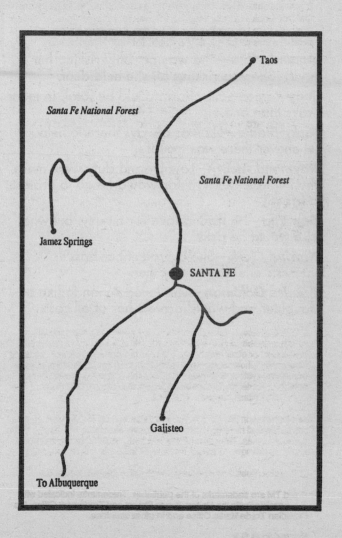

CAST OF CHARACTERS

Amanda Vila—She was not only risking her heart. She was risking all she held dear.

Tony Ramos—His charm could be fatal, in more ways than one.

Ricky Biddle—He was always there to help whenever there was trouble.

Raymond Atcitty—Loyalty and duty were more than words. But how far would he go to protect a friend?

Ron Vila—He traded love for money, but what else would he risk?

Katrina Clark—She'd protect her boss's interests one way or another.

Bernice Goldman—She loved Amanda like a daughter and would protect her at all costs.

Prologue

Lynn Ramos heard the screen door slam behind her as she walked outside onto the moonlit porch. She'd meant to adjust that annoying spring latch many times, but had never quite gotten around to it. Quickly, she glanced down at the soft bundle in her arms. The baby stirred, yawned without opening her eyes, then drifted back to sleep. Lynn smiled, relieved. Six-month-old Carmen could sleep through most anything.

Lynn drew her daughter closer, protecting her from the winter evening as she walked around the Bureau sedan to their own car. She fastened the baby into the car seat, then glanced back through the kitchen window. Tony was still on the phone. Everything in their lives always seemed to take a distant second to his career in the FBI. As usual, that had been the focus of their argument tonight.

Lynn drove down the narrow two-lane highway, tears streaming down her face. She wondered if Tony had even noticed she'd left. The thought that he might not have noticed cut deeply. She stared ahead stubbornly, turning onto the mountain road that led toward her sister's house.

As she followed the sharp curve in the road, she heard something shift on the floor of the car. Lynn glanced down for an instant and saw a paper sack jutting out from beneath the front passenger's seat. Without taking her eyes off the road, she reached down. As she picked it up, a small stuffed raccoon fell out of the sack, tumbling onto the seat beside her.

Lynn recognized the toy she'd meant to pick up for the baby. Her throat tightened as she realized Tony had made time to go by Toy Mart and buy it for Carmen. A rush of warmth swept over her, dissipating her anger. Tony's dedication to his job was infuriating at times but, in her heart, she knew that he loved her and Carmen deeply.

Lynn took a deep breath and let it out slowly. Her hair-trigger temper had certainly been working overtime tonight. What on earth had she been thinking? She watched the snow flurries pile up on her windshield, then get swept to the side as the wipers kept up their steady rhythm. She should have never gone out on a night like this.

Hearing the soft gurgling coming from Carmen, she turned up the heater a click, making sure the car stayed warm enough for the baby.

"Okay, little girl." She smiled, looking at her daughter in the rearview mirror. "Mom blew a gasket, as usual, but we're going back home now."

Lynn began searching for a place to turn the car around. Narrow shoulders plagued this mountain highway east of Santa Fe. She slowed down, pumping the brakes carefully on the icy road as she rounded a switchback curve, careful to avoid picking up more speed than was safe for this stretch of pavement.

Suddenly, out of the gloom ahead she saw a pair of blinding headlights coming straight at her. The driver was on the wrong side of the road!

Lynn pulled the wheel hard to the right, barely missing the other car as it shot by. She fought the steering wheel and brake, trying to bring her car back under control on the glaring ice covering the road.

Lynn screamed as the car skidded off the pavement and hurtled down the hillside into a dark abyss. Something smashed against the windshield, and she was instantly covered with chunks of glass. The car plunged into a steep ravine, flipping end over end.

As the car finally came to a stop, Lynn struggled to hold on to consciousness, but it was a losing battle. One by one, her senses began to fail. First, she couldn't feel anything, not even the cold. Then silence enveloped her as if her ears were stuffed with cotton. As her sight gave way, surrounding her with a soupy blackness, she tried to reach out and touch the car and panicked as she realized her arm wouldn't move.

Then, suddenly, the darkness lifted, and a sense of peace filled her. There was no reason to fear. Her child would be all right. Freed, she surrendered to the light.

FLASHLIGHT IN HAND, the solitary man staggered drunkenly down the snow-covered slope toward the car. What had he done? The cold wind stung his face, sobering him up.

Though he didn't want to climb down into the arroyo, something compelled him to keep going. He slowed down, trying to stay on his feet, but the going was icy and rough, and he kept slipping and falling.

If there really was a hell, he was sure the Almighty had reserved a special spot for him. He should never have taken that first drink tonight, much less the fourth. Or was it fifth? He knew better. But it was too late to think about that now. He had to concentrate on damage control.

Maybe there was still a way for him to get out of this mess without losing everything. One thing was clear, there was no way he could report the accident. The police would smell the whiskey on his breath three miles away. They'd jail him, and he'd be ruined.

As a sliver of moonlight edged out from behind the clouds, he saw the car clearly for the first time. Dear God, nobody could have survived that! It was right side up, but the top was caved in like a soda can that had been stomped by a heavy boot.

He turned around, ready to climb back out, when he heard a soft mewling cry. A cat? He glanced around, trying to clear his thinking, but his thoughts seemed strangled by the thick cobwebs the liquor had left behind. He stood motionless and listened, still not wanting to approach the car. If the driver, by some miracle, was still alive, he'd phone in and report the accident anonymously.

Hearing the soft cry again, he forced himself to go closer to the wreck. The body of the driver was slumped to the right of the steering wheel at an odd angle. One look told him she was dead.

His attention shifted as he heard the cry again. It was coming from the back seat. Aiming the flashlight beam, he saw an infant in a car seat. An embroidered blanket lay on the floor beside her. The child's pink-and-white sleeper was covered with tiny cubes of glass, but she appeared unharmed, except for a few slight scratches on her face.

His gut tightened. This was the last thing he needed. Unless he got the kid out of there, she wouldn't have a chance. The cold would finish what the accident had started. He went to the rear door, grabbed the handle with both gloved hands, and pulled hard. His feet slipped on the frozen ground, sending him sprawling backward. He fell hard into the snow.

All he wanted to do was get out of this place, but he couldn't leave the baby. He staggered back to the door and stared at the child inside. The baby's gaze seemed focused on the beam of his flashlight, and strangely enough, she'd stopped crying.

He glanced around. No help was in sight; it was up to him. The driver was dead, and the snow was intensifying. It would be hours before help could arrive. What the hell was he going to do?

Almost as if guessing his thoughts, the baby reached out with one tiny hand, her fingers opening and closing, seeking contact. He watched her, avoiding her touch, trying to decide on a course of action. As if suddenly impatient, the baby let out a long wail.

"Shut up, kid." He held his hands over his ears. His head felt as if it were exploding, and the high-pitched crying was torture. Why did this have to happen to him?

Then abruptly the child stopped crying and stared at him, expressionless. That scared him into action. He pulled at the broken window and managed to break away most of the remaining glass. As he brushed the baby's face with one finger, he realized the child was ice-cold. Leaning through the opening, he quickly freed her from the car seat.

The infant made a soft, gurgling sound and then smiled.

"You're a smart little cookie, aren't you?" he muttered, picking her up and maneuvering her through the window.

The child's eyes closed, but he knew she'd be okay. All she needed right now was to get warm. The heater in his car would take care of the problem. His gaze drifted to the body of the woman behind the wheel. He couldn't help her, but he'd take care of her baby. He owed her that much.

He reached into the car one last time for the baby's blanket and wrapped it around her. Then he placed the child inside the folds of his jacket and began to plow back up the hill, ignoring the torrent of snow stinging his eyes. There was only one way for him to protect himself and still keep the kid safe. He knew exactly what to do, and he would do it.

Chapter One

Amanda Vila stood by her window, watching the children playing outside in the shade of the large cottonwood. The bells of St. Francis Cathedral, in the heart of Santa Fe, mingled with the happy squeals and laughter of the preschoolers outside.

Starting this day-care center had taken all Amanda's savings, and then some. But it had been worth it. She was finally back home, her business was thriving, and for the first time in over a year, she felt on top of the world.

She watched her own daughter outside, playing with the other children under the watchful eyes of her staff. She was proud of Los Tesoros Day School. When she assured parents that her day-care center was the best around, she knew it was no idle boast. She'd worked hard to make it a place she felt safe entrusting with her own treasured child.

Hearing her door open, Amanda turned around just as her assistant and friend, Bernice Goldman, came into the room.

Bernice was fifty-five. Her salt-and-pepper hair made her look slightly older, but she refused to color it, stubbornly maintaining she'd earned each and every one of her gray hairs. Life hadn't always been kind to Bernice, Amanda knew. A lifetime of struggles had imprinted a certain harshness on her features, but that always disappeared in a burst of warmth the second she smiled.

"Mail came," Bernice said. "All of it is routine, except this," she added, placing a padded envelope on Amanda's desk. "It was marked Personal."

Amanda glanced at the hand-lettered envelope, noting there was no return address. "Strange," she said and started removing the staples that sealed the edge. "I hate things like this that come out of nowhere. I'm always certain it's going to be bad news."

"I've known you all your life. I even baby-sat you when you were your daughter's age. You're pretty tough. You'll handle whatever life throws at you."

Amanda extracted a small white sheet of paper and a cardboard box, the kind inexpensive jewelry comes in. Scanning the typed note quickly, she glanced up. "We've got trouble, all right," she said, brushing back a strand of her shoulder-length brown hair. "You know Tony Ramos?"

"The guy who got fired from the FBI after his daughter was kidnapped a few years back?" Seeing Amanda nod, Bernice shrugged. "Of course. Everyone does. He's some sort of self-appointed vigilante nowadays. Wasn't he thrown in jail recently?"

"He's been released. He must have come by here last week," Amanda said. "I saw the updated computer-generated image of his daughter on our bulletin board, which means he found a way to get in again. You'd think he'd understand why I left word for him to simply mail the flyers and not drop them by in person. We can't have someone like him coming around when children are here. Parents would get worried. Let's face it, he was fired from the Bureau for excessive force, and now with that arrest for brawling in a bar, it's obvious he's living on the edge. His reputation is gone."

"Maybe it's just a matter of his wanting to pin it up there himself to make sure it's done," Bernice suggested. "He goes to all the area day-care centers personally, I'm told."

"I only wish I knew how he's getting in here. Our staff categorically denies helping him, and I believe them. On the other hand, there are never any signs of a break-in, so that's not the answer." Amanda sighed. "Now I've got to contact him. Fate's having a laugh at my expense. Can you bring me his latest flyer?"

Bernice left the office and came back a moment later. "Here it is. What's going on?"

"I can't tell you yet, but I will as soon as I can. Count on it."

Amanda waited until Bernice had left her office, then dialed Tony Ramos's number. Ramos's voice was gruff. From the sound of it, she was willing to bet she'd awakened him even though it was almost noon.

Amanda quickly told him about the packet she'd just received. "The note says they have news of your child, and I was to contact you but say nothing to the police. That's exactly what I've done so far. I figured you'd want to handle things yourself."

"Correct assumption." His voice had changed and was now completely alert. "I'll handle it my own way. Anything else?"

"There's a small box that came in the envelope. Shall I open it?"

"No, I'll take care of that. I'm on my way over now," he said.

"No. Let me meet you elsewhere." Amanda's thoughts were racing. Trouble seemed to follow Tony Ramos, and her business didn't need his kind of publicity. "I'll meet you in the little park north of the cathedral. How much time do you need?"

"Fifteen minutes."

"I'll be there."

Amanda leaned back in the chair, trying to collect her thoughts. Why was she being used to contact Ramos? The only connection between them that she could think of was the flyer that he left here every few months. But he left an identical one at every other day-care center in the city, as well as many other places. Perhaps none of the other day-care centers could match the reputation for excellence hers had acquired. Or maybe it was just that hers was the largest ad in the Yellow Pages. At this point, it was just too hard to venture any reliable guesses.

Ten minutes later, Amanda picked up the envelope on her desk. As she started toward the door, the buzzer on her desk sounded. Ignoring it, she continued out to the reception area. "Whoever it is will have to wait, Bernice. I've got to leave right now."

"No, you don't. I've come to you," a deep, masculine voice said.

Amanda saw the tall, dark-haired man stride around Bernice and come toward her. Nothing could have prepared her for the raw, muscled masculinity and vitality this man exuded when seen up close. For a moment, all she could do was stare.

"I was about to tell you," Bernice said, "that Mr. Ramos had arrived."

"We should talk privately," Ramos said, then, maneuvering past Amanda, led the way into her office.

As Amanda watched, Tony stalked across the room and sat in the chair across from her desk. Anger and disbelief mingled disturbingly inside her. With great deliberation, Amanda walked around to face him but didn't sit down. Trying to look as intimidating and commanding as he did, she leaned against her desk and regarded him boldly.

Instinct told her that he was a man who was used to getting his way. He lived in a world of violence where his wits and his fists were his two best allies. Amanda couldn't afford to let him get the upper hand. She fixed him with an unblinking glare, and he gave her an arrogant half smile, as if he knew precisely what she was doing. Every inch of her body began to tingle. She felt as if lightning were about to strike.

"Mr. Ramos." She forced herself to use that special tone she'd found particularly effective against people who challenged her authority.

"Please, sit down and relax," he said cordially. "I'm really quite harmless." Ramos's voice was surprisingly soft. "You said you had something for me?"

"Mr. Ramos, I asked you *specifically* not to come here."

"I was in the area, and I wanted to save your valuable time," he countered evenly.

"I appreciate that, but you should have respected my position." She slid the padded envelope over to him. "Here's what arrived in our mail today."

Ramos read the note, then pulled out the small package inside the envelope. As he opened the box, an infant-size gold ID bracelet slipped out. His hand shook briefly, then stopped.

The tiny bracelet had affected him, but he brought himself under control in the blink of an eye. Amanda couldn't help wondering what kind of life would require that a man develop such complete emotional control.

"Exactly when did you get this?" His gaze was shuttered as he glanced up, his voice low and steady.

"Less than half an hour ago. I called you right after I read the note." Amanda looked away from the coal black eyes that were now trained on her. Ramos's attention made her feel nervous and self-conscious. She glanced back at him furtively, noting the way his shirt clung to his broad shoulders, accentuating his muscular build. Sensual awareness flickered to life within her. The unexpected reaction took her by complete surprise. She couldn't remember the last time she'd felt the primitive surge of desire. She suppressed it quickly. This kind of hormonal rush was the last thing she needed now.

"Has anyone called you and followed up on the note since we spoke? I expect someone will call to confirm whether or not you received it."

"I haven't heard from anyone." She could feel the anger he kept in check with his iron will. She suspected it wouldn't take much to have it come crashing to the surface.

He studied the closed box. "This bracelet belonged to my daughter. I recognize the little nick over the letter *C*. My father inscribed it for her. His hands shook at the time. Parkinson's," he added, glancing up. His gaze drifted down her body, lingering for a moment on her throat, then her breasts, searching and gaining knowledge far too intimate for strangers.

On impulse, Amanda used the silence stretching out between them to study him as thoroughly as he'd done her. She had to fight not to smile when she saw the glimmer of surprise on his face.

Ramos quickly drew back into himself, growing somber. "After all these years, the kidnappers finally get in touch. But the real bottom line is that they've chosen to contact me through you. Why do you think that is?"

"Maybe they want someone less . . . shall we say, unpredictable to deal with? I'm known in this town and have a very solid reputation as a businessperson and an active citizen."

"Meaning I don't." He smiled, but it never reached his eyes.

Amanda shrugged. "You asked for a guess. I gave you one."

Tony's eyes were as dark as a summer storm. Finally he moved over to the window and glanced at the children playing outside. "I hope you're playing straight with me, Amanda." His tone made his words half prayer, half threat.

The way he said her name made a shiver course up her spine. "I am." An unspoken challenge charged the air between them. She tried to appear in control, but her heart was racing with excitement. "I've told you all I know."

"Good, because I can be *very* unpleasant when someone crosses me." Ramos turned and trapped her gaze. "Given a choice, that's not the way I'd like things to be between you and me."

Amanda forced herself to remain very still. "Tell me, Mr. Ramos, which part of that was a threat, the first or the second?"

The corners of his mouth twitched, but he didn't crack a smile. "You don't rattle easily."

"I can't afford that luxury. I run a day-care center filled with toddlers," she said, reminding herself to stay cool. Despite his charm and soft voice, he was a man of violence. She couldn't allow herself to forget that.

"I wish I could tell you that I know precisely what being around toddlers is like, but I can't. *My* child is gone, and that's a situation I intend to rectify, no matter who I have to walk over or how long it takes."

Amanda heard, as well as felt, the steel-hard determination in his voice. She was a good judge of character and, right now, all her instincts were telling her that Ramos meant trouble. He would do whatever was necessary to get his child back, regardless of the consequences. She could understand that, even support it, but she had to make sure he didn't run roughshod over her and jeopardize everything she valued in the process.

Tony eased the note and the box back into the envelope and picked it up by the edges. "I'll be back after I run this by a few of my sources."

"No, you won't. You can *call* me here, but I do *not* want you coming by again. Is that clear? I won't refuse to help you, though your reputation precedes you. However, I cannot afford to have the parents of the children in my care getting nervous."

"The more people I make nervous, the sooner I get my little girl back," he said coldly.

After Tony left, the room felt oddly empty. His intensity and rough manner should have repelled her, yet she couldn't remember ever feeling so drawn to a man. Her body was still trembling with excitement. Tony Ramos exuded an aura of supercharged maleness that practically took her breath away.

Bernice knocked and came into the office without a pause. "Well?"

"He's a bit cool and very forceful, but not as bad as his reputation makes him out to be. But then again, in his profession, I'm sure he's learned to wear many masks. In this particular case, too, he's fighting to get his child back. I'm sure he's prepared to become whatever he needs to be to get her back. If Hope was taken from me, I know I would."

Bernice gazed at her speculatively. "I know a bit about him, but it's mostly from newspapers and gossip I've picked up. Are you interested?"

Amanda nodded.

"His wife was involved in a terrible accident three years ago, killed almost instantly. Ramos was the one who found her, but by the time he reached the accident site, his daughter had already been taken. A massive search got underway, but the accident took place during a winter storm so there were almost no clues. Heavy snowfall had obscured the tracks of the person who took his child."

"He lost his wife and daughter at the same time?" Amanda's stomach tied itself in knots. "That certainly explains a lot about him."

"But not everything. There have been questions about Tony Ramos for a long time. He's been more or less unemployed for the past three years, but his style of living hasn't noticeably changed. He's never short of money, it seems. And he hangs out with real scum—crooks and cut-throats of all sorts." Bernice exhaled softly. "He comes in a nice package, but he's bad news from what I've heard."

"I don't doubt it for a second. I still feel for him, though. What mother wouldn't? I'll do what I can to help, but I've got my own daughter to think about. I intend to keep my association with Tony Ramos as brief as I can—and as far from Hope as possible."

Bernice stood as the phone on Amanda's desk began to ring. "Amanda, one more thing. I'm not sure exactly what's going on here, but I gather it has something to do with his daughter. If that's the case, I wouldn't wait for him to call the police if I were you. He may not, and you need to protect the center on this. If the newspapers ever get hold of this story, you're going to want it known that you took all the proper steps."

THE REST OF THE AFTERNOON went by with agonizing slowness. Amanda had expected to get a call from the police. The fact that none came made her think Bernice had been right to suspect Tony wouldn't tell them. Uneasiness spread through her and she began to regret her agreement to let him handle things his own way. Tony was obviously unafraid to take the law into his own hands. The thought of him acting on his own, answering to no one and perhaps giving in to his violent side, frightened her. Foreknowledge meant she'd share responsibility for his actions.

Amanda picked up the phone ready to call the police, then set it back down. She wanted to give him a chance to play it his way. Any parent searching for his or her child deserved that much. More important, at this point, he was only checking with his sources. The police certainly hadn't helped him much, judging by the results. Her gaze fell on the photo of Hope on her desk. She couldn't even imagine being without her daughter, living in that uncertain limbo Tony had dwelt in all this time. She'd give him a chance, but if by tonight she hadn't heard from the police, then she'd step in.

Several more hours crept by before Amanda finally cleared her desk, ready to leave. It was almost five, time to pick up Hope in the nursery and go home. The time she spent with her daughter in the evenings was her favorite part of the day, and thanks to Bernice, she now had even more time. Bernice had taken over the job of staying late and locking up after all the children were gone.

Amanda stepped into the outer office and spoke to the older woman. "Hope and I will be going now. We'll see you tomorrow." As she reached the door, the telephone rang. Amanda stopped and waited, wondering if the police had finally decided to call.

"It's for you," Bernice said, putting the caller on hold. "The voice sounds funny somehow. It's a woman, I can tell that much, but she won't identify herself. She says it's urgent. I tried to put her off, but she says she knows you're still here."

"I'll take it in my office." Puzzled, Amanda returned to her desk and reached for the phone, identifying herself quickly.

"I'm the one who sent you the bracelet," the woman answered, her voice pitched higher than ordinary, like an audio tape playing at the wrong speed. "Now listen carefully, because I won't be on long. Tell Ramos I know where his kid is. I *will* give him the information, but first I have certain chores for him. He can start by going to the FBI office here in town and getting a copy of the file on the Henderson case."

"But he's not an agent anymore," Amanda countered, wondering how any local person could be unaware of that, as she wrote the woman's demands down on a notepad.

"He's still got connections. He'll manage. Just tell him he's got two days to meet my first demand, or he can kiss his kid goodbye forever."

"Why don't you deal directly with him? Why are you telling me?"

"You're our ace in the hole in case we need someone to put a leash on Ramos. You see, we know all about you, too, Ms. Vila. You're the perfect choice, because you have a secret...and something to lose."

"What do you mean?" Amanda silently denied the words had any connection to her life as she struggled to understand the woman, whose strange voice was clipped and harsh, probably because it was being electronically disguised.

"We know your daughter was adopted, and that you've tried to keep that from everyone. If you don't do whatever we say, we'll make sure you regret it. We can alter adoption records, even make sure that the age-progression software Ramos is using starts producing an image that looks just like your kid. We can set it up so that there'll be no doubt in his mind that she's his little girl. Once he's convinced, it won't matter what anyone else thinks or says. Official approval or not, you know he'll stop at nothing to take her away from you."

That threat had the ring of truth. Having met Tony, Amanda couldn't deny it. She felt her blood turn to ice. "Breaking into the state's computers can't be easy. How do I know this isn't just some kind of bluff?"

"Check it out. We've set up a little demonstration. There is no longer any computerized record of your daughter's adoption. We've eliminated it from the data banks completely."

"I still have the original documents," Amanda answered, unable to suppress the fear that came through in her voice.

"Nothing exists in the computer's memory to back them up. Ramos could claim they were phony."

"You've obviously been digging deeply into my life. Why? What do you want from me?"

"Just do what you're told and *don't* go to the police, not unless you want to be responsible for the death of his child, and the loss of your own. And don't even think about running. If you do, we'll make sure Ramos tracks you down wherever you go. In the end, we'd be off the hook, he'd have your child, and you'd have nothing."

"Blood tests would prove my daughter isn't his," Amanda argued back angrily.

"And not yours, either. Are you willing to give up the girl to a welfare agency while the courts decide the case? That could take months, years maybe. I'll bet the press would like to know about it, too. Imagine how a story like this could affect your business. Who'd trust an accused baby snatcher with their own precious darlings?"

"You're bluffing," Amanda uttered in disbelief.

"Check the state computer for the adoption records if you doubt us. We're very capable of backing up our threats." The line went dead.

Bernice walked into the office and gave Amanda a startled look. "You're white as a sheet! What's going on?"

Amanda's hand shook as she hung up. "Does your friend still work for Social Services?" Amanda asked.

"Sure. She's been there for years."

"I need a favor. I was hoping to keep this story from you. In this situation, knowledge is dangerous, but I need your help and you have a right to know." After telling her friend about the kidnapper's threat, she dropped back into her chair.

"How could they know Hope was adopted? The only ones who knew were Ron, his sister, you and I, and a few clerical workers at the agency who handled the adoption. If I remember correctly, Ron made you promise never to tell anyone. He was always afraid that the child's father would return to harass his sister about giving up Hope for adoption. Did you change your mind and confide in anyone else over the years?"

Amanda shook her head. "Of course not. I would never have risked it."

"Maybe the birth father is behind this scam, or at least in league with the people responsible. Somebody obviously talked to the woman who called."

"Maybe. First things first, though. Get hold of your friend and have her search the computers. See if the adoption record is still there. I have to know if it's just a bluff."

Bernice glanced at her watch. "I may still catch her. She usually works late. I'll be back in a minute."

Amanda sat down to wait, then, on impulse, decided to call Ron. She'd need to know if he'd told anyone about the adoption, and also to find out all she could about Hope's birth father. It would definitely be tricky. She couldn't afford to tip her hand. If Ron knew the whole story, it was possible he would insist on getting involved. Yet she knew he'd be doing it out of pride—not love for his daughter—and that meant that he would be willing to take the kind of risks she'd never condone. He'd likely complicate things rather than solve them.

Gathering her courage, she dialed her ex-husband's office. Katrina, his longtime paralegal assistant and secretary, answered the phone.

"Hello, Katrina? This is Amanda. I'd like to speak to Ron, please. It's important."

"He's with a client, Amanda. I'll take your number and have Mr. Vila return your call." Katrina was cold and excessively polite, as she had been ever since the divorce. She made it a point to be difficult whenever Amanda called. Katrina was undoubtedly acting on Ron's instructions.

"Sorry, Katrina, this can't wait. Tell Ron it's about Hope, but it doesn't concern his money or his time. That should put his mind at ease." Amanda couldn't understand why Katrina was so loyal to Ron. It certainly wasn't because of a romantic attachment. In two years of marriage, Ron had proven to be the most unemotional man Amanda had ever known.

Katrina put her on hold without another word. After five minutes, just when Amanda was getting really angry, Ron picked up the line. As usual, Ron seemed more annoyed than pleased to hear from her. After a curt greeting, he urged her to get to the point.

"I need to get in touch with your sister," Amanda said, "but I don't have her telephone number."

"Why do you want to talk to Louise?"

"Hope has a little friend who's adopted, so Hope is now filled with questions of her own. I thought this was the perfect time to start introducing Hope to the idea that she's adopted, too. But I don't want to do it if there are still problems with her birth father."

"Louise hasn't heard from that guy in years. In fact, last Christmas when I saw her, she said he'd moved to Mexico. Louise is married now, so don't go calling her and dredging up the past. Her husband doesn't know about the baby. Besides, don't you remember that you and I agreed not to tell anyone Hope was adopted? Try to keep your word for the sake of my sister, and leave me out of it, too. I've got important work to do."

She heard a click, then a dial tone. Some things never changed. To Ron, Hope had never ceased to be a reminder of his inability to father a child. Frustration and anger rippled through her, making her insides tie into a knot.

When Bernice finally came into Amanda's office twenty minutes later, Amanda scarcely dared to breathe as she waited for the news.

"There's no record of the adoption," Bernice said in a muted voice. "Everyone was gone, so Jenny was able to access several different data banks. She checked everything she could think of, but the adoption records are just not there. They must have been erased somehow."

Amanda felt the blood draining from her face. "Then it's not a bluff. They've tampered with the state records."

"So what now?"

"I call Tony, pass on their demands, and keep quiet about the rest. For now, that's the only thing I can do. I don't want to risk losing my daughter, even if it would only be for a while."

"You're a fighter, Amanda. You won't be able to stand this for long. When your patience runs out, what will you do?"

"I'm not sure, but I do know I can't just sit back and trust this caller to keep her end of the bargain. I'll need some leverage of my own sooner or later."

Amanda managed to keep her hands from shaking as she finished dialing. To her disappointment, she only reached Tony's answering machine. Frustrated, she decided to leave a sketchy message and wait to give him the details later. They were in this together now, though for different reasons; allies, yet not.

As she finished speaking to the machine, she considered giving him her unlisted home number, but then decided against it. She didn't want him calling her at home, possibly frightening Hope. "I'll call again later so we can discuss this at length," she added.

Bernice watched her. "You've got to talk to someone... the cops or a lawyer. You can't handle this by yourself."

"I can't go to anyone yet. And you can't say anything, either. Promise me. I've got to have something on these people in order to safeguard Hope and myself. The only way I can get that is to play along for now."

"I understand, but—"

"No, no buts. This is the way it's got to be."

Bernice nodded. "I'll do everything I can to help you. I don't know how much good I'll be, but you won't go through this alone."

Amanda toyed with a pencil on her desk, trying frantically to get a handle on the situation. "Wait a second. Did you tell me the caller *knew* I was here?"

"That's what she told me."

"How could she know that—unless she's watching?" Amanda walked over to the window and pulled the curtain aside to glance up and down the street. Finally she allowed the curtain to fall back into place. "There are cars parked all the way down the street as usual, but I didn't see anyone sitting inside one."

"Maybe they know your car."

"I suppose that's possible." She took a deep breath and let it out slowly. "I'm going outside to take a look around. I don't want to leave here with Hope and have someone follow me home."

"I'm going with you."

Amanda nodded then changed her mind. "Maybe I'm overreacting, but I'd rather you stayed here on guard. I don't want to take any chances with the children."

As she walked out of the building, she looked around cautiously. There were plenty of people just getting off work. She'd be safe.

The narrow cobblestoned streets adjacent to the Santa Fe Plaza made it difficult for anyone to hide. She passed a mural of Saint Francis of Assisi painted on the crumbling wall of an old adobe building. The saint's ability to talk to the animals was a link between Pueblo beliefs and the modern-day Santa Fe natives, who saw their city as one in perfect harmony with nature. Trouble of any kind here seemed impossible, but the facts were inescapable.

As she headed back, Amanda noticed an off-white sedan parked in the shadows of a narrow alleyway. From there, the driver would have a clear view of the day-care center. Amanda allowed herself a furtive glance. There was definitely someone in the car, but the driver's face was masked by long, sculpted shadows that made it impossible to distinguish facial features.

Amanda slowed her steps, trying to get a better look. Suddenly, the vehicle sped out of the alley, heading north, away from the center. The license plate was from New Mexico, but Amanda couldn't make out the letters or numbers. She hurried back to the center.

She pulled Bernice into her office. "That person was definitely watching us," Amanda said. "I wish I'd managed to get a look at the driver's face."

"Maybe you're safer not knowing who it is," Bernice said slowly.

Amanda felt her skin prickle. What on earth had she been drawn into? She thought of Hope and her heart began to hammer. No matter what happened, she had to find a way to keep her daughter with her, out of danger.

Amanda went directly to the phone and called the police. She reported the car she'd seen watching the day-care center, but she avoided mentioning anything concerning Tony or the kidnappers.

Bernice shook her head as Amanda hung up. "You should have told them the whole story."

"I can't. But this way at least, the police will keep an eye on the center, and make sure that creep stays away from here." Amanda took a deep breath and gave Bernice a worried look. "It's getting late, but I'm still not sure it's safe to take Hope home."

Bernice moved to the window. "You'll be okay. That car's long gone. Go home. Just remember my house is less than a mile away. If there's a problem, come over immediately. Winston's the best guard there is. He'll make sure everyone's safe."

"Winston!" Hope, a small dark-haired girl with large brown eyes, ran through the open doorway and launched herself into Amanda's arms. "Are we going to see Winston, Mommy?"

"Hello, Peanut." Amanda gave Doris, the nursery attendant, a nod, assuring her that Hope's unexpected entrance was okay.

"I like Winston, Mommy! He's my friend."

Amanda smiled. "Yes, I know." Winston was Bernice's gargantuan bullmastiff. When he stood on his hind legs, he could see over the top of Amanda's head. Nobody ever gave Winston a hard time. Though the dog rarely growled, he had a habit of standing directly in the path of anyone he didn't know and licking his chops, as if making dinner plans.

Amanda glanced at Bernice. "I may ask to borrow Winston before this thing's finished."

"Yippee! Winston can sleep over."

Bernice laughed. "You're welcome to him anytime."

As AMANDA DROVE HOME, her eyes continually darted to her rearview mirror. Nobody was following her, she was certain of that. She soon let Hope's incessant chatter divert her fears and began to relax.

As her daughter sang a nursery rhyme, Amanda's thoughts strayed to Tony. She'd be calling him tonight after Hope fell asleep. The prospect sent a rush through her. Although she told herself quickly that it was only the product of all the extra adrenaline still pumping through her, she knew there was more to it than that. Tony's appearance in her life had reminded her that she'd suppressed her womanly needs far too long, concentrating solely on being a mom. That aspect of her feminine side she'd so neglected was starting to demand her attention.

Forcing Tony from her thoughts, she focused on enjoying the drive with her daughter. This was their time, and she wouldn't let anything encroach on it.

As they left the city behind, Amanda felt more of her tension melt away. She liked country living. Her house was on the southern outskirts of Santa Fe, nestled in a rural area dotted with small, territorial-style adobe houses. Here, prices were more reasonable, and she could afford to give Hope a huge yard to play in.

"Mommy, look! We have company!" Hope pointed ahead.

Amanda felt her breath catch in her throat. A pickup was parked in the shadows of the Russian olives that grew wild along one wall of her house. If the driver's intentions had been good, he wouldn't have been hiding there. Sensing danger, she made a sudden change of plans.

"Hang on, Peanut. We're not going home after all." Amanda stepped on the gas pedal, shot past her house, and sped on down the road.

Chapter Two

Amanda's car responded instantly, but the dirt road made high speed precarious, and the rear end of the vehicle fishtailed before Amanda brought it back under control. Fear slammed into her as she raced toward Bernice's home. Phil, Bernice's husband, would be there and so would Winston.

"Wow!" Hope squealed. "This is fun, Mommy!"

Despite the thick cloud of dust she left behind, she could see the pickup had shot out after them. She wasn't sure what was going on, but there was no way she was going to let anyone catch up to her, not with Hope in the car.

Amanda followed the bend in the road, staying away from the edges where she knew the sand would be soft. She hoped the pickup would get bogged down, but the other driver stayed right with her. For the first time since she'd purchased her home, she regretted the distance between houses.

Suddenly, Ernestine, her nearest neighbor's miniature goat, stepped out into the road.

"Hold on tight, sweetie!" Amanda pumped the brakes and turned the wheel sharply to the right, narrowly missing the animal.

Just then she saw a motorcycle ahead going her way. Amanda raced to catch it, recognizing the driver as Ricky Biddle, who lived about two miles farther down the road.

He'd help her out. She honked the horn and saw Ricky turn his head, then start slowing down.

She came up behind Ricky, pulled over to the right and stopped, far more confident now that she wasn't alone. As Ricky halted his motorcycle a short distance in front of her, the pickup pulled up alongside.

Amanda's temper flared as she saw Tony step out of the pickup and walk around the front of the vehicle toward her. "Are you okay?" he asked.

"Mr. Ramos!" Amanda got out, anger spiraling through her, robbing her of breath. "I should have expected something like this from you!"

Ricky, a sandy-haired young man in his late twenties, headed toward Amanda, removing his red motorcycle helmet as he walked. "Is this man bothering you?"

Towering over Ricky, Tony transfixed the younger man with an uncompromising stare. Ricky took a step back, realized what he was doing, then held his ground.

"It's okay, son. The lady's safe with me."

"I'm sorry, Ricky. I made a mistake. I didn't recognize Mr. Ramos for a moment. I can handle this."

Ricky looked at Amanda. "Do you want me to go find a cop?"

"No, that's not necessary," Amanda said, noting Ricky hadn't offered to stay. Not that she blamed him. Tony's face was set and he looked about as friendly as a stone gargoyle. "I'll explain later, okay?"

Ricky glanced at Tony, then at the ground. "Um, okay, Amanda. Call me later. Do you still have my number?"

"Sure. It's right by my phone," Amanda said. "Thanks for stopping."

"I'll be home the rest of the evening. I'll stop by later to check on you."

"No, please don't bother," Amanda said, hating what she'd started. Ricky was a nice guy, but she didn't want him hovering around, which he had a tendency to do. "I'll be talking to you soon, okay?"

As Ricky restarted his motorcycle and rode away, Amanda glanced to make sure Hope was still safely in her car seat, out of earshot, then glared at Tony. "You owe me an explanation. What were you doing by my house? I don't recall giving you my address."

Tony looked at her and smiled. "I took it upon myself to find it."

"You're a pain in the neck, Mr. Ramos."

"Call me Tony. Once you calm down, you'll see you have no reason to be angry. We do have some very important business to discuss, and this *is* away from your day-care center. You said you didn't want me going there."

He was being so reasonable—and so polite—she felt outclassed as she struggled to keep her temper in check. "I'll meet you back at my place."

"Mommy, aren't we going to go play with Winston?"

"Not now, honey. Maybe later." Amanda tried to get her pulse to slow down. He was so charming, it was hard not to trust him. Yet no matter how controlled and well mannered he seemed to be, his reputation told a different story. She had to be careful around this chameleon-like man.

She drove home slowly, postponing the inevitable confrontation. By the time she pulled into her driveway, Tony was already there. She had no idea how he'd found her address, but she had to make sure he didn't feel free to stop by whenever he wanted, bringing his problems here to her home. He was a man with a cause she could respect, but she would not allow him to compromise her daughter's safety.

"I have to talk to this gentleman, Peanut," Amanda said, taking Hope inside. "Will you go to your room and play for a bit?"

"Can I take some cookies?"

"One."

"Two?"

"Ah, you're learning all about counting, are you?" she said, smiling. "Well, I suppose two, but that's it."

Amanda took Hope's hand in hers. Glancing back at Tony, she gave him *the look,* a warning for him to keep quiet. To her surprise, it worked as well on him as it did on the kids at the day-care center.

"I'll get my daughter settled, then you and I will talk," she said in a glacial tone.

As Amanda poured a cup of milk and fished two cookies out of the jar in the kitchen, Tony walked up to Hope and crouched down beside her. "Hi. I'm Tony. What's your name?"

Hope smiled. "I'm not supposed to talk to strangers, and I don't think Mommy likes you," she said.

"You're absolutely right on both counts, Peanut, but I need to talk to this stranger myself. Now here are three mini chocolate chip cookies for you to take to your room."

Hope's eyes gleamed as she noted that the cookie count had suddenly been increased. "Yeah!" She took the cookies and followed her mother out of the room.

TONY GLANCED AROUND the living room while he waited for Amanda to return. The woman had Spartan tastes. Everything was meticulously clean, but there wasn't much in the way of furniture. A simple wood-framed sofa with plain off-white cushions stood in the center of the room. Two straight backed chairs that looked like something left over from the Spanish Inquisition had been placed across from it.

He turned around, hearing Amanda's returning footsteps on the baked-tile floor. Steely anger was clearly etched on her features.

"Mr. Ramos, how dare you show up here at my home? The fact that I'm willing to help you does *not* give you that right. And while we're at it, how *did* you get my home address?" she demanded, searching his face with all the warmth she'd reserve for an insect that had crawled out of her cupboard.

"I have friends who help me from time to time." He summoned his best smile, hoping to thaw her. Most women considered him handsome, and he wasn't above using his looks to get their cooperation when the situation called for it. Considering how angry Amanda was, he certainly needed any edge he could get with her. "I'm not as impossible to deal with as you might think," he said. "Why don't you give me half a chance?" He kept his gaze steady, penetrating, and locked on hers, a gesture meant to disarm. He'd been told before that it packed a sexual wallop that made it particularly disconcerting to the fairer sex.

Amanda continued to glower at him, apparently unaffected. "Oh, I *see*. So you obtained my address behind my back and that's supposed to be okay with me?"

So much for sexy looks. "Well, no, not exactly." Tony gave her a chagrined half smile, and quickly changed tactics to reasonable concern and an apology. "I'm sorry if I've upset you, but after your last call, I felt it would be best for us to talk in person. I came by, saw that your home was secluded, and figured it would be okay for us to meet here. Everything would have worked out fine, too, if you hadn't panicked."

"So it's *my* fault? You have a lot of nerve!"

Tony looked at her admiringly. She was beautiful in a girl-next-door kind of way, all gentle curves and softness. Right now, fury made her look radiant. Her cheeks were flushed and her hazel eyes sparked with life. "I don't know how to make you understand," he said in a conciliatory tone, or as close to it as he could ever come. "It's obvious how devoted you are to your own daughter. Think how awful it would be for you if our positions were reversed."

He deliberately moved closer to her, standing near enough to hopefully shake some of her self-assuredness. He knew he had to play on her emotions, because if she backed out now, he'd lose his only lead to Carmen. With that in mind, he glanced around. He needed ammunition. Spotting what he was searching for, he walked over to a shelf and picked up a Christmas photo of Amanda and Hope. He smiled sadly.

"Hope looks just like you. She has your eyes...and your smile. I envy you." He saw her start to thaw.

Amanda moved to the sofa and motioned for him to take a chair. "I *will* help you, Tony, but if you continue to act like a Neanderthal, I'll treat you like one, even if it means beating you over the head with a club to prove I mean what I say. Is that clear?"

He blinked. No one had spoken to him like that since Mrs. Trujillo in sixth grade. "Er...sure."

Amanda gave him the details she could afford to divulge about the call she'd received, then told him about the car she'd seen near the day-care center. "I called the police to ask them to stay on the alert for that vehicle, but I didn't tell them about you or the messages from the kidnappers. I just told them someone was watching the center."

He nodded thoughtfully. "The kidnappers—and I think it's safe to assume we're dealing with more than one person here—left you no other option. You did what you had to do to protect the children in your care."

"Right. So what's next? Like it or not, we're in this together. Is there any way to stop them? My life, by your standards, might be dull, but I like it. I want it back." Amanda was determined.

"So you want to go on the offensive?" Tony asked, surprised.

"I didn't pick on them, they picked on me. I don't want any trouble with these people. They scare me. But if we go strictly by their rules, they have no incentive to keep their word. I don't think we can afford to put any faith in their assurances."

Tony watched Amanda carefully. Something about her had changed and instinct told him that it had something to do with the reason she'd been chosen as intermediary. "This goes beyond your trying to protect the reputation of your day-care center. You're holding something back."

"Don't underestimate how much my day-care center means to me. By encroaching on it, they declared war."

Tony watched Amanda. From her expression, especially her eyes, he could tell she was terrified of something. Yet she was not about to tell him what it was. He wouldn't get answers by asking, either. Good thing he still had several tricks up his sleeve. "Their primary interest isn't your day-care center. That stakeout was focused on you. I'd bet my last dime on it."

Amanda shrugged, nervously searching for an answer. "It's not your money you're betting. That day care is *part* of me. The question remains. What are we going to do?"

"I want to attach a tape recorder to your phones, here and at work. If the woman calls again, I want to hear her voice, disguised or not."

"All right."

Tony studied her telephone. What he needed in addition to the recorder was one well placed bug hidden right in the middle of her living room—one she'd know nothing about. He had one in his surveillance kit in the car. A little gem like that would allow him to hear anything Amanda said, either here or in the adjacent room. A receiver and tape recorder hidden outside in the hedge would ensure it.

He turned around abruptly and caught the unguarded expression on Amanda's face. She was frightened and trying hard to keep the lid on her fears. She was doing a pretty good job of it, too. He wondered what was going on inside her head. He had to know what secrets Amanda was keeping locked away—the stakes were too high to allow her any privacy. At the first opportunity, he'd set up his equipment and lay her life bare before him. As he contemplated the thought, it twisted in his mind. Passion sent a furnace blast of heat flashing through him.

Forcing the distracting thoughts away, he took out a tape recorder from his pocket and made a show of setting it up. He felt Amanda coming up behind him a few minutes later.

"What good will it do to use that little tape recorder? Surely you can come up with something more sophisticated?"

"Not without getting the phone company and local law enforcement involved."

"You've decided not to do that, I take it."

"I have a friend in the FBI, my former partner. He'll help me *and* keep it unofficial."

"Good." She knew that there was no way he could elicit official help, but this way at least there would be someone there in case the kidnappers turned ugly. "You're too close to this emotionally, and I have no experience with this kind of thing. It was a bad idea for us to try and handle this on our own."

Tony sat down in one of the chairs. "I've dealt with this kind of animal before. Bringing the FBI or the police in officially is what will blow it. Believe me, that's what happened before." He remained silent, his bitterness hanging between them. Finally he continued. "After my daughter's disappearance, the kidnappers contacted me within a day. The woman asked me for quite a bit of money. I didn't have it, but I knew I could raise it one way or the other.

"While I was getting the money together, I continued to go after them through official channels. I was one hundred percent certain that I would succeed in getting my daughter back. I was well trained, with all the Bureau's resources at my disposal. But something must have scared them away. They never called me back with instructions for the drop-off, and this is the first time I've heard from the woman since."

"Did you ever find out why?"

"I always suspected a leak at the Bureau, though I never did find evidence to support it." Tony shook his head, then met her gaze. "All I know for sure is that my daughter and my wife, everything that really mattered in my life, vanished. Carmen was only a baby, and it was snowing and very cold that March. I have no idea if Carmen is even alive. There's no evidence one way or another. This is the chance I've been waiting for, and I won't blow it this time."

"I'm fighting for everything I value, too, Tony. If this situation became public knowledge, people would start wondering why the kidnappers chose me as go-between. You certainly did. I'm blameless, but the implications alone would ruin me. Without my income from the day care, I'd have nothing except debts. How could I support my daughter? We need trained people on this job, people who can be trusted and who can find answers fast. We can't cover all the possibilities alone."

"I understand you're trying to safeguard your livelihood. But what about your husband, if you don't mind me asking? Wouldn't he take care of his own daughter?" As he watched Amanda, Tony sensed a battle going on inside her. She wasn't just afraid of bad publicity.

"I don't need Ron, and it's a good thing. He never comes to see Hope, and he pays only minimal child support. He's barely spoken to me since the divorce. You see, he didn't want us to split up. It wasn't because he loved me or Hope, or even because he wanted us to stay together as a family. It was just that he couldn't stand the thought of publicly failing at anything. I was the well-dressed, attractive woman he kept on his arm to show off. Not having me there like a trophy hurt his pride."

Tony watched her speculatively. She wasn't asking for his sympathy, despite her bitterness. She was a strong woman. It would take one heck of a man to claim her heart now—she'd encased it so protectively in steel. Yet something told him that she'd be worth the effort. But he had other priorities now. He had to make sure he remained focused on finding the kidnappers. He needed all the information Amanda had, not just what she chose to give him.

Amanda stood and paced restlessly around the room. Finally she turned around and looked at him directly. "You frighten me, Tony. You want to find your daughter so badly, you're not going to allow anything to get in your way. I won't let everything I value become a casualty."

Tony nodded. She was right to protect herself. The more he got to know her, the more he liked her. Under different circumstances, they might have been one helluva team. But he couldn't afford to be a team player. "I *will* get them, Amanda. I won't rest until I do."

"How about this old partner of yours? How much can he help us now?"

"He's going to be involved soon enough, one way or another. I can't get the file they asked for without his help."

Amanda walked to the portable phone on the wall and handed it to Tony. "Call him right now. Ask him to meet you here. If he's going to get involved, I want to meet him. While you're doing that, I'll go check on Hope."

Tony dialed Raymond's number as Amanda walked out of the room. The die had been cast. There was no turning back now.

AFTER AN HOUR OF PLAYING with Hope and putting the whole kidnapping mess out of her mind, Amanda left Hope with her favorite video, a hot dog and fruit salad. This was usually their time together, and she hated leaving her daughter to her own devices. Yet, although she felt guilty, she knew this was the best way to handle the situation. After meeting both men, Amanda had decided she didn't want Hope to spend much time around either of them. There was a darkness about them that spoke of a side of life where despair and sorrow were always the victor. She was determined to shield her daughter from people who might give her a glimpse into a world no child should know.

"Sorry to keep running out on you," she said, returning to the kitchen. Tony's ex-partner, Raymond Atcitty, a Navaho, appeared almost cherubic, with his round face and slightly protruding belly, but his eyes were hard and cold.

"There's a state-of-the-art voice-activated tape recorder attached to your phone now," Raymond said. "All you have to do is pick up the phone, and it will start recording. We'll do the same for the one in your office. I'll also get hold of one of those caller ID machines. Once we find the woman who's contacting you, your part in this will be over. We'll take it from there."

Tony studied the recording device, then stepped over to join them. "We have your word that you'll keep this out of official channels?"

Raymond met his gaze and hesitantly nodded. "For now, I'll let you call the shots. That's all I can promise."

Tony shot him an icy glare. "For as long as it takes."

Raymond didn't answer.

Amanda watched the Navaho. She had a feeling Raymond would blow the whistle if he felt that either Hope or she was threatened. She took comfort in that thought. Where Tony had an edge that came from his lawlessness, Raymond was methodical and, from all appearances, a careful man who did not believe in taking unnecessary chances. Protecting and serving the public seemed to be far more than mere words to him.

"We'll be leaving now, Amanda, but don't worry," Tony said, "I've left a card on your counter with my home number and address, my pager number and my cellular. If you need to talk, just pick up the phone."

Raymond walked back into the room. "Let me show you one more thing. You need to know where I placed extra tapes in case you need them." He glanced back at Tony. "I'll be with you in a minute." Raymond reached into the drawer beneath the phone and showed her the tapes. "You're all set. Just remember one thing," he said, dropping his voice. "Be careful how you play things out. My old partner has had to contend with more pain than most of us. He's on the edge. He's been there for a long time. Just make sure he doesn't get pushed out of control."

As Amanda walked with Tony and Raymond to the door a car pulled up. Bernice quickly opened the rear door and Winston catapulted out. The bullmastiff bounded to the front door and stopped less than three feet in front of Tony.

Tony froze. Raymond backed up a step, but hearing the ominous throaty growl that came from the dog, stopped dead in his tracks.

"He doesn't like either of you," Bernice said pleasantly, walking up to the porch. "He always blocks the path of people he takes a dislike to. I wouldn't do anything too quickly right now, gentlemen," she added pleasantly. "And for your sakes, please don't even think of sneezing. He might not understand."

"It's all right, Bernice," Amanda said quickly, trying not to laugh. Both men appeared to have stopped breathing. She crouched and called Winston, but the animal continued to stare at Tony.

"Winston, heel!" Bernice said. The dog went to Bernice's side, but his gaze stayed fixed on Tony. "I'm sorry, but as I said before, he doesn't like you."

"Occupational hazard," Tony muttered, then edged around the dog, never turning his back. Raymond followed. "See you later," Tony said.

Bernice waved at them sweetly. "Goodbye, gentlemen." As the men drove off, she quickly turned to Amanda. "I came by to make sure you were okay, but I didn't expect to find Ramos here with a friend. What the heck was that all about?"

As they stepped inside the house Winston loped past them running straight to Hope's bedroom. The little girl squealed with delight. Used to this routine, and certain the child and dog would be safely occupied for some time, Amanda and Bernice went into the kitchen.

Amanda gave Bernice the latest news as she brewed a fresh pot of coffee and made a bedtime snack for Hope. "I'm terrified of going up against these people, but I can't just sit tight and do nothing. If they make good on their threat I have no doubt I'll have to fight Tony. If that happens, the more I know about him, the better off I'll be."

Bernice shook her head. "Amanda, listen to me. Ramos is nobody's fool. The kidnappers wouldn't be able to trick him into believing Hope was his for long. A simple blood test would establish the truth."

Amanda placed two cups brimming with hot coffee on the table, then sat down. "The problem is, he would *want* to believe them. Given the lack of documentation at the state level, thanks to the kidnappers, he might not even stop to question it. At that point, he could do anything. He might even take off with my child. He's already proven that the law is something he's willing to bend to suit his own purposes."

"But surely that's a bit drastic, even for him," Bernice said.

"Maybe, maybe not. He's desperate to find his child. Who knows? And if he makes the authorities suspect I obtained Hope illegally, even if he didn't take her, it might take months of legal action and cost me everything to get her back. And if word leaked out to the press, the publicity could damage my credibility as the owner of a day-care center. Even if that didn't happen, there could still be a problem. When Ron and I took custody of Hope, we promised never to reveal that she was really his sister's child. There could be problems in the family, especially since Louise's husband knows nothing about the baby. And even though Ron told me his sister hasn't heard from the father for quite a while, he could turn up and claim he wants her back, if only as a way to extort money from me." Amanda shook her head. "I won't risk it. I've *got* to stay one step ahead of everyone else."

The quiet that descended over them was interrupted only by enthusiastic squeals from Hope, who was still happily playing in her room with Winston. Amanda rose to take her empty coffee cup to the sink, when suddenly a monstrous crash erupted from the front of the house. As a gust of wind blew through the kitchen doorway, Amanda heard Hope scream. Spikes of fear pounding through her, Amanda raced to her daughter.

Chapter Three

Tony sat sipping a cup of black coffee in the corner booth of the small café. Though most other people couldn't read Raymond, years of practice had made Tony proficient at it. He knew without a shadow of a doubt that Raymond was really ticked off. "Buddy, I wouldn't have asked if there was any other way, but I really need that file. It's payback time."

"Don't pull that crap on me. You and I have been through a lot of close calls. I think the score's about even," Raymond answered through a clenched jaw.

"That's true while we were both agents. But I wasn't an agent last year, and if it hadn't been for me, the perps you ran across in the parking lot of Santiago's would have killed you."

"Do you really think I'd be doing you a favor by loaning you that file? Think about it," Raymond snapped back. "You, of all people, should know that it doesn't pay to negotiate with kidnappers."

The words hit him as hard as Raymond meant them to. Tony swallowed, but maintained his confrontational gaze. "Don't become my enemy on this."

"I'm not your enemy, you jackass." Raymond leaned over and lowered his voice to a growl. "I'm only telling you what you already know. You need a few cards up your sleeve, and the only way you'll get them is if we talk to the S.A.C."

"The special agent in charge?" Tony looked at Raymond as if he'd lost his mind. "*No way.* After that fight we had right before I quit, he wouldn't give me a glass of water if I were dying of thirst." He leaned back. "You're either with me or against me, buddy. That's the way it's got to be. I've never been convinced that it wasn't a leak somewhere within the Bureau that made the kidnappers bolt."

"I looked into that. You're way off base there." Raymond stared at him for several long moments. "I'll get you something that looks real, but not the genuine thing. The substitute will have to be altered. Deal?"

"Okay, but I'll have to see the original file."

"I can arrange that, but you'll have to come to my office tomorrow morning at six before anyone else gets there. The S.A.C. is at the Albuquerque office, but I still don't want you to show up while the support staff is present."

"I'll be there." Tony felt as if a great weight had landed on his shoulders. He knew what he had to do. Although he'd never betrayed a friend before, he had no choice now. He wouldn't risk blowing everything by giving the kidnappers false information.

"By the way, once I get you inside, remember to duck your head. I don't want your mug showing up on the surveillance cameras. All I'll have to say then is that you're one of my more nervous informants."

"No problem."

Raymond stared pensively across the room. "Have you considered the possibility that pursuing this lead could take you someplace you don't want to go?" Raymond asked quietly. "Are you prepared to face the worst, if it comes to that?"

Tony met his friend's gaze, using all the willpower he had to shutter his emotions. "You still don't believe she's alive."

"No, I don't. If she were, they would have used her before now."

Recognizing the grain of truth in Raymond's words made his gut clench, but he knew he had to see it through. "I've got to know either way." Tony stood up. "One more thing. I'd like you to do a full background check on Amanda Vila."

"Good idea. I was about to suggest it myself."

As they reached the door, Tony's pager went off. He glanced down. "It's Amanda's number." Tony spotted a public phone near the cash register and went directly to it. Amanda picked up the phone on the first ring.

"Did you get a description of the car?" Tony asked after hearing her story. "Okay, don't worry about it. Sit tight. I'm on my way."

Tony glanced back at Raymond. "We've got trouble."

TONY ARRIVED ALONE at Amanda's less than fifteen minutes after her call. Raymond would come by shortly after handling a few necessary details. As he glanced around the living room, he measured the damage. The center of the wood-framed picture window that faced the front yard had been reduced to a pile of glass shards scattered over the tile floor. A large rock lay near the wall, where it had come to rest. The rough, porous surface of the volcanic rock left him convinced no prints could be lifted from it.

Tony glanced up at Amanda. Her face was gray, as if someone had dusted it with ashes, but she was still very much in control of herself. His admiration for her grew. "Do you ever have any vandalism in your neighborhood?"

Amanda shook her head but remained silent.

"Well, actually we do, but nothing like this," Bernice volunteered.

"What do you mean?" Tony's gaze fastened on Bernice. "If you know something, don't hold back now."

Bernice nodded, then continued reluctantly. "Last week someone slashed my tires. Right in front of my house, too. I thought it was Jerry, my neighbor's son, since he and my husband had argued about his speeding down the lane."

"Does he know you and Amanda are good friends?" Tony asked.

"Yes, but I doubt this had anything to do with that," Bernice said. "It's just too far a stretch."

Amanda put her hand on Bernice's arm. "I think the same would apply to us linking this to the kidnapper. It doesn't make sense, not in that context."

She started to say more, when a knock sounded on her open door. "Are you okay, Amanda?" Ricky Biddle came into the room. "I was out for a run, and I saw all the cars and the broken window."

"Hello, Ricky." Amanda forced a thin smile. "We're all fine. Thanks for asking."

"You're going to need help fixing that," he said, glancing at the smashed window. "I can call my brother's hardware store. It's late, but he'd open up for me. I'm sure I can get everything you need delivered, and we'd have a new window up in no time."

Amanda looked tempted by his offer, but she hesitated. Tony watched her for a second, then his gazed shifted to Biddle.

Tony could sense the guy was interested in Amanda and wanted to get her attention. Though it was perfectly obvious to Tony that Biddle wasn't her type he decided to step in anyway. "Don't worry, Mr. Biddle. Amanda will have plenty of help here this evening."

Amanda shot Tony an angry look. "I can speak for myself."

Tony clamped his mouth shut realizing he'd made a tactical error and hoping she wouldn't invite Biddle in just to spite him.

Amanda glanced back at Ricky and smiled. "I appreciate your offer, but it's really not necessary. I can tape something over the opening for tonight. There'll be time for a thorough repair tomorrow during daylight. I'll have someone come and fix it."

"But..."

Tony approached Ricky, eyeing him carefully. The guy bugged him. His neat blue jogging suit had been chosen more for style than practicality, and if the guy had ever actually worked up a sweat in it, Tony would have been surprised. "Do you always go jogging at this time?"

"Oh, yeah. I work mainly in the mornings and goof off in the afternoon and evenings."

"What do you do for a living, Mr. Biddle?"

Ricky gave him a suspicious look. "Who are you? The IRS?"

"It's okay, Ricky," Amanda said. "He's a friend."

Ricky's shoulder sagged slightly. "I develop and program computer games. Have you ever played Cannibal Cafeteria?"

Tony stared at the guy, wondering what, exactly, he found so irritating about him. "No, I'm not much into games."

"Well, Cannibal is one of the most popular simulations on the market," Ricky said with a shrug.

"Did you happen to see someone hanging around here earlier, or maybe notice an unfamiliar car speeding down the road?"

"No, I wish I had." Ricky glanced at Amanda. "I'll come by and check on you every once in a while, if that will help."

"Thanks, but it's really not necessary, Ricky," Amanda answered. "I'm sure this was an isolated incident."

Tony watched Biddle. He was continually glancing around, unable to stand still, like some hyperkinetic kid. Tony schooled his face into polite neutrality and used his best authoritative tone. "Everything's under control here, Mr. Biddle."

Amanda led Ricky back toward the door. "Thanks for stopping by, Ricky. I'll make sure to call you later, okay?"

"Do that."

"Okay. It'll be just as soon as I have a free moment."

Once Ricky left, Amanda went over to Tony. "What exactly were you trying to pull? Didn't you think I'd have enough sense to know that Ricky would be in the way if the kidnappers called?"

"I was taking charge of the situation *before* any problems cropped up." That was only a partial reason. The fact was he didn't want Biddle around Amanda, though he was at a loss to explain why he'd taken such an instant dislike to the guy.

Bernice began working pieces of glass loose from the window frame in preparation for covering the hole. "Ricky makes me nervous every time I see him."

"He's okay," Amanda said with a thin smile. "He just tries too hard. The poor guy works and lives all alone. All he seems to have for company is that rottweiler of his. He's probably just lonely."

Tony shrugged. "Does he come by your house often?"

Amanda shook her head. "Not that it's any of your business, but I haven't encouraged that."

Tony nodded, relieved to hear it. His possessive feelings surprised him. He certainly had no personal claims on Amanda. Yet somehow she'd managed to get under his skin in a way no one had for a very long time.

As Bernice left the room to find a broom and dustpan Hope came into the room. Amanda smiled at her reassuringly. "It's okay, Peanut. I'll be in your room in just a few minutes. Will you wait for me there?"

Hope nodded wordlessly then ran down the hall. Amanda's gaze stayed on her as if she was torn between making her home safe for her daughter or rushing to her side.

Tony placed a hand on her shoulder, and as their eyes met, blood thundered in his veins. "Go take care of your daughter. I'll clean up the glass."

Tony bent down, gathering the pieces into his palm. He needed to put some distance between himself and Amanda. He was finally starting to hope he'd get his daughter back and his brain was going soft from the strain. The last thing he needed was any complications. He needed to stay focused on Carmen. That was all there was to it.

As Raymond's car pulled up outside, Amanda returned and met him by the front door. With a wave of the hand, she invited him in.

"I stopped at a friend's house and borrowed his caller ID device," Raymond said. "Let me get it set up for you, okay?"

"Sure." Amanda showed him to the phone in the living room.

Hearing footsteps and the clicking sound of a dog's nails against the tile floor, Amanda turned around. Hope was standing in the hall wearing her pajamas, hanging on to Winston's collar. The dog stared at both Tony and Raymond, then took a step forward, positioning himself in front of Hope.

"Mommy, come back. I'm scared," Hope said, big tears running down her cheeks.

Amanda hurried over to put her arms around her daughter. "Don't be. There's nothing for you to be frightened of," she said softly. "We're okay, Peanut."

As Tony looked from Amanda to her daughter, a knot formed in his gut. Amanda and Hope belonged together. The love they shared marked them as a family. They shared something he would have given everything to have—something he'd quite possibly lost forever.

A slow ache continued gnawing at his insides as he heard Amanda comforting Hope. To his surprise, he found himself walking around the dog, despite a throaty warning growl, and crouching down beside them.

"Hope, honey, please don't cry," he said gently. "Sometimes bad people act mean, but there are always good people around to make things come out okay."

Out of the corner of his eye, he saw Raymond's surprised face and Amanda's expression of disbelief. Even Bernice had stopped looking for glass and was watching him. Well, what the hell. They could think whatever they pleased. Hope had stopped crying.

"You're a good guy?" she asked, looking up at his face.

"Yep, I sure am. Though sometimes people don't know that right away."

"Why?" Hope moved away from Amanda and toward Tony.

"I guess it's because I'm not always polite and nice," Tony said softly. "But if they look past that, they find I'm okay to have around."

Hope smiled at Tony, then gave him a hug.

Tony saw Amanda's jaw drop. He felt as stunned as she looked. "We're friends?"

"I like you, Tony." Hope disentangled herself and looked up at Amanda. "He's not a stranger anymore. And he looked like he needed a hug. It's okay, right? You told me that grown-ups need hugs sometimes, too."

Amanda smiled. "It's okay, Peanut."

"Can we play?" Hope looked at Tony.

"In a little bit, all right? Let me fix this window for your mom first."

Bernice moved next to Tony as Amanda took Hope back to her room, Winston by their side. "You may have convinced Hope and Amanda," she whispered, "but I'll be watching you, mister."

No longer needed, Raymond excused himself and left. Bernice, on the other hand, seemed determined to remain as long as Tony was there. They worked side by side, removing every trace of glass and taping together pieces of cardboard shoe boxes to repair the window.

Tony finished the section he'd been working on, aware of the way Bernice was watching him out of the corner of her eye. When he glanced past her, he noticed Amanda was standing by the phone, lost in thought. "What's wrong?"

"I think I should report this incident to the police. It'll make it easier to file a claim with my homeowner's insurance."

Her unspoken question came through to him clearly. She didn't want to jeopardize the situation if he thought this was connected to the kidnappers. But it was more than that, too. She was being careful around him, like someone would be around a ticking bomb. The knowledge knifed at him. It didn't seem so long ago that people had turned to him for assurance.

"Go ahead and call," he said. "It can't hurt anything at this point, though I don't think the police will be able to do much except file a report."

Tony continued working with Bernice as Amanda called and answered routine questions over the phone. The bright patchwork of cardboard they had put together effectively covered up the hole.

"Well, it's colorful, that's for sure. I wish I had found some sturdier cardboard, but the shoe boxes will do for now," Bernice said.

Amanda finally hung up the phone. "They said they'd be here in thirty minutes to take a report, but the officer said that they don't generally have much luck tracing acts of vandalism."

"That's the same response I got when my tires were slashed," Bernice said, shaking her head. "I guess all these cuts in the city budget are beginning to take their toll."

Amanda saw Bernice glance at her watch and knew what was on her friend's mind. "Why don't you go home, Bernice? I know Phil's going out of town tomorrow, and you've got things to do."

"It's just one of his overnight business trips. Why don't you and Hope come over and keep me company?" Bernice asked.

Amanda shook her head. "I can't. I've got things to do here." She gestured to the front window.

"Then let me take Hope with me. She can sleep over. You know how much Phil and I like having her. And she loves having Winston sleep with her."

Amanda laughed. "I can't really say that's a selling point with me, but okay. It'll give me a chance to make sure I find all the pieces of glass."

It only took a few minutes to pack an overnight bag for Hope. The little girl gave Amanda a hug and a kiss, then turned to Tony and gave him a hug, too. "Take care of my mommy, even if she's crabby. She's really nice, once you know her."

Tony laughed. "I'll do that."

"You just mind yourself," Bernice said, her glare icy as it focused on Tony.

Tony nodded, his expression neutral as he watched Hope, Bernice and the big dog walk out to the car. "That woman obviously doesn't like me," Tony said to Amanda as soon as they were alone.

"Do you blame her? She's protective about me." Her gaze strayed to the tape recorder next to her phone. "You should come with a warning label."

"The choice to have you involved wasn't mine." Those words brought to mind the one question that continued to prey on his mind. Tony didn't believe in coincidences, he never had. Amanda was tied into all this somehow, and he didn't have much time to figure out what her connection was. Maybe the bug he'd decided to plant just as soon as he had time alone would reveal what he needed to know.

As Tony helped her search for stray pieces of glass, his eyes scanned the room, always vigilant. "You have a terrific kid," he said, hoping to make Amanda relax. Maybe then she would lower her guard and reveal more about herself. He needed to get a handle on her that didn't involve the one weak point he'd seen—her daughter. He and Amanda had one thing in common—their determination to keep children safe. He just didn't bother to pretty things up with a lot of fancy, useless rules and regulations.

"Hope is a wonderful little girl," she answered, "but she's so very vulnerable. She needs protection and love. I intend to see that she gets both."

She was warning him off, like a lioness protecting her cubs. She'd do whatever was necessary to keep him away from her child. In that one respect, they were more alike than she knew. "Hope is one very lucky little girl."

"I think you better be going, don't you? The police will be arriving soon."

"I can handle them. I'm here with your permission."

"Yes, but I'd rather not have anyone link you and me, particularly with you here at this hour. This police department is a small one and rumors travel fast. Two of the parents at the day school are cops, and I don't want them to get wind of this."

Amanda's telephone rang just as she finished speaking. Tony felt the hair on the back of his neck stand on end—a sure sign he'd learned never to ignore. "Remember to write down the number that flashes on the caller ID," he said, automatically moving toward the extension. "The system will store the number in memory, but it's better to have a hard copy."

She glanced at the number marked Pay Phone that appeared on the LED display. She jotted it down.

With a nod, Tony picked up the extension at the same time Amanda did. The electronically altered voice had the same effect on him as fingernails on a chalkboard. He heard

Amanda argue briefly as the woman moved up the deadline they'd given him to get the file. Now she wanted it by the end of tomorrow. Amanda protested, but the woman hung up abruptly.

Amanda gave the phone a hostile glance, then slammed it down. "So much for trusting them to keep their word."

"I had a feeling she'd call tonight and find some way to keep the pressure up. These variations of routine and changes of plans are meant to keep us off-balance. This person knows what she's doing."

"Can you get the file they want?"

"I think so." Tony dialed Raymond's direct number. "Track this pay-phone number, will you?" he said without identifying himself. He read out the number, then added, "Use my cellular when you call back." Tony hung up and glanced at Amanda. "I'm going to take the tape with me—"

Flashing red lights suddenly could be seen through the smaller side windows that hadn't been broken. Amanda's eyes grew wide. "It hasn't been twenty minutes! What a time for them to become efficient! Now what?"

"I'll duck into your garage and wait there. My pickup's in your driveway, so with luck, they'll assume it's yours," he said, deciding to leave the tape where it was for now.

Through a crack in the door, Tony watched Amanda greet the officer and usher him inside. The officer stepped in, looked around, and then asked her a few routine questions meant to give him some leads. Getting nothing useful, he held out the report while she signed it.

"I'm afraid that we have very little to go on," he said. "Our chances of catching the person or persons connected to this are slim."

"I know," she admitted.

"We'll increase patrols in this area, and if you have any more problems, give us a call."

Tony waited until Amanda closed the front door before coming out. His patience was strained to its limit. Glancing out the front door to make sure the officer was gone, he went to his car and retrieved his cellular phone. He joined her back inside a moment later.

Amanda gave him a worried glance. "What if Raymond already called you?"

Tony shook his head. "It takes longer than that to track down a number, particularly at this time of night. We have a few minutes more to wait." He walked to the tape recorder and rewound the message. "Help me listen for background sounds. See if there's anything significant." In his own mind, Tony blocked out the dialogue, concentrating. Finally he shut off the recorder.

"All I could hear was what sounded like traffic," Amanda said.

"Same here."

His cellular phone rang just as he finished speaking. Raymond confirmed that the number matched a pay phone and gave him an address. "Let me go over there," Raymond said. "Maybe I can dust for prints and get something."

"No, no way. They may be watching the booth, waiting for my next move. They expect me to have some contacts. Finding out I traced the call shouldn't come as too big a surprise. Seeing me there won't be, either. On the other hand, having my former partner show up might scare them off. I don't want them to know you're involved. And, again, don't tell anyone at the Bureau about any of this. We don't know who might feed information to these bastards," Tony said, writing down the address. "I'll take care of this. All I need you to do is meet me tomorrow so we can go to your office, as we agreed." Once again, regret flooded over him. His planned betrayal could cost him the best friend he'd ever had.

"I'm going, too," Amanda said, looking at the address he'd written down.

"Why? There's no reason for you to come."

"That address is about a block from my day-care center. If someone's throwing rocks at my house, they might have done something worse at the center. Don't try to talk me out of it. I'm coming," she answered flatly.

Tony decided against arguing. The lady had a mind of her own. If he said no, she'd probably just follow him. He didn't really have a choice, and at least this way he could keep an eye on her. He'd find out nothing useful unless she relaxed. Maybe pretending to confide in her would help.

As they got underway, he glanced over at Amanda. He had to find some way of getting her to lower her guard around him. "I don't think we're being followed, and that's a good sign. I don't expect to find anything at the phone booth, but I've got to make a show of going there to look around and dust for prints. These people will expect me to have a few tricks up my sleeve and connections to check out things like fingerprint records. If I don't act as they expect, they'll get nervous, thinking I've got some master plan in the works or something."

"I wonder how they'll react to my coming along?" Amanda's voice was hesitant, as if she had suddenly become unsure of herself.

"How else could you keep an eye on me?" Tony suggested, watching her reaction carefully.

Amanda glanced at him, startled. "Does an intermediary do that?"

"Sometimes."

Tony gave her an appraising glance, then focused his attention back on the road. He could see the lines of worry that sharpened her face in response to the thoughts she was keeping hidden from him. Amanda seemed determined to keep him at arm's length, though he was doing his best to disarm her. He knew women found him attractive, and he'd always managed to get what he wanted. Until now. He fought the urge to pull over to the side of the road and kiss her until she went soft in his arms, her reserve shattered.

The thought suddenly gave way to another realization. That impulse had nothing to do with finding a key to making Amanda more cooperative with his investigation. Exasperated with himself, he clenched the steering wheel tightly.

"You don't allow yourself to need anyone, do you?" he asked.

She shrugged. "Certainly not people I don't know."

"Like me?"

"All I know about you is that in one day you've turned everything in my life upside down."

She had a point. "If you want to know anything about me, ask."

He saw the questions crossing her face. She studied him for a moment, then with a more guarded expression, shook her head. He couldn't be sure, but her reluctance made him think that she'd decided making him angry was not to her best advantage. "You're a man of secrets," she said. "I know the type, believe me. I could ask you a million questions and never get any genuine information."

"Your ex was like that?" he asked, neither confirming nor denying her accusation.

Amanda nodded. "After we'd been married a while, I realized we never really talked about things that mattered. He never shared anything that was important to him or wanted to talk about what was important to me. His job was far more interesting to him than I ever was."

That last line, so close to what his wife, Lynn, had said to him so many times, stung, flooding his brain with bitter memories. "Some men don't always know how to show or even talk about what they're feeling. It doesn't always come to us as easily as women want."

Amanda gave him a long, guarded look. "Well, at least you've told me something about yourself, though in a roundabout way," she said.

Tony realized that, if anything, his being open had made her more suspicious of him. Regret filled him as he acknowledged that, had circumstances been different, he would have wanted her to know him, just as he would have wanted to know her—in every possible sense. Aware of the danger of entertaining those thoughts, he drew back into himself. Nothing could get in the way of his finding his daughter and punishing the creeps who had taken her away from him.

Tony pulled up next to a public phone beside a convenience store. "Wait for me here." Tony retrieved a fingerprint kit from the back seat and walked up to the booth. Though he went over every inch of it, there were no prints. It had been wiped completely clean. As he turned to look back at her, he saw Amanda coming out of the convenience store. Muttering an oath, he rushed up to her. "What are you doing?"

"Making myself useful. I went inside to talk to the clerk, thinking he might have seen something."

Tony transfixed her with his coldest glare. "You know absolutely nothing about questioning a witness! You may have ruined any chance we had."

"He didn't see anything," Amanda protested.

"And I supposed you asked him really nicely?" he scoffed.

"Of course I did. I wanted him to help me, not call the police! Being polite doesn't hurt," she argued.

Tony stared at the ground, trying to control his temper. "Intimidation works better, particularly with a reluctant witness." Though he forced his tone to remain calm, he saw the cautious look that flickered in Amanda's eyes. Her inability to predict his reactions seemed to frighten her at times, though she tried to hide it. The problem was, he didn't particularly like having her treat him like a wild animal, afraid of the violent nature that so many believed was part of him. "Calm down, Amanda. I know what I'm doing."

The young man inside seemed annoyed when Tony forced him to put down the mystery novel he was reading. Unable to elicit any satisfactory answers, Tony slammed his fist down hard on the counter, picked up the novel, and tossed it across the room. The startled clerk sat up abruptly.

"Now that I've got your attention . . ." Tony purred.

"Look, man, I don't know nothing. I've been reading. An entire army could have used that booth."

Tony leaned toward him menacingly. "Try harder. From what I can tell, you have a clear view of the booth."

The young man slid off his seat and took a step back. "Look, I'm just here to pick up some extra cash in the evenings. It's quiet, so I use the time to read and relax. I'm not concerned with what happens outside unless it disturbs our customers."

Amanda followed Tony as he stalked back to the pickup. "I gather you found no fingerprints?"

"They cleaned the booth until it shone," he growled, disgusted.

Tony glanced around. After business hours, this neighborhood was like a cemetery. There were two cars parked inside a private parking area next to a government building ahead. One, a cream-colored four-door, reminded him of his first Bureau car. He smiled, recalling its habit of breaking down. Silently he wished the owner of the sedan better luck than he'd had.

"Let's go try the front doors on that building," he said. "They'll probably be locked, but it's worth checking out." After finding the building sealed up, they walked back to the pickup. "Let's drive around the area a bit."

"What are we looking for?"

"Basically I'm going through the motions in case they're watching, but who knows? We might get lucky. Keep your eyes open. Maybe we'll find a street person who caught a glimpse of our caller. Anything."

"Go by the day-care center, too, okay? I need to make sure everything is all right there." She glanced at the cream-colored sedan. "That reminds me of the car I saw watching the center," she said, then explained.

"There are thousands of cream-colored sedans in this area. That's not much of a lead."

He drove around the Plaza, hoping he'd pick up a tail. All he needed was one break.

Amanda glanced in the side mirror. "That same sedan is back there. But I can't tell if it's following us or not. It's several car lengths behind us."

He spotted the light sedan behind them, weaving through traffic. It was the same car he'd seen next to the government building. He slowed down, hoping to draw it close. The car, however, persisted in keeping its distance, allowing other cars to slip between them. Whoever was back there was either trained in surveillance or a natural. He considered the possibility of a Bureau-trained agent, possibly one who'd gone bad. Tony speeded up slightly, causing the other car to lag behind. Then, as they reached the corner, he stopped for the light. "Is your seat belt on?"

"Sure. Why do you ask?"

Not waiting for the green light, Tony looked both ways, then stepped on the accelerator. He rounded the next corner with a screech of tires, leaving behind the stench of burning rubber.

Amanda's breath came in short gasps. "What are you doing?"

He glanced in the rearview mirror. His tail wasn't behind them anymore. He wheeled down a narrow alleyway, then doubled back.

"Hang on." Tony made another sharp turn, heading up a deserted street. "We'll catch the guy tailing us in a moment. Then he's going to have to answer a few questions."

Amanda gripped the dashboard tightly. "But first, we have to survive this ride."

Chapter Four

The driver of the cream-colored car noticed them seconds after Tony burst out of the narrow street adjacent to a hotel. The car shot away from them, heading toward an old residential area where there were no streetlights. Only their headlights probed through the darkness.

The sound of a hymn from a church organ could be heard in the distance, and Tony tightened his grip on the wheel. "Wednesday-night services are about to end. Traffic should pick up again soon, and he'll have a better chance of losing us."

"It's too dark here. You can't see where you're going, at least not clearly. Let him go," Amanda urged.

"Not a chance." Tony called her attention to the speedometer. "See for yourself. He's slowing down. He can't see any better than we can. But look just ahead. See that lighted parking area?" He pointed down the street. "I'll lay odds he ducks in there to hide."

Suddenly the red taillights they'd been following seemed to disappear. Amanda leaned forward, straining to see through the soupy darkness. "Where is he?"

"He's gone into the church parking lot, where he can blend in with the other cars and leave with them once the service lets out," Tony said.

"That's that then. You certainly can't follow him in there without having someone call the police."

"Sure I can. Look for yourself," Tony said as he slowed the vehicle and pulled into the lot. "Nobody's out here yet. They're still inside."

"What if he went inside, too?"

"Doubtful. He wants to get away, not deal with a lot of citizens who would notice a stranger. He's out here some- where, hoping to give us the slip." Tony parked beside a large van. "Stay inside. I'm going to take a look around."

"You can't be serious! There are no lights back here. I can't tell one light-colored sedan from another, and there are at least fifty cars around us."

"I'll handle it. Just stay put." Without waiting for an answer, he stepped noiselessly out of the truck and disap- peared into the shadows.

Amanda watched for a moment, wondering what she should do. Tony was like a loose cannon where the search for his daughter was concerned. She really wasn't at all sure they'd been tailed in the first place, though the car they'd followed did look like the one she'd seen earlier outside the center. But pulling up behind someone in a light colored se- dan, and then wildly chasing after them, just might have scared the life out of some innocent person, frightening him into making a run for it.

Amanda opened the pickup door and looked out. Tony's aggressiveness left a lot of room for error. As she searched for some sign of him, she caught a glimpse of a shadowy figure moving inside one of the parked cars near where she'd last seen him. The realization that he'd been right hit her like a bolt of lightning. She had to tell him what she'd seen.

Amanda left the vehicle quickly and walked in the direc- tion Tony had gone. She found him a moment later.

"Tony, wait!" she whispered harshly.

He turned around, still in a crouch, and motioned for her to get down. Suddenly, the car door next to him flew open.

It slammed hard against Tony, hitting him squarely in the head and knocking him to the ground.

Amanda rushed toward Tony as she heard the car's engine start up. Grabbing his arm, she dragged him between two cars, narrowly avoiding being run over as the vehicle backed up with a screech of tires. Crossing the sidewalk, the sedan hurtled over the curb and bounced into the street, making a clean getaway before Amanda could spot the license plate.

Tony rose to his feet, rubbing his temple. "Hard pavement. Good thing I've got an equally hard head."

"No argument there," she muttered, trying to catch her breath.

"What the heck were you doing out here? I told you to stay in the car."

"I came because—" Amanda stopped abruptly. There was no way now she could tell him that she'd been afraid he was terrorizing an innocent person. Even in the dim half light, she could see that the bump on the side of his head was beginning to swell at an alarming rate. "I came because I saw someone lurking inside one of the cars. I figured you needed my help."

"Yeah? Well, you didn't exactly save the day, did you?"

"It could have been worse. I kept you from being run over, didn't I? Let's face it. You were right next to him, yet you had no idea he was there."

"That's why I was being careful," he snapped. Tony gingerly touched his temple with his fingertips as they walked back to his truck. "Now we're back to square one."

As they reached the pickup, Amanda walked to the driver's side and nudged him out of the way. "Let me drive. I don't give my passengers heart failure."

"Of course not. You have your own inimitable ways of finishing them off," he grumbled sourly.

She looked at the angry red bruise on his temple. "Maybe I better take you to the hospital. You should have that checked."

"Forget it. I'm fine and I'm driving." Tony stepped around her and slipped behind the wheel. "I don't see double, and there's no gushing blood. I'll live. Do you still want to go to the day-care center like we planned?"

"If you're up to it."

"As I said, I'll be fine."

Fifteen minutes later, they arrived at the center. Amanda searched the exterior of the building, then breathed a sigh of relief to see everything was intact. She left the pickup, rummaging in her purse for the keys, but after several seconds, Tony edged in front of her.

"Let me help. If the cops are patrolling this area, they're going to spot us here. I don't feel like answering half a million questions and as you said, you don't want to be seen with me." He slipped a skeleton key in the lock, then using something that resembled a nail file, jiggled the mechanism. A second later, the door swung open.

Amanda's mouth dropped open. "I don't believe you. Is that how the photo of Carmen kept showing up on the bulletin board even though nobody ever knew how it got there?"

He gave her a quick half smile. "Hurry and do your check," he said, not answering her. "That's my truck out there, and a patrol car might run the plate and come in to see what's going on."

Five minutes later, satisfied that nothing had been disturbed, Amanda returned to the pickup with him. "I don't want you to *ever* use that key to get into my day care again. Or my home," she added quickly.

"Sorry. I only make promises I'm sure I can keep."

Amanda thought of Hope and the other children. Anger gave her courage. "If you get caught in here, I'll press charges. If you're in a jail cell, you're not going to be much use to your daughter.''

He remained quiet for several moments, then finally nodded. ''All right. But that means I'll have to personally bring in the computer-generated image of Carmen whenever there's an update on it. I know you understand how important that is to me.''

She sighed. He was being so perfectly reasonable about it; she was the one who sounded unreasonable. Yet what was so unreasonable about asking someone not to break and enter? ''Mail it, then check the following day. You can always call me. I guarantee that if it doesn't arrive within twenty-four hours, I'll go get it from you myself.''

''All right.''

As they drove back to her home, Amanda's thoughts raced in a multitude of directions. There were so many questions, and so few answers! ''What's in that file the caller wants so badly?''

''I'll know by tomorrow.''

''Tell me as soon as you do.''

''I'm not sure that's a good idea. The more you know, the more of a threat you'll be to them. You'd be better off letting me handle that.''

It would have been wonderful to be able to trust Tony enough to feel confident about his using his experience to keep Hope and her safe. Only that couldn't be. Tony's priority was his daughter Carmen, not Hope—and definitely not her. ''No, we're both involved, so we'll share the information. We may be working together, but our priorities are totally different. There's no way I'll relinquish responsibility for my well-being or that of my daughter to you.''

He stiffened as if she'd slapped him. ''You have a right to mistrust my abilities.'' He glanced at her, his face taut and expressionless. ''I wasn't good enough to protect my own wife or child. But I'm tougher and smarter now than I was back then. Life's taught me the hard way. I'm the best ally or the worst enemy you could ever possibly have. Believe it.''

''I don't doubt your abilities, just your priorities.''

Tony pulled into her driveway. ''Well, at least we each know where we stand.'' He switched off the ignition.

''What do you think the kidnappers will do now?''

''They want the file, so I don't think they'll do anything providing I deliver it.'' He gestured toward her front door. ''Come on. I'll walk you to the door, borrow some aspirins, then be on my way.''

''You ought to come in for a few minutes and clean up those cuts and scratches all over your face,'' she said, depressed by the unbridgeable gap that separated them.

''All right.''

She opened the front door and let him in. ''The bathroom is down the hall to your right. After you wash up I'll put some disinfectant on those cuts,'' she said. Then, with a tentative grin, she added what she always said to her daughter, ''Don't worry. I've got the ouchless kind.''

''That makes me feel infinitely better,'' he countered in a tone that left little doubt he thought she'd lost her mind.

As Tony disappeared down the hall, Amanda picked up the phone and called Bernice, needing reassurance that Hope was fine. That accomplished, she retrieved the first-aid kit from the kitchen drawer.

She tried to tell herself that she'd only extended hospitality to Tony out of courtesy, but she knew that wasn't the truth. Every time she saw his cold, withdrawn expression, she felt the need to reach him somehow, find a way to ease his pain. She shook her head, exasperated with herself. She was much too old for these fantasies. She didn't believe she could kiss a hurt and make it better, and she definitely didn't want to be Tony's mommy.

Hearing Tony step into the room, she turned around. Her pulse began to race as her gaze fell on him. He looked uncompromisingly strong, his face set as if it had been chiseled from the hardest stone. Yet it was that very strength that seemed to cry out for a woman's tenderness. Her tenderness.

"Have a seat."

Standing beside his chair, Amanda carefully dabbed the scratches just below his bruised temple with disinfectant.

Tony held himself still. "You have gentle hands."

"Thanks." His words made her melt inside, arousing an impossible longing to touch him everywhere, to soothe, then excite him. Chiding herself for the sudden turn of her thoughts, she forced herself to concentrate on the job at hand.

As she leaned forward slightly, taking special care around his eyes, her breast brushed against his shoulder. Every nerve ending in her body was suddenly jolted awake. She glanced down at Tony, wondering if he'd even noticed. His own obvious reaction stole her breath away.

Amanda fought the tremor that spiraled through her as Tony captured her gaze. He grasped her wrist and tugged her toward him, and it seemed as if the world suddenly shifted into slow motion.

He gathered her into his arms and held her steady. "You're playing with fire," he whispered. Slipping his fingers through her hair, he brought her mouth down to meet his.

His kiss was like the man he was, filled with purpose and determination. He urged her lips apart, then stroked her tongue with the length of his. Excitement arose deep within her, like curls of flame that spread out, sparing no part of her. She couldn't think, she couldn't breathe. Her world became a kaleidoscope of fire and velvet. Tony eased his hold to allow himself greater access, then buried his head at the nape of her neck, tasting the soft flesh there.

A war raged within Amanda, torn between what she wanted and what she knew she must do to protect herself and her daughter. As her eyes flashed on a photo of Hope on the wall, she pushed away from him and stood up.

"I shouldn't have let this happen." Amanda questioned her sanity. This wasn't the time to lose control.

"Something special is happening between us, Amanda, despite the situation we're in. Don't deny it."

Amanda wondered why he was so eager to convince her. Still, evasions seemed pointless. There was no denying the truth. But for once she didn't have a ready answer.

Tony obviously took her silence as denial. "I better go," he said, standing up. "If you need me, I'm only a phone call away. I can be back here in no time at all."

"I won't need you," she said quietly, mostly for her own benefit. "And Tony, I really don't think you should come here again. It's likely we'll lose any advantage we might hope to gain if the kidnappers think we're working closely together. It'll be far better if they believe they're in total control and have us pitted against each other. I'm sure they're counting on your resenting having to go through me, and my resenting being put in this position." At least she had been truthful about that part of it.

"You may have a point. I'll give it some thought and see if I can find a way we can work around it," he said. He looked at her searchingly for a moment before he left.

His answer infuriated her. Of course her idea was sound. What was there for him to think about?

Amanda watched the path his pickup truck traveled long after the taillights had disappeared into the night. Longing inexplicably filled her. She turned away from the side window and went back into the kitchen, feeling more alone than she'd ever felt in her life.

SHORTLY AFTER SUNRISE, Tony met Raymond outside the large commercial building containing the local Bureau office, as well as half a dozen independent real-estate and legal firms.

Tony had made careful arrangements for this meeting. With any luck, Raymond would never know for sure what had happened right under his nose. He'd suspect, but never be able to prove anything. That suspicion could well destroy their friendship as trust vanished between them, but it was the only way he knew of not risking his chances of getting his daughter back.

Raymond watched Tony, studying his bruised face as they walked around to a side entrance. "What happened to you?"

"It's a long story."

"Then it'll wait. Come on. I want to get this taken care of before the rest of the staff gets in. I'm passing you off as one of my informants to the security guards on the closed-circuit monitors, so whenever we pass a hall camera, remember to duck your head."

"No problem. And thanks."

Raymond led the way to his office, a tiny partitioned area within a large room. He walked to the file cabinet and pulled out a thick file. "This is the Henderson file. Henderson is still a fugitive. After he pulled off that armored truck heist five months ago, he went underground and we haven't been able to flush him out. He's still in the area, though. We're sure of that." Raymond took off his jacket and hung it on the hook near his desk.

Tony noted the act with satisfaction. Old habits died hard. "Question is, how does Henderson tie in with my daughter's kidnapping?"

"He may not. You know as well as I that they might be using him as a red herring to cover up something else, or they could be asking you to steal a file on a high-profile case so they can blackmail you later on and increase their hold."

Tony studied the file, biding his time. The phone should ring soon. If his informant let him down, he'd personally kick his butt to the border.

A moment later, the phone on the desk began to ring, and his ex-partner picked it up. Raymond's expression changed, then he glanced at Tony. "It's one of my contacts. He's a block down the street. I need to go talk to him. It's urgent." Raymond pulled out another file from his bottom drawer. "Here's the copy I've made for you. It's virtually the same, except for the leads we're currently following up on. It'll pass a civilian inspection, I'm certain of it."

"Give me a moment to compare them, okay? Go talk to your contact. I'll stay right here." Tony saw the flicker of suspicion in Raymond's eyes. "Come on, buddy. Copying this would take more than a few minutes, that's *if* I could make it past the surveillance cameras in the hall *and* come up with a valid user code for the copier."

"I'm going to trust you on this one. Don't screw with me."

"Go. I'll be right here."

As soon as Raymond left, Tony pulled out a miniature camera. He focused carefully, then snapped photos, one after the other. The entire process took less than thirty seconds. He then slipped the camera inside Raymond's jacket.

Tony had returned his attention to the file and was comparing the duplicate to the original when Raymond walked back in. The agent's eyes mirrored distrust. "I'm going to have to frisk you, buddy. I'm sorry."

"Go ahead."

After searching Tony, Raymond stood back. "I really regret doing that. But I couldn't take a chance you'd pulled a fast one."

"You better escort me out of the building. I've got an appointment in a half hour I have to keep."

"Anything I should know about?"

"It's with a lawyer who works for me," Tony said. "A little matter about a guy whose face I rearranged in a local tavern. It made the newspaper."

Raymond shook his head as they headed out the side door. "You were a good agent once. You've thrown it all away."

"That's your way of looking at it. To me, nothing is more important than finding my kid."

Tony opened the driver's-side door and, as he stepped into the pickup, purposely allowed the edge of his jacket to get closed in the door. As he raised his arms to the steering wheel, the fabric was torn lengthwise in a jagged line.

Tony muttered a curse, throwing the door open again in disgust. "I'm about to try to convince a judge that he shouldn't throw my butt in jail, but I'm going to go in looking like a total loser. Some days it doesn't pay to get up."

"Here, take mine," Raymond said, shrugging off his jacket. "I don't want to see you in jail. I can't afford to bail you out."

"Thanks, buddy." Tony slipped off his coat and tossed it onto the seat. "I'll bring this by your house later."

As Tony slid behind the wheel, he caught the look on Raymond's face. It was impossible to tell for sure, but he could have sworn his old partner had just realized what had happened. No. That was just his guilty conscience. Had he known, Raymond would have stopped him. He started the engine, preparing for a fast getaway.

"Good luck," Raymond said calmly and stepped away from the truck.

Tony watched him for a second, then nodded, still unsure. "I'll catch you later."

As he drove away, he had the feeling that he'd taken the first steps down a very dangerous road. And this time, there would be no turning back and no friends who'd stand with him at the finish line.

Next, he planned to hide electronic bugs at Amanda's office and home. If she found them, it would guarantee his losing any trust he'd gained from her. But it had to be done for Carmen's sake. It was certainly his day for betrayals.

Tony was halfway to his home when his cellular phone began to ring. He expected it to be his contact, demanding the rest of his money, but it was Amanda. A sudden chill enveloped him as he heard her voice. There was trouble.

"You're going to have to come over. It can't be avoided this time. I was just getting ready to go to work when I got a message, but not by phone this time. I need you to see this for yourself. Bernice will take Hope to the center. I'll wait for you here."

"I'm on my way." His heart went cold at the irony of the situation. His first chance to betray Amanda had come when she needed his help.

TONY ARRIVED AT AMANDA'S a short time later. As he pulled up, she opened the door and stood at the entrance, waiting. She was wearing slacks and a soft-looking, form-fitting white pullover. Desire, strong and urgent, tightened his body. His hands clenched and unclenched as he struggled to bring himself under control. A moment later, he stepped out of the pickup.

As he walked toward the door, Tony saw fear in Amanda's eyes. "Are you okay?" he asked quickly.

Wordlessly, she led him to the backyard, then pointed to Hope's sandbox. Someone had written in the sand with a stick or other sharp object.

Tony crouched to read the block letters, "'Don't play games. You'll lose.'"

"That's got to be from the kidnappers," she said, her voice taut.

"When did you find this?"

"Right before I called you. I came out to hang Hope's quilt on the clothesline. I always wash it after Winston comes over, because he gets on the bed with her. He sheds."

Tony studied the writing in the sand. "It looks like the wind's started to fill in some of the letters. But there was no breeze to speak of last night."

She glanced down, following his gaze. "It's clear enough," Amanda snapped. "What can't you read?"

"No, you don't understand. This message may not have been left last night. When were you out here last?"

"Two days ago, I think. We've had long hours this week at the center. If I remember correctly, I was out here Tuesday morning with Hope, and there was nothing unusual then."

As much as he hated to alarm her, Tony couldn't discount the possibility that this had nothing to do with his case. "Is it possible you may have made an enemy, someone you're not aware of? How about a noncustodial parent who hasn't been allowed to pick up his child at day care, or an old boyfriend, or anything else along those lines?"

"The parents and my day-care staff have always worked closely together. Noncustodial parents haven't been a problem for us so far, though I know from reading the newspaper that they can be. And I have no boyfriends." Amanda shook her head. "This is from the kidnappers," she said. "I can feel it."

"What you feel is fear. It's natural, but you can't afford to jump to conclusions because of it," Tony answered calmly. "Do you have a camera?" He'd used up all his own film. "I'd like a photo of this." Tony watched her step inside the house. She was still too close for him to be able to plant the bug. The windowsill would pick up too much outside noise and interference.

She came out a moment later holding a Polaroid camera. "Moms always have cameras, but never enough film. There are two shots left."

Tony snapped off the shots. He slipped the prints into his jacket pocket trying not to notice the bug he also had in there, waiting to be placed in her house at the first opportunity. "Why don't you go on with your morning schedule? I'll follow up on this and do some investigating on my own this morning."

"Let me know if you find any leads to the creep who did this, okay?"

"You've got it."

Tony left her home, headed down the street, parked behind some trees and waited. Moments later, Amanda drove by. Tony followed her into town, staying well back so she wouldn't notice him. Once Amanda was inside the day-care center, he turned around and wheeled the truck down an alley. Hidden from view, he stepped into some gray overalls marked with the logo of a courier service he'd invented to complete the disguise. After posting a sign on the side of his truck with the service's name, he drove down the street from the day-care center and settled back to wait. The only lead he wanted to pursue right now was Amanda herself. Instinct told him she was somehow the key to all this.

He made himself comfortable, leaning back against the seat. Surveillance. It had been a while since he'd done this type of work, but he had no intention of letting Amanda out of his sight. Sooner or later, someone would tip his hand.

AMANDA GAZED FROM her office window at the toddlers playing outside, but found her thoughts drifting to Tony. He was so alone and desperate in his search for his daughter! That made him vulnerable. But when that happened to a man like Tony, it generally only served to make him more dangerous. Although it was difficult for her to think of him as a violent man, judging from what she'd heard and from what she'd seen of him, she couldn't afford to lower her guard around him for even a minute.

Leaving the confines of her office, Amanda walked outside. Every once in a while, she really needed to get away from the paperwork and be with the kids. As she entered the playground, a little blond-haired boy with big blue eyes walked up to her, dragging a small athletic bag.

Amanda crouched as he approached. "Hello, Brian," she said softly.

He smiled broadly. "Hi! I found this, and Mrs. Brown said to bring it to you since it has your name on it."

"Really?" she said, her curiosity piqued since she had never owned an athletic bag. "Let me take a look."

As Brian pushed it in front of her, Amanda saw the tag. Strangely enough, it did have her name on it, neatly hand lettered in capital letters. "Where did you find it?"

"Over there," he said, pointing toward the swings. "By the tree. If you don't want it, can I have it?"

"We'll see, okay?"

Brian glanced over his shoulder, hearing one of the children calling out to him, then smiled at Amanda. "Gotta go, okay?"

"Have fun!" Amanda picked up the bag, noting how light it was. It wasn't hers, and she couldn't recall ever having seen it at the center. With so much going on around here these days, there was no way she was going to risk opening it in front of the kids. Carrying it by the handle, she returned to her office, trying to ignore the prickly sensation at the back of her neck.

Amanda set the blue-and-white bag on her desk, unable to decide whether or not to call the police, when a soft sound captured her attention. Leaning forward, she heard a muted ticking coming from within the bag.

Just then, Bernice came into her office and Amanda jumped. "Hi. Sorry I surprised you. I just—"

"Have a fire drill right now!" Amanda interrupted. "Make sure all the kids are out of the building!"

"What—"

"Just do it!" Amanda stepped away from the bag, grabbing the phone simultaneously. Fear gripped her as she dialed the emergency number.

"I may have a bomb on the premises," Amanda said quickly. "Send someone over to Los Tesoros Day School *now!*"

Chapter Five

From his vantage point in the pickup, Tony saw children being led quickly out of the day-care center. Picking up the binoculars beside him, he noticed the anxious expressions on the adults' faces. This was no ordinary fire drill.

He hurriedly left the truck and jogged down the street. As he reached the crowd of preschoolers and staff gathered in the parking lot, Tony glanced around for Amanda. She was nowhere to be seen.

Anxiously he rushed past the children and adults and made his way to Amanda's office. He found her there seconds later, pushing a tall file cabinet toward the window. "What's going on?"

Amanda noted his uniform, but there was no time to comment. "A bomb," she replied, and gestured to the athletic bag on the desk. "I have no idea how powerful it is or how long we've got, but I intend to block the window with everything I can find. This is a crowded neighborhood. It's not just my kids I'm worried about."

"I'll take care of it. Go."

She looked at him with a determined gaze. "I'm not going anywhere. Help me or get out of my way."

"If it is a bomb, you could be turning that file cabinet into a missile. Leave it where it is." Tony stepped around the file cabinet, maneuvered past the corner of the desk, and stopped in front of the athletic bag. "Where did it come from?"

"It was discovered outside. One of the kids brought it to me. My name is on it."

Tony peered inside a portion of the zipper that had worked open. "It doesn't seem to have any obvious booby traps, like a wire attached to the zipper. I need a flashlight and a small mirror."

Amanda reached into her purse and retrieved her compact and a penlight. "Will these do?"

"Perfectly." Tony slid the light inside the bag, then angled the small compact mirror.

As he studied the contents of the bag, a man wearing an armored vest and helmet, visor up, came into the room. The bomb-squad officer, with a name tag announcing he was Baca, glanced at Tony in surprise.

"Ramos, what the heck are you doing here?" Baca demanded in a gravelly whisper. "And what's with the get-up?"

"I was on my way to a costume party, when I was suddenly invited here," Tony answered sharply.

"He's helping me," Amanda added.

Tony stepped away from the bag. "Relax, Baca. It's a hoax."

"Since when did you become an expert?" Officer Baca snapped, moving around Tony to take a look for himself.

"It's obvious, unless you think an alarm clock, three wooden dowels painted red and a hand-lettered sign that says 'Boom' is the real thing."

After studying the bag's contents with his own curved mirror, the officer removed his helmet. "You're right. But you shouldn't have opened the bag. You're not the Bureau's golden boy anymore, Ramos. Far from it." Baca glanced down at the athletic bag. "I hate crap like this. We've got better things to do with our time. What's your part in this?"

"I'm working for Ms. Vila on an unrelated matter," Tony replied, wishing Amanda would stop glowering at him. It wasn't his fault Baca had recognized him. He'd tried to come anonymously.

Baca stared coldly at Tony. "I won't have you interfering with my investigation of this incident. If you do, I'll throw you in jail. Is that clear?"

"Get the answers the lady needs, and I'll be glad to stand back," Tony said smoothly.

Officer Baca met Amanda's gaze, holding it. "We'll take this athletic bag to the lab so the techs can check it for evidence. But that'll take several days. You could help me out a great deal by answering some questions."

"Let's go outside to my reception area," Amanda suggested. "I'd rather not sit next to that bag, harmless or not."

Baca smiled, nodding his understanding. "Not a bad idea at all."

Amanda led the way to the adjoining room. After reaching it, Tony and Officer Baca stood glaring at one another. "Don't you have something to do?" Baca demanded sharply.

"If you're questioning my client, I should be here. I may be able to give you answers she can't."

"No doubt, but I'm only interested in the truth."

Tony glanced at Amanda. She was okay now, though furious that his involvement in something connected to the day-care center would now be known. With a stone-cold look at the cop, Tony strode out of the room.

AMANDA ANSWERED Baca's questions as calmly as she could, but the phony bomb had rattled her. Although she was certain the kidnappers were behind it, she couldn't figure out why, and that worried her even more. But of course, she couldn't mention them to the police.

"Someone wanted to frighten you, Ms. Vila. That leaves only two possibilities. You have an enemy, despite what you may think, or someone is trying to create a diversion. Our records indicate you've had other problems lately. You reported a suspicious car here yesterday and there was vandalism at your home last night. Are you sure there's nothing else you can tell me?''

"What would all this divert me from?"

"The real target. Maybe a noncustodial parent did this hoping he could snatch his kid in the confusion, or that his kid might be moved to another center where security isn't so good."

She jumped to her feet. "I never considered that, but I'm going to take a head count right now."

"I'll go with you."

All the children, including Hope, were soon accounted for, and Amanda felt a flood of relief. "Everyone's here and safe."

"I'd still advise you to stay alert," Baca said, taking her aside. "The watcher in the car that you reported yesterday could be tied in to this. I'll ask for patrols to be increased in this area."

"I appreciate that." Amanda considered telling him about the sandbox message, but uncertain if the kidnappers were behind that, decided to remain quiet. For now, she'd trust Tony to follow up on it. "Is there anything else you need?"

"I'd like to speak to your staff members individually. Is there someplace private where I can interview them?"

"The staff lounge is at the end of the hall. I'll have my assistant arrange to have each of them meet you there."

"Excellent idea."

Amanda made the arrangements with Bernice, then went into her office. Tony was there, standing by her desk, waiting. "How did it go?" he asked.

"He thinks it may be the work of a noncustodial parent," she answered. "But you and I know differently."

"I'm still not convinced this has anything to do with the kidnappers," Tony said. "They have nothing to gain from drawing attention to themselves."

"In that case, maybe I should tell the officer about the message in the sandbox."

Tony considered it. "That's up to you, but I'd advise against it. The more they poke around, the more there's a chance of their spooking the kidnappers."

"All right. I'll keep quiet about it, providing you'll keep digging into it."

"I will. Don't worry. This type of thing is meant to annoy, not to do any damage."

"Oh, it'll do damage," she argued. "This kind of publicity can ruin my business."

"You have an enemy, Amanda, whether you like it or not."

"Maybe someone hates the fact that you're around. Officer Baca certainly did." Amanda returned to her desk.

Tony stiffened as if she'd struck him, but his voice remained calm and controlled. "If I'm the reason this happened, I'll get to the bottom of it. But this time I don't think so."

"This time?" Amanda repeated, puzzled. "What happened before?"

"Some officers had a theory that my wife's accident and my daughter's kidnapping were caused by someone who wanted to get back at me."

Amanda felt her stomach tighten. This man carried enough nightmares for a lifetime. But any sympathy she might have felt vanished when she saw the dark, deadly intent in his eyes.

"You're hiding something important, Amanda," he said. "We can't find the truth until you start to trust me."

"The police don't trust you, and according to community members, you're a vigilante. You can't deny your lifestyle lends itself to more questions than answers. And every time we've met so far, it's been disastrous for me. How can you expect me to have faith in you?'' She shook her head.

"You'll do what you think is right, but there are a few more things for you to consider first. Your precious day-care center is being threatened in a major way, and unless you're straight with me, I have no chance of stopping whoever is doing this to you. There's also another matter to take into account. If I'm right and these incidents aren't related to the kidnappers, the ones making the demands are bound to get nervous and tighten their grip when they hear what's been going on. Then we'll be at war on two fronts, with everything to lose. By being honest with me, you'll at least give us a fighting chance.''

"I've been honest,'' she said. "I have no idea who's behind any of this. If I did, I'd tell you. I want this to be over just as badly as you do.''

"Maybe, but you *are* keeping something back, and I'll find out what it is, with or without your cooperation.'' Tony turned and strode from the room.

Amanda watched Tony leave, then gathering her courage, she went into the reception area to meet with Bernice. All the phone lines were ringing. Bernice glanced at her. "The backlash has already started. News travels fast.''

"I'll split the calls with you,'' Amanda said and returned to her desk.

Time dragged by as parents and members of the press called in for the story. By the time five o'clock came, Amanda was exhausted, but satisfied that she'd managed a fair amount of damage control. Only one student was being withdrawn from the center—the other parents were reassured, at least for now.

"I'm going to pick up Hope and go home,'' she told Bernice at last.

As they drove home, Amanda noticed that Hope seemed undaunted by the events of the day. To her, it had only been one of many games she'd played. A fire drill was routine, nothing to get excited about. Amanda found herself envying her daughter's innocence.

After a quiet dinner and an hour playing together, she and Hope settled in front of the small television set in Hope's room, and Amanda held her daughter as they watched a cartoon. She closed her eyes and started to drift off to sleep, when the sound of a vehicle pulling up startled her into alertness. Leaving Hope still enthralled with the cartoons, Amanda went into the living room, turned on the front light, and pulled back the curtain slightly from her newly repaired window. A van with a TV repair sign was parked in her driveway, and a man wearing blue coveralls and a baseball cap was walking up to the front door, toolbox in hand.

"Company, Mommy?" Hope had come into the room in her pajamas and turned to run toward the front door.

"Don't open that," Amanda warned quickly. "It's a TV repairman, but I didn't call one."

Amanda had recognized the name of the company emblazoned on the side of the van, but the impromptu arrival made her nervous. "Go back to your room, Peanut. I'll be in shortly to finish watching cartoons with you."

"Mommy, can he fix my TV? People look green."

"I'll take care of that myself. Now go on, please."

Amanda placed the chain on the door, then opened it just a crack. "Can I help you?"

"Sure you can," said a familiar voice.

Amanda stared at the low-slung bill of the baseball cap that obscured his face. "Tony?"

"The one and only. Now let me in, and let's make this look good. I'm playing your handy-dandy TV repairman."

Amanda took the chain off the door and let him in. "What on earth do you think you're doing?"

"We both decided that we shouldn't be seen together, remember? But we still have things to do. After today, in particular, we need a chance to have an uninterrupted talk."

Hope came out to the hall, paused uncertainly, then smiled broadly and ran to Tony. "Hi, Tony!"

Hope took Tony's hand. "Are you really a TV man? Will you make the people not green?"

"Sure," Tony said, allowing Hope to lead him by the hand.

A shadow passed over Tony's face as he thought of his own missing daughter. "You're a lucky woman, Amanda." Tony crouched by the TV set and opened his toolbox as Hope ran out into the hall to pick up a doll she'd left on the floor out there. "You know, everytime I look at Hope, I can't help wondering what Carmen looks like today."

Amanda felt a chill run through her and, with effort, suppressed a shudder. Grateful that Tony's attention was on the TV controls, she struggled to gather her wits.

"No, that's even worse!" Hope wailed, running back into the room. "Now they're orange!"

Amanda walked around Tony, pushing him to one side. "Allow me, Mr. Fix-It." A moment later, the colors were correctly adjusted.

Tony gave her a sheepish smile. "I've never been good with television sets."

"Do you like popcorn?" Hope asked Tony. "Maybe Mommy would fix us some, then we can watch cartoons!"

"I love popcorn," Tony said, laughing, then glanced at Amanda.

"You just had dinner!" Amanda smiled at Hope. "How can you be hungry again?"

Hope shrugged. "Popcorn's *good.*"

"Okay, I'll fix some. Then after the cartoons, it's time for you to go to sleep. Agreed?"

Hope nodded. "Okay, Mommy."

Tony picked up a bear puppet and began to talk to Hope in a deep voice. Hope squealed with laughter as Tony pretended to have the puppet hoard her toys and hide them beneath the bed.

Amanda watched them for a moment. Her child was safe with Tony. She'd never have imagined him so gentle and loving as he was right now with her daughter. Confident she was leaving Hope in good hands, she stepped out of the room and returned a short time later holding a small bowl filled with popcorn. "Here we go, you two."

Tony made the hand puppet tickle Hope as she reached for the snack, and the little girl tried to tickle him back, laughing and squirming. Tony picked up Hope, then lay back on the floor, holding her aloft while she giggled and tried to reach down to him with her tiny arms.

Amanda watched them, unsure of her feelings. She should have been happy that Hope was having so much fun, but she'd never realized until now how much Hope was missing by not having a father around the house. She'd never roughhoused with Hope, nor even suspected her daughter would enjoy it.

Amanda sat down to watch them, and her eyes soon focused on Tony. The muscles of his chest rippled as he kept Hope up in the air. Longing ribboned through her. She forced her gaze away immediately. This was ridiculous. Tony was the last person on earth who should have been able to rekindle her desire. She wanted the kind of traditional family life she'd never known as a child, and this man was a perfect example of what to avoid in a potential parent and mate—unpredictable, potentially dangerous, and altogether too good at concealing his true feelings.

As Tony rolled to his side and gently placed Hope down, a thick roll of money fell out of his pocket. Amanda stared in shock at the rubber-banded stash. If the bills were all one hundreds like the one on the outside of the roll, there must be thousands in that bundle!

Tony noticed the look on her face and quickly shoved the money back into his pocket. "I hate writing checks. I always deal in cash."

As Amanda remembered what Bernice had told her, questions rose again in her mind. Tony seemingly hadn't been employed for a long time. Where would he get that much money just to carry around?

When Hope settled in before the television, popcorn in hand, Amanda quietly led Tony down the hall. "Now tell me what you wanted to discuss with me," she said, waving him to the sofa.

Tony leaned back, stretching out his legs. "Although I don't expect a repeat of the bomb incident, I think you should consider hiring a security guard. He wouldn't have to be in uniform if you're worried about how the parents will react."

Amanda weighed the suggestion for a moment, then nodded. "You're right. I have to make sure no one threatens the safety of my kids. Can you recommend somebody?"

Tony nodded and wrote down a number. "This is the man's home phone. I've known him for years. I can't remember his firm's name, but he's a former cop and he'll give you the best for the money. Joey's got an excellent reputation with both law-enforcement people and the business community."

"I'll call him later tonight, after spending some time with my daughter. We both look forward to our evenings, when I can read to her or we can play."

"I didn't mean to interfere with your family life," he said quickly. "I'll tell you what. I'll make the phone call for you right now and set it up. You can work out the details with Joey later tonight or tomorrow."

"Fine. I better go check on Hope now. I get nervous when she's too quiet," she added with a ghost of a smile.

Tony's cellular rang as Amanda started down the hall. She stopped and turned around, but he smiled and nodded, letting her know everything was okay.

Amanda stopped in a doorway just out of sight. She hated nosy people, but circumstances were forcing her hand. She needed to know what Tony was up to.

Amanda heard her name, but Tony's voice was too low for her to make out the rest. Edging out, she crept back down the hall.

"She lived in California? That's interesting. So it may not be local talent at all," he said.

Amanda felt her temper rise. He was checking *her* out? How dare he! He should be concentrating on the kidnappers, not wasting his time on her.

Tony suddenly turned around and caught sight of Amanda. Trying to act casual, she shrugged and walked past him to the kitchen. She would never have made it as a spy.

He came to look for her moments later. Hearing his footsteps, she met him in the hall and returned with him to the living room.

"If you want to know what I'm doing," he said, taking a seat across from her on the sofa, "why don't you just ask me instead of trying to eavesdrop. It would be simpler and far more effective."

"Only if you told me the truth," Amanda countered. "That doesn't seem to come easily to you."

"You're the one holding back."

"And that's your excuse for invading my privacy by checking up on me?"

"Why does that bother you? Do you have something to hide?"

"No. It's just a colossal waste of your time. There are far more important things you could be doing."

"I'd be a fool not to find out all I could about you. And I'd be willing to bet you've asked someone about me."

Remembering her talk with Bernice, Amanda looked away. "I didn't go to such major lengths as you apparently did."

"Probably because you didn't have the right source." Tony smiled. "Ease up, Amanda. I'm on your side even if you aren't sure you want me there. I play to win and that's exactly the kind of ally you need. We will win, Amanda, believe that."

The timbre of his voice sent vibrations throughout her body. He reached out, caressing her face with his palm. His tenderness wound past her defenses, melting away her resistance.

"I'm not the monster you think I am," he said softly.

Amanda felt the warmth of his palm searing through her. His eyes seemed to be pleading with her for understanding. Instinctively she leaned into his palm.

He sucked in his breath. "You're so incredibly beautiful."

When he pulled her into his arms, she didn't resist. She wanted to lose herself in the warmth of his embrace, to take comfort from his strength.

"Mommy?" Hope's voice echoed down the hall.

Hearing her daughter's voice, Amanda jumped back. What on earth was she doing? Dear heaven, the man could scramble her thinking in no time flat. "I've got to take care of my daughter."

She strode quickly down the hall hoping he wouldn't notice that in reality she was running away from him. She didn't want to deal with the questions her own feelings continued to raise in her mind.

Amanda stayed with Hope for more than an hour, playing a favorite game, then reading bedtime stories to her. When she went out to get her daughter a drink of water, she heard Tony on the phone with the security guard, arranging for his services. When Amanda finally turned the last page, Hope's eyes were heavy and she blinked sleepily.

"Mommy, will I ever have a daddy like other kids?"

"You have a daddy, Peanut. But he works very hard and that's why he doesn't come to visit very often."

"My daddy's not like Angie's daddy or Teri's. He doesn't like to play. I like Tony better. He even likes to dress up funny."

Amanda almost burst out laughing. She could just imagine the story going around that Tony liked to "dress up funny and play pretend." "You mustn't tell anyone that Tony came here dressed up like a repairman, Peanut, okay? It's got to be our secret."

"Mommy, are you in trouble?"

Amanda felt her mouth go dry. She'd never lied to her child before. "Don't worry, Peanut. There are some grown-up things I have to take care of. Everything's okay."

"Will Tony help?"

"I hope so."

"After you finish, can he be my daddy?"

"Now that's an idea," said a masculine voice from the door.

Amanda turned around and glared at him. "No, but Tony could stay our friend, providing he learns to behave himself."

"Is Tony naughty?"

Tony grinned. "I can be. But your mom sets me straight real fast."

Amanda stared at Tony. *"Do you mind?"*

"Good night, Hope." With a chuckle, Tony turned and went back to the living room.

Hope looked at Amanda. "Mommy, you *do* like him! I can tell. You're just teasing."

Amanda smiled at Hope. "Let's keep that our secret, okay?"

"Okay." Hope buried her head deeper into the pillow. "'Night, Mommy."

Amanda met Tony back in the living room. "In the future, I'd appreciate it if you didn't interfere when I'm talking to my daughter in private."

Tony felt a stabbing pain somewhere around his heart. If she only knew how little privacy she'd have from now on. He'd left a listening device just beneath the molded edge of her kitchen cabinet. With that in place he'd be able to hear any conversations she had in either the kitchen or the living room. Earlier today, after the bomb threat, he'd placed one on the bottom of her office desk.

"I guess I'd feel that way, too, if she were mine. Some things are meant to be shared only by family."

"Did you get in touch with your friend who owns the security service?" Amanda asked, obviously anxious to get down to business.

"He'll have someone there tomorrow. They'll cover the day-care center as long as you need them. The man he sends will leave a list of references for you, so you can check out their firm."

"Thanks." Amanda sat down on the sofa. "Now what? Did you figure out a way to get the file the kidnappers wanted?"

"I have it already." He looked away, unwilling to meet her gaze. Amanda liked playing by the rules, and that was something he seldom did.

"What have you done?" she asked softly.

"What I had to," he said in a clipped tone.

"I'm not trying to pass judgment on you. I just need to know. Everything you do impacts me directly as long as I'm involved."

Tony took a deep breath. "Let's just say I made the necessary moves. No matter what my relationship with Raymond is, I can't afford to work with the FBI. What I'm doing is more in line with working around them. I've always suspected a leak," he said, explaining briefly. "I can't afford to risk it now."

"Yet you still miss being an agent, don't you?" Amanda observed. "It seems like you invested a lot of yourself in your career. It couldn't have been easy for you to walk away.''

"I didn't walk away. I was forced out," Tony admitted, his voice cold and hard. Amanda could read more into him than he believed possible. That knowledge bothered him. "I called in sick often, following up leads in my search for Carmen. Finally the Bureau chief gave me a choice. Either stop searching for my daughter or leave. That discussion got out of hand fast. Let's just say that he lost face in front of quite a few agents. When I quit, he took my resignation gladly."

"Maybe someday all that can be straightened out."

"No. There's no turning back. Not anymore." Tony glanced at his watch, then the phone. "I really thought you'd be contacted again tonight, but it doesn't look like that's going to happen. I better go now, otherwise my cover as TV repairman won't hold."

After a quick goodbye, Tony walked out and, as nonchalantly as possible, bent over and activated a receiver/recorder inside the thick hedge bordering her home. He did it in one smooth motion and simply continued on into the van.

The black demons from his past were always there, molding him, forcing him along paths he would never have walked down on his own. He glanced in the rearview mirror at the warm lights of Amanda's home as he drove away. He was tired of being alone, of having to lie and trick people all the time. But he'd been doing this for so long now— first in undercover work, then on his own—that he wasn't sure he could be any different.

Slamming his hand against the steering wheel, he welcomed the night that crowded in around him. Amanda was of the day, a woman who thrived in the sunlight. These days he was more comfortable in the shadows of darkness. It was there he belonged.

AMANDA SAT ON HER SOFA, working absently on a crewel design she'd been given two Christmases ago. Someday she'd finish it.

Hope was asleep. The house was quiet. And for once, she shut out all the disturbing thoughts that circled in her mind. Then a car turned into the driveway.

Hearing Bernice's familiar knock, five quick raps followed by two, Amanda answered the door. "Come in. Is everything all right?"

"When I was driving to the supermarket, I saw a TV repair van pulling out of here. If your set's on the blink, you're welcome to borrow my portable. Shall I bring it over after I put my groceries away?"

Amanda started to tell Bernice the truth, but then stopped. The more Bernice knew, the greater the possibility that someone else could find out that Tony had been here. Amanda decided to protect Bernice as best she could. "It's okay now. It wasn't a big deal. Hope was kind of upset because the people were green."

Bernice laughed. "Well, I can see how that could get annoying."

Amanda led Bernice to the kitchen. "How about some cocoa?"

"Sounds good to me. The groceries will be okay for a little longer." Bernice opened her purse. "By the way, I went to the library today. I looked for stories about Tony Ramos written at the time his daughter was kidnapped. One article in particular caught my attention." She slid it across the table toward Amanda.

Amanda read the headline. Local Fed Fired—Excessive Force Charges Dropped. She scanned the article quickly, aware that the report conflicted with what Tony had told her. The story claimed Tony had attacked a fellow agent and been fired from the Bureau.

"This doesn't sound right," Amanda said.

"In what way?"

"It seems to be more innuendo than anything else. Notice how the reporter fails to mention any names except Tony's? And while he says that his information came from reliable sources, it's not confirmed by anyone in an official capacity."

"The reporter was protecting his informants," Bernice answered. "Don't you think it sounds plausible, though, knowing what you do about Tony?"

Amanda didn't answer. Tony was unpredictable and stubborn, but he didn't seem the kind who used violence unless someone used it on him first. But if the article was accurate, then it raised other important questions. If Tony had lied to her about that—something said in conversation and really not that important in the overall scheme of things—what else was he lying about? The more she learned about Tony's past, the harder it was to trust him. Still, just being around Tony made her feel more alive, more of a woman, than she had in years.

With a heavy heart, Amanda slid the article back to Bernice. "Thanks for showing this to me."

"Keep it. I have a feeling you'll need it as a reminder from time to time." Bernice rinsed out her cup. "I better go."

Amanda walked her friend to the door and said goodnight. After locking up, she went down the hall and listened to the soft breathing coming from her daughter's room. Amanda peered inside, and saw that Hope was still sleeping peacefully. She was exhausted after a full day of playing at the day-care center and then with Tony. Remembering her daughter's words, Amanda wondered if Hope was starting to get too attached to Tony. The danger existed—for both of them. As nice as it would have been for Hope to have a real, stay-at-home daddy, Amanda knew it couldn't be a man like Tony. He loved his own daughter and seemed good with hers, but he wasn't a domesticated, family-man type. Ignoring the protests of her heart, Amanda went to her empty room.

Chapter Six

Amanda stood at the kitchen counter, struggling to come awake as she filled the small coffee machine with water and then turned to stir Hope's oatmeal. Nightmares had kept her up all night. Now it was morning and time to get breakfast for her daughter. Unfortunately, all she wanted to do was crawl back into bed.

Hearing the telephone ring, she walked into the living room, bypassing the phone in the kitchen. It was probably Bernice needing a ride to work. Her car was, at best, temperamental. Amanda glanced down at the caller ID. The screen indicated a private caller. That meant it wasn't Bernice. Steeling herself, she picked up the phone.

Amanda immediately heard the electronically altered voice. Perhaps it was the early morning hour or the silence of the house that made the voice even more ominous, but it took all her willpower to keep her own voice steady. "I know it's early, dear, so you better take notes," the caller said, as if speaking to a child. "We've decided you're going to be our courier."

"Me?" Amanda's mouth went dry.

"That's right. *You.* Now listen carefully. You're to get the file from Ramos and bring it to Las Tiendas Mall at noon today. Go to the west side. There's a corridor right next to the rest rooms. Bring Ramos's cellular phone with you and wait there. We'll contact you." The line went dead.

Amanda placed the phone back on the cradle just as Hope ran into the room. "Good morning, Peanut," she managed, trying to sound cheerful.

"Mommy, a pretty lady said I can have a new daddy."

Amanda groaned softly. "It was just a dream, Peanut."

"No, Mommy! She's my angel. She said it when I was sleeping."

Amanda smiled. A few months ago, Bernice had given Hope a print of a guardian angel guiding two children over a bridge. For a while, Hope's interest in angels had soared, but then, like most children, she'd gone on to other interests.

"She likes you, Mommy. She told me."

"I'm glad." Amanda worried that perhaps this was Hope's way of coping with what had been happening. Maybe her daughter wasn't as oblivious to the dangers surrounding them as she'd thought.

"Did she tell you who your new daddy will be?" Amanda almost hated the trick question, but if Hope mentioned Tony, then she'd know her daughter was using her imagination to deal with the situation.

"No, Mommy, but she said we would be happy."

Amanda breathed a sigh of relief and went into the kitchen with her daughter. It had just been a dream after all. She placed a bowl of oatmeal on the table in front of Hope. "It's the way you like it, with fresh strawberries."

Amanda picked up the phone. She would have to be careful what she said in front of her daughter, but she had to call Tony and let him know what had happened.

Tony's groggy voice greeted her. "Ramos here."

"Good morning," Amanda said. "Hope and I are just having breakfast, but I wanted to let you know that I received a call this morning. The number had been blocked, though."

"So much for tracing it, then. Any instructions for the drop?" he asked, instantly alert.

"Yes. Noon at Las Tiendas Mall. They want *me* to bring it," she answered, measuring her words carefully.

"You mean they want you to deliver the file?"

"Yes. We'll have to meet. I'll call from work to discuss it."

"Take the tape with you. I'll want to hear it. Did the caller ID come up with a number?"

"No. It just said private number, that's all."

"Okay. See you shortly, then."

"Who was that, Mommy?"

"Just business, Peanut."

Amanda replaced the tape with a fresh one and slipped the used one in her purse as she watched Hope finish her breakfast. Looking forward to another day at school, Hope began chattering about the games she'd be playing today with the other kids. More determined than ever to protect her daughter from danger, Amanda mentally prepared herself to face the day.

By the time Amanda arrived at the day-care office, Tony was already waiting, disguised as a maintenance man. His hair had been powdered to look almost white, and he was wearing blue workmen's pants and shirt with a tool belt and harness.

Despite his change in appearance, his demeanor hadn't altered. He was pacing back and forth in the reception area like a caged tiger.

Bernice gave Amanda a frustrated look. "Look what the ill winds blew in," she said, cocking her head toward Tony. "The maintenance man."

"We're wasting time," he growled, staring at Amanda.

As Amanda's gaze drifted over him, her pulse began to race. Despite his change of hair color, he looked spectacular. His broad shoulders and flat stomach were accentuated by the military-style shirt, making him look fit and ready for physical action. His day-old beard gave him a rugged look she found appealing.

Forcing herself to ignore her body's instinctive reaction, Amanda unlocked her office door and led him inside. "What kind of plan have you come up with?" she asked, shutting the door as he crossed the room.

"First, I'd like to hear the tape." Tony placed a small tape recorder on her desk. "I brought this in case you don't have a player here at the center."

Amanda took the microcassette from her pocket and placed it into the machine. They both listened to the exchange that had occurred earlier. "I've got to tell you, I wasn't prepared for that at all," she admitted after the recording ended.

"I could hear it in your voice." He exhaled softly. "Do you have a speakerphone?"

"Sure."

"I think we need to have Raymond in on this, and it'll be easier for us to coordinate if he's on the speaker while we talk."

Amanda dialed the phone number Tony gave her, then when Raymond answered, pressed the button to put him on the speaker. Tony quickly recapped the situation.

"I was afraid something like this would come up," Raymond said. "I'm about to leave on another case. I've got to back up another agent when he makes an arrest today. I'm sorry I can't help you. If you'd agree to let me tell the boss what's going on—"

"You know that won't work. Forget it. I'll handle this on my own."

"If you change your mind, let me know. I'll do whatever I can to find someone else to give you backup."

"No chance."

Amanda hung up the phone when their conversation abruptly ended. "Do you think it'll be safe to handle this ourselves?"

"It's not the ideal situation, but we'll be okay. There's no way I'd want anyone else but Raymond involved. We can handle this if we work together. I'll give you my cellular and be your backup. We'll play it by ear, but I'll be the one who gets . . . let's say creative, if it's necessary. Agreed?"

"I don't know. . . ."

"I've got more to lose than you do if something goes wrong, so believe me, I won't take unnecessary risks. If I blow it, they won't be back. I think this is a test of sorts, a trial run. They want to see if we'll both play by their rules. They'll be watching, giving you last-minute instructions and seeing how we handle it."

"No way are you planning to play by anyone's rules except your own, Tony. I know you that well already. What have you got up your sleeve?"

Tony reached into a pouch of his leather tool belt. "This is a two-way radio. I have another one. We'll stay in touch. I'll follow you to the drop site and when they show, I'll tail them. With luck, your part in this will be over by this evening."

"Even if you catch the kidnappers, they still may not tell you where your daughter is."

His eyes turned the color of a moonless night. "They'll tell me everything, Amanda. Believe me."

She did. Tony's expression was now cold and deadly, and she fought to suppress the shiver she felt building at the base of her spine. She almost pitied the kidnappers when Tony finally got his hands on them.

"You won't see me again this morning, but if anything comes up, call my pager number. I'll get to a phone. And I'll be at the rendezvous point. You can count on it."

Amanda glanced down at the cellular and the two way radio. Fear slammed into her. "I wasn't cut out for this kind of work. I'm a teacher, not a spy."

"Are you frightened?" he asked softly, reassuringly.

"Terrified," she admitted.

He gave her a quirky half smile. "I think what you need is a distraction."

Without warning, he pulled her into his arms, then lowered his mouth to hers. His kiss was hard and hungry. Her body turned into molten wax and her knees threatened to buckle. She could feel the barely leashed power in him. Need, powerful and primitive, demanded she yield to this man. She had to fight to keep her willpower from shattering under the gentle assault.

"I won't let anything happen to you. These are *my* enemies. I'll deal with them," he whispered in her ear.

Amanda stepped away, suppressing yet another shiver that this time his heated breath had sent spiraling through her. The steel-hard determination she'd come to associate with Tony alarmed her. She'd always hated violence, but the underlying darkness she sensed within Tony was the closest she'd ever really come to it. Up to now, the violence in her world had consisted mostly of three-year-olds fighting for a toy.

She took a deep breath. "I can do whatever's necessary," she said, trying to bolster her own courage.

"I know you can, Mandy."

Amanda was startled by the nickname. "My mother was the last person to call me that," she said, smiling, remembering better days.

"It suits you somehow. Do you mind if I call you that?"

"No," she answered.

"Good."

As he started out the door, she heard him whisper two words. A special warmth ribboned through her, making her heart race. There was no way to be sure, but she could have sworn he'd said "My Mandy."

AMANDA ARRIVED at the shopping center a bit before noon. Walking confidently—she'd read somewhere that to appear weak invited being victimized—she entered the corridor the kidnappers had selected.

Minutes ticked by slowly. Tense, she kept alert, but she didn't spot anyone who looked particularly interested in her. Amanda walked back into the recesses of the narrow hall, wondering how long they planned to make her wait. She leaned back against the wall, grateful that at least for now her own child was safe. As the noon crowd grew in size and volume, she heard the cellular ring. Amanda opened the handset quickly and answered it.

"You've done well," the electronically altered voice told her. "Now go to the east side of the mall. There's a noisy group of people gathered around a karaoke singer. In the corner to the singer's left is a big planter containing a phony ficus tree. When you're sure nobody's watching, set the file beside the tree trunk and walk away. *Don't look back.*"

"But what if—"

"We'll worry about the what ifs. All you have to do is follow our instructions."

Amanda heard a click, then the dial tone. She fought the urge to yell in anger at the caller, who was issuing orders like a drill sergeant. Composing herself, she quickly threaded her way through the crowd. If only Tony would catch these sick people and get them out of their lives!

The music led Amanda to the singer, who was belting out the worst rendition of an old Beatles tune she'd ever heard. Despite the off-key wailing, everyone around Amanda appeared to be having a good time. For one brief moment, Amanda smiled, envying their carefree attitudes.

Slipping through the gathering, she approached a realistic-looking, ten-foot tree nestled in the corner. Praying that a synthetic leaf blight would be passed on to the kidnappers, she laid the file in the planter. Though sorely tempted, Amanda resisted the urge to glance back. She simply walked away. Now it was up to Tony.

Amanda walked into the nearest store, then headed for the ladies' room, a small cubicle designed for only one person. She locked the door and waited for Tony to contact her. Only a few minutes had passed before she heard the beep on her radio.

"I need your help," Tony said quickly. "Two women walked by the planter at the same time. Either one could have made the pickup. One's heading your way now. Come to the front of the store and follow her. She's about your height, with short black hair and a floppy hat. She's wearing a light blue windbreaker and jeans. She's carrying a big tote bag. Stay well back, but don't lose her. Of course, if you see anything that indicates she's the one who made the pickup, contact me immediately."

"I'm on my way."

Amanda left the rest room and stopped outside the store entrance, pretending to examine the window display. A moment later, the woman Tony had described hurried past, moving around the shopping carts lining the center aisle. Amanda stayed with her, alert and cautious, ignoring the way her stomach did flip-flops. If this was the person they were after, Amanda wouldn't let her get away.

TONY KEPT HIS EYES on the woman ahead of him. She'd been closest to the planter and was juggling three large plastic clothing sacks. Any one of them could easily conceal the file. If she was the woman who'd made the pickup, as he suspected, the kidnappers had chosen well. The lady was about as nondescript as anyone could get.

As the suspect stopped by one of the store windows, Tony hung back. He didn't want her to see his reflection in the glass. Just then someone bumped him from behind. He turned his head for only a second, but when he glanced back, the woman was gone.

Tony hurried toward the small shoe store with the display she'd been looking at and wandered inside as if browsing for bargains. After a brief moment, he found his suspect in the back. She was alone, still carrying the three shopping bags.

The woman turned around, coolly met his gaze, and then walked right past him. He'd been made. He followed, giving her plenty of room, but she kept glancing back, searching for him in the crowd as they walked through the mall.

Knowing the game was up, Tony hurried forward, ready to force a confrontation. Just then, the woman whirled and raced into the largest store in the mall.

Tony shot after her, losing sight of her for a moment. As she proceeded into the women's-wear department, a security guard suddenly stepped out from behind a column. The man grabbed Tony's arm and, twisting it, threw him against the wall. "Assume the position, buddy," the burly guard snapped, taking Tony's gun. "Whoa. Carrying a gun too. You're in a heap of trouble, mister."

"I don't have time for this," Tony said, pushing abruptly back against the guard, a move meant to give him room to disengage himself, but the guard countered with a quick hand-to-hand combat maneuver that sent Tony against the wall again.

"I'll crack your head open on that wall if you don't settle down," the guard said, his tone low. "Now we don't want to alarm all these nice people by getting blood everywhere, so chill out."

The woman he'd been following stepped out from behind the counter. "Thank you, officer. He's been following me all around the mall."

"I'm on a stakeout," Tony mumbled, aware of the cautious crowd gathering around them. "You're blowing it sky-high for me."

"Yeah, you're a cop, and I'm Prince Charles," the guard retorted.

"Why else would I be carrying a two-way radio and a gun?" Tony countered. "Look in my jacket pocket."

"You're a thief working with a partner," the guard accused, glancing at the radio Tony had indicated.

"If you'll look in that woman's bags, you'll see an unmarked manila envelope. Inside is a file taken from the FBI."

The woman's eyes widened. "That's just not true." She quickly opened all her bags and showed them to the guard. "And look, my purse only has a hairbrush, my wallet and some keys. See for yourself."

"She's telling the truth," the guard said, cuffing Tony and turning him to face the woman.

Tony's gut clenched as he realized that he'd either followed the wrong woman, or she'd somehow passed the file on to someone else.

The lady stepped forward, an angry frown on her face. "I'm not who you think I am," she said. "My husband is the manager of this store. Why would I steal a file from the FBI?"

The woman's indignation seemed sincere and Tony decided he believed her. He turned his head toward the guard, who stood like a rock wall behind him, holding on to one of his arms. "That means my partner is following the right person. She'll need my help. You've got to let me go. Reach into my pocket. My ID and gun permit are in my wallet."

The guard extracted Tony's wallet from his pocket. "All I see is a business card for some P.I. agency that anyone could have made up and your driver's license, and a permit that's so creased and worn, it could be a forgery. We're going to the security office."

"It was an honest mistake," Tony told the woman, giving her an apologetic look and his best smile, hoping he could charm her. "Believe me, I'm after some very dangerous people.'' Tony saw the doubt that still lingered in her eyes. ''If you delay me any longer, you could cost me the chance to find the people who have threatened a family.'' Sometimes the naked truth worked better than anything else, and at the moment, he could think of nothing else to try.

''I don't want to press charges. That would just create bad publicity for the store,'' the woman said calmly, then shifted her gaze to the guard. ''But I don't want him to follow me anymore.''

''No problem, ma'am. He's coming with me. Even if you don't press charges, the mall might.'' He led Tony out of the store, toward the mall's security office.

''Give me a break, will you? My partner could be in deep trouble,'' Tony insisted as they walked past curious shoppers.

''No chance.''

''At least let me use the two-way radio.'' It was a risk—the beeper could go off at precisely the wrong time—but Tony had to let Amanda know that she was following the right suspect.

''If your partner's in danger, tell me where she is. I'll send help.''

Tony shook his head, knowing that his intervention could alert the kidnappers and insure even more trouble.

''That's what I thought you'd say.'' The guard smiled. ''Now sit down while I run a make on you. I'm not taking the cuffs off until I check you out. Make yourself comfortable. We may be here a while.''

Tony shifted, contemplating making a run for it, handcuffs and all.

The guard smiled mirthlessly. ''You're tough, but so am I. Before you reach the door, I'll have you down on the floor.''

Tony remembered the combat moves he'd learned at Quantico, the Bureau's training school. Even with his hands in cuffs, he could do the guard some serious damage. But then he'd face charges that would put him in jail. He'd been there before, but he didn't have the time for that now. Tony remained seated, realizing it was his only logical option. "Get to it, then. Don't waste my time or yours."

AMANDA DIDN'T DARE USE the two-way radio to call Tony. The woman was still ahead, but staying with her was taking all the ingenuity she had. She was certain the woman hadn't spotted her, but at this rate, she wasn't sure how long it would be before the woman disappeared in the crowd.

The woman moved as if she'd been trained to dodge people. She was very careful, stopping abruptly from time to time and checking the area behind her, but so far Amanda was holding her own. She didn't think the woman knew she was following her.

Amanda threaded her way through the coat and sweaters section of a large clothing store, keeping her suspect in sight. Suddenly, the woman turned and sprinted out the side entrance. Amanda rushed after her, but as she neared the door, she slowed down. She could see the woman standing on the sidewalk directly outside.

Amanda moved cautiously, slinking along the wall beside the glass door. She peeked out the door just in time to see a large blue van pulling up. The woman climbed in, and before Amanda could get outside for a look at the license plate, they had wheeled behind a row of cars.

Amanda ran across the street, but the van disappeared around the corner. Mumbling a rarely employed curse, Amanda hastened to follow, in an effort, to relocate the vehicle, but the search was fruitless. She knew then that the matter was far from settled.

Amanda walked back through the mall, glancing around for Tony. Not seeing him anywhere, she tried to raise him on the two-way radio. An unfamiliar voice answered.

Amanda shut it off quickly. Something had gone very wrong. If she'd been following the person who'd picked up the file, what had happened to Tony? They had decided to meet at his pickup if they became separated, so she headed to the prearranged spot. If he was all right, he'd find his way there eventually. If he didn't show up soon, then she'd call Raymond. He'd know what to do.

Amanda walked across the parking lot. Within minutes, she'd located Tony's pickup. She walked briskly toward it, then suddenly froze abruptly. A shadowy figure was crouching by the front fender.

Chapter Seven

Amanda stood and watched for a moment, trying to figure out what the person was doing to the truck. She started forward, staying behind other vehicles as much as she could while she approached.

She needed to get a clearer look before doing anything drastic, but it was definitely suspicious behavior. Gathering her courage, she edged forward slowly, trying to make out the person's face or determine his actions.

Amanda grabbed the shoulder strap of her purse firmly. If he was up to no good, she'd swing the bag right at his face. As heavy as it was, that would at least buy her some time and, of course, she'd let out a scream that would have people rushing to her in seconds.

She crept even closer, ready for action. Then, as if warned by some sixth sense, the figure spun around, reaching underneath his tan jacket.

A heartbeat later, she saw Tony's face. Relief swept through her, and the sudden release of tension almost made her knees buckle. Amanda gratefully eased the death grip she had on her purse. "Relax, it's just me," she said, then glanced down to see the flat tire on Tony's car.

Tony pulled his hand out from under his jacket. "Things got really fouled up." He explained his run-in with the guard. "I have a license for my weapon, otherwise, I would have still been cooling my heels back there." Tony's gaze shifted to the tire. "Then, as soon as he released me, I came out here to this. Looks like my tire's been slashed."

"Are you sure it's not just a flat?" she asked.

"Look for yourself." He pointed to a long slice in the tire's sidewall. "A knife did this. It's a good cautionary method on their part. They found my pickup, and disabled it just in case I planned to follow them. They expected me to do more than just meet their demands. This is getting to be like a giant chess game."

"Between equals?" Amanda asked. "Like two FBI agents?"

"No. If I'm right about the leak within the ranks of the Bureau, this sure doesn't have the Bureau stamp. These people aren't with the Bureau. They're not cops, either, unless I miss my guess. They're just very good at reading me. They did exactly what I would have done if the roles had been reversed."

Amanda felt herself begin to shiver, but she took a deep breath and then proceeded to describe her pursuit of the other woman and the escape in the blue van. Tony reached out and covered her hand with his own. "You did your best. No one can ask for more."

Amanda felt the warmth of his touch reach into her soul. Desire as intoxicating as it was foolish spiraled through her. She struggled to finish her story but didn't pull back her hand. The tenderness of his touch was too powerful a temptation to resist.

"Don't be afraid of them. I *will* beat them at their own game." There was a deadly calm in his voice.

His certainty frightened her. Tony was a man so intent on finding his daughter that he would never stop to consider the damage he might do along the way. At this moment, she was more afraid of him than of them. The kidnappers had only one real hold on her. If they could convince Tony that Hope was his child and not hers, it would threaten the very meaning of her life.

"What's on your mind?" Tony asked.

"I'm worried about the next step. They will take one, won't they?"

Tony looked more determined than ever and assured her he'd be ready, whatever that next move was.

Feeling more confident, Amanda allowed herself to relax somewhat. "Shall I drop you off someplace?" she asked.

Tony glanced at his watch. "I'd appreciate it if you'd give me a lift to the Palace of the Governors. I have some business to do near there and I'm already late. I'll call a garage and have them bring a tire and change this one. I punctured my spare a while back, and I haven't gotten around to fixing it."

Twenty minutes later, Amanda pulled up next to the curb, dropping Tony off where he'd asked. "Here we are."

"Thanks for the ride," Tony said, then walked away.

Amanda watched Tony in her rearview mirror as he strode away, heading into the midst of the crowd around the Indian Market. Trying to find a way around a stalled car in the Plaza, she cut through a narrow street behind two government buildings.

Two figures standing in the shadows at the end of an alley caught her attention as she passed slowly by. Her gaze drifted over the pair, and she suddenly recognized Tony. The man with him was dressed in a well-cut Western suit. A Stetson shielded his face.

Amanda watched the man hand Tony a large envelope. Tony placed it in his jacket pocket and walked away without looking back. Questions filled her mind as Amanda continued down the street. What kind of business did Tony conduct in an alley with someone that well dressed? And what was in that envelope?

Of course these questions made her realize just how little she knew about Tony. There were so many secrets between them! The reality of the situation left her feeling lonely and more than a little frightened. Whatever comfort she might derive from Tony's touch was, at best, a fleeting pleasure, because they lacked what was the foundation of any good relationship—trust. And who was to say that if the secrets were all divulged, they wouldn't find even more insurmountable barriers separating them? Tony was certainly capable of being charming, but the real Tony might be someone she would despise.

By the time she entered the reception area outside her office, Amanda's spirits were at rock bottom. She went past Bernice's desk, aware of her friend's speculative glance.

"I gather things didn't go all that well," Bernice observed, rising and following Amanda into her office.

"They sure didn't. What's been happening here since our big scare?" She motioned Bernice to take a seat.

"Three more parents withdrew their kids. They're sending them to Casa de Los Amigos now."

Amanda tried to maintain a confident front, despite the tightening in her chest. "Well, it's their loss. This is the best center in town."

"I'm afraid more parents are going to follow suit."

"Has it been that bad?" Amanda forced back the disappointment that showed in her voice.

"I've been getting calls all morning. I kept telling everyone that the phony bomb was just some crank's idea of a joke, but the parents are still very disturbed about it."

"I can't blame them."

Bernice went to the window and glanced outside. "Nothing else can happen here at the center, Amanda, or we're in for *big* problems."

"I know that. Did you talk with the plainclothes guard I hired?"

Bernice nodded. "He came in this morning, introduced himself, and left a list of references before he started patrolling the grounds. I put his personal information on top of the file cabinet."

The phone on her desk rang, and Amanda picked up the receiver automatically. The now-familiar, electronically altered voice greeted her, and she froze for a moment. Recovering immediately, Amanda started the tape recorder Tony had attached to her office phone. "I'm listening," she said, noting Bernice's raised eyebrows.

"Tell Ramos not to try to match wits with us again. It's pointless. We know how he thinks."

"Is that all?" Amanda said coldly. Betraying fear to people like this was like inviting them to use it against her.

"Tell Ramos we want the names of all the agents and informers involved in the Gage forgery investigation. Tell him to use his own network of informants if he can't access the information from the Bureau directly. And as payback for his little games at the mall, we want this in *two* days. We'll give you a time and a place later. You might remind him that we are now in possession not only of information about his daughter's whereabouts, but of a Bureau file he stole, as well. We won't hesitate to send a copy to the newspapers and credit him with the theft. If he's in jail, he'll have a hard time finding his kid or us. You might keep that in mind since it concerns you, as well."

"What do you mean by that?"

The electronically distorted laugh sent a chill up her spine. "By delivering the file, you're an accomplice to his crime. I wonder where your daughter will stay while her mommy's in prison?"

Amanda stiffened as if ice water had suddenly been poured down her back. "I've done what you want. You have no need to threaten me."

"Just remember, we have several ways of insuring that you'll lose your daughter for good."

"You've made your threats abundantly clear," Amanda snapped. She heard more distorted laughter and then, abruptly, the dial tone.

"What on earth did they say to you?" Bernice came around her desk and placed a hand on Amanda's shoulder. "You're as white as a sheet."

"I don't think I should tell you this. I'd be placing you in jeopardy, legal and otherwise." Amanda shook her head, seeing Bernice start to protest. "All I can tell you is that they've threatened to use Tony to start a chain of events to insure that Hope will be taken from me."

"Amanda, think it through. Nobody could do that. Public sentiment would be on your side if all this came out."

"But look at what they've done already. The callers knew Hope was adopted, even though I've kept it a secret out of deference to Ron and his sister. They said they would convince Tony that Hope was really his daughter by manipulating the adoption records. I pointed out that a blood test would prove otherwise, but they said any publicity could still result in my losing my daughter for weeks, maybe months, and they proved their clout by erasing Hope's adoption records." Amanda couldn't keep the fear from her voice.

"I know it would be a tough battle," Bernice acknowledged, "but Tony wouldn't get your child."

"The publicity could bring Hope's birth father into the picture, however. He might fight for custody if he thought there was money to be made. Even if he hasn't been heard of for some time, he could become a big problem. He *is* her father."

"The courts would never award Hope to him! He walked out on Hope's mother before she was even born."

"I don't want to gamble on what the courts may or may not do. They've taken children away from loving couples who've raised them from infancy and given them to strangers who'd abandoned them."

"Amanda, you've got to go to the police. This is getting more complicated by the minute."

"I've already broken the law, Bernice. These people have got me over a barrel. The only thing I can do is fight them if I get a chance...and make sure none of this touches Hope."

Amanda dialed Tony's pager number to ask him to call her, then sat back in her chair to wait. It wasn't easy for her to face the fact that her only ally was a vigilante with a tragic past and a shady future.

TONY WALKED THROUGH the doorway a short time later. He was dressed in the brown pants and shirt of a deliveryman, and he was carrying a parcel. She was astonished at the easy way he adapted to each disguise. It made her wonder how much of what he'd said she dared believe.

He set the parcel on the floor and sat down across from her. "Are you okay?" he asked when she remained silent.

Amanda shrugged. "You need to listen to this tape," she said, depressing the Play button.

After the recording ended, he looked at her thoughtfully. "What else have they threatened you with? The woman said something about 'several ways' of making you lose your daughter. Do you know what she's talking about?"

"If this day-care center goes down, and we're already losing kids, then I won't be able to support my daughter. I'd probably lose custody of her to my ex-husband, or worse, I'd be so broke I wouldn't even be able to afford food for Hope. I couldn't bear that," she said, her voice a mere whisper. For now, that was all she could tell him.

Amanda watched Tony pace, moving like a predator searching blindly for his prey in the dark.

"I can't access this forgery information they want me to deliver. Snitches are protected, revealed only on a need-to-know basis. Even if Raymond could steal that information, which he won't, the most he'd find would be code names totally unrelated to their identities. Yet, somehow, I've got to do what they want.''

"Are you sure it's wise to give them any information at all?'' Amanda said cautiously. "Innocent people could get hurt.''

His dark eyes, always so disturbing, now shone with a turmoil that was frightening in its intensity. "The agents on the case are trained to confront trouble, and the informants are in the business of selling people out for money. There are no innocents involved, except my daughter.'' Tony challenged her with a stony gaze, then turned and walked out of the room.

A dark despair filled her. She was struggling to keep the child that was rightfully hers, and Tony was fighting for the daughter that had been taken from him. Yet in order to keep her own child safe, she had to withhold information that might lead Tony to his.

Confused, miserable and frightened, Amanda stared absently at her glass. In her heart, she felt as cold as the layer of crushed ice floating at the top of her tea.

AMANDA STARTED to straighten up her desk in preparation for the end of the day. As soon as Bernice came back, she'd pick up Hope and head for home. As she placed the files for the children who were being withdrawn back into the cabinet, Amanda heard a knock on her open door. She turned and saw Raymond standing there.

"Your receptionist is gone. Mind if I come in?''

"Not at all. Is something wrong?'' Amanda couldn't read the man's expression at all.

Raymond shook his head. "I was planning to meet Tony in another thirty minutes at his home. He's on the way there now, but I can't get a hold of him to cancel. He's not answering his pager.'' He set a file on her desk. "It's important he look at this tonight, so I can have it back tomorrow.

It's a collection of mug shots and rap sheets of women con artists. He asked for it after your run-in at the mall. A positive ID could give him a solid lead."

"This is more than a con, though," Amanda said.

"Yes, but we need a place to start. The kidnappers we have on file are either behind bars, or they have nothing ostensibly to do with this case. Tony's already familiar with all that information."

Amanda took the file and slipped it inside her tote as Raymond drew a small map showing how to get to Tony's home. "It's a bit tricky. Some of the street signs are missing, but this should help."

"Thanks. I'll see that he gets the file. You want it back tomorrow?"

"First thing, if possible. He can meet me before work at my place. If he wants to talk to me sooner, tell him I've gone to Taos on a case, but I should be back by midnight or thereabouts. Okay?"

"No problem."

Amanda couldn't deny feeling a rush of excitement at the prospect of seeing where Tony lived. A home always revealed quite a bit about the person who lived there. She knew very little about the things that really mattered to Tony, and this seemed like a golden opportunity.

After picking up Hope, she followed the directions Raymond had given her. Hope sang "Three Blind Mice" over and over as Amanda drove. She smiled at her daughter, comforted by her presence in the car and not the least bit annoyed by the singing. No matter what happened, Amanda knew she couldn't allow anything to separate the two of them.

Her thoughts drifted to Tony. The kidnappers really had him in a stranglehold. Worst of all, he was acting with her knowledge so she would share his guilt if they were caught.

"Mommy, can Tony and I play at his house?"

"No, Peanut. We won't be there long. I just have to give him something."

"Oh."

Amanda took two wrong turns but finally found the gravel road on Raymond's map. After passing a run-down garage and laundry, she arrived at a wood-frame-and-stucco apartment building that, from the looks of it, had seen better days. Hope had finally tired of her song and was slumped in her booster seat, chin on her chest, asleep.

Amanda was just pulling in when she noticed a tall, skinny young man with gang colors standing by the side of the building. The garish headband contrasted sharply with his black T-shirt and baggy pants.

As Amanda slowed down, she saw Tony come around the corner. He grabbed the surprised youth by the collar, then threw him backward against the wall. Tony hit the stunned kid in the stomach, then stepped back and tossed what appeared to be a roll of bills at him. Then, as the young man lay there on the ground, moaning, Tony strolled casually away.

As soon as Tony was out of sight, the young man got to his feet, ran to a low-rider sedan parked nearby, and sped away.

Amanda stared, unable to believe her eyes. The boy had been no match for Tony. Did he coerce his informants, paying them only after he'd roughed them up in order to get the information he wanted?

Amanda drove down the street, rethinking her visit. She glanced down at the file sticking out of her tote, then at her sleeping daughter. No matter what her personal feelings were, there was no denying that her child's welfare was at stake.

Needing time to compose herself, Amanda circled the block twice, then finally returned to Tony's. By the time she arrived, Tony was standing alone by the rear of his pickup, tools in hand. From the dust all over his jeans, she surmised he'd just crawled out from under the vehicle. She studied the tan T-shirt he wore. His sun-darkened skin contrasted with the paleness of the material, and the hardened planes of his body were barely sheathed by the thin material.

Feeling the jolt of a large pothole in the parking lot, Hope stirred awake, and Amanda's attention focused back on her daughter.

"We're at Tony's, Peanut. This won't take long."

Hope looked out her window and waved at Tony, who came over to join them as they got out of the car.

"This is a surprise," he said with a pleased grin. "And good timing, too. I just put my spare back into place under my truck."

"Raymond left something with me for you and asked that we go over it together tonight. He wants it returned first thing tomorrow," she said, not explaining in too much detail because of Hope's presence.

"Come in," Tony said, leading the way down a long hallway.

Amanda walked inside, holding Hope's hand. The apartment was meticulously clean, if small. The furnishings were old and tattered, and at a guess she expected they'd come with the apartment. The whitewashed walls were barren, giving the place an impersonal feel.

"You could use a few hanging plants," she said.

"This is just someplace I eat and sleep. Without my daughter, I haven't got a reason to make any place home."

Aware that Hope was getting restless, Amanda glanced around and noticed a small, portable television set. "Do you mind if Hope watches TV?"

Tony switched it on as Hope settled on the couch. "Would you like to select what she watches?"

Amanda turned the dial until she found a rerun of an old family Western. "Here we go. It's your favorite—the one about the little house." Amanda pulled a coloring book and a small box of crayons out of her tote bag. "Here. You can do some coloring, too."

Leaving Hope occupied, Amanda walked to the table and set the bound folder down. Tony offered her a chair and sat next to her, looking at the file's contents.

Amanda could feel the warmth of his body searing through her clothes, making her vibrantly aware. His breath tickled her neck each time he commented on a photo, and she had to fight to suppress those telltale shivers that started at the base of her spine.

"Nothing here," he said at last, closing the folder.

As his hand brushed hers, Amanda held her breath. Needing a distraction, she stood and wandered around the living room, looking for clues to the man. She could feel Tony's gaze on her, but she tried to remain nonchalant.

"Would you like to see the rest? Not that there's much to see, but you seem curious."

"Of course I am," she replied with a smile.

"In that case, let me give you the grand tour. It should take about twenty seconds." He went to his right and pushed open a door. "This is my bedroom."

The words made a flush of heat spread through her, but with a burst of will, she curbed her thoughts and walked inside. The room was imprinted with the masculine essence he wore. It seemed to surround her, filling her senses and weaving a spell of seduction.

She'd avoided looking at the bed, but as she turned, the intricate quilt that covered it captured her attention. It had a delicate, feminine touch that told her it was handmade. She walked over to it for a closer look. The patchwork formed a motif for each month of the year. "This is gorgeous."

"It was a gift from my grandmother. She made it the same year I joined the Bureau."

"Does your family live here in Santa Fe?"

"I come from a small farming community in southern New Mexico. Just a wide spot in the road, my father always said."

She walked to a tiny silver framed photo he kept on the dresser. She'd almost missed it altogether in the shadows of the one low-powered light bulb. The photo showed Tony standing with an older man who shared Tony's eyes, square jaw and handsome features. "Your dad?"

"That was taken the day I graduated from the FBI Academy. My dad was so incredibly proud of me! Of course, that all changed."

Amanda set the portrait back down. "When you left the Bureau?"

He shook his head. "When I lost my family."

She glanced once more at the man in the photo, then at Tony. "I don't understand. Why?"

"I come from a very traditional Spanish background. Above all else, a man is expected to protect his family. It's a matter of honor. Yet even with all my training, I failed. In their eyes, I was less of a man because of that. My father died last year, asking to see his granddaughter. My mother will never forgive me for that."

"What happened to your wife and child wasn't your fault!"

"*My* family was *my* responsibility. That's the truth of it." He walked to the doorway, silently urging her to continue the tour.

Amanda followed him out. She'd never known what it was like to grow up in a real family, but after listening to his story, she began to suspect that her life had been far simpler because of it.

"This is my study," Tony said, opening the other door off the living room.

For the first time, Amanda caught a glimpse of Tony's world. This room mirrored his personality. A black silhouette target of a human torso was taped on the far wall. All the rounds were clustered tightly in the center of the head and the heart.

He followed her gaze. "I'm a good shot, always have been, but that target was one of my best. I kept it as a souvenir. I have marksman status. Or I did anyway."

Amanda walked to the cork bulletin board over an old wooden desk. Snapshots of young children filled it.

"I keep track of any child in the state of New Mexico who is reported missing. Most of these cases are attributed to noncustodial parents, so I concentrate on the ones that seem to have no explanation. I'm convinced that one of those will furnish a lead to Carmen someday."

"This last photo, the snapshot of this mother and child isn't very detailed." Amanda looked at him and saw the haunted look on his face. "Your wife and child?"

"We never had time for proper pictures," he answered in a taut voice.

On a small table between two file cabinets, she saw a large, blue, stuffed brontosaurus with a bright red bow tie. She stared at it in mute surprise.

"I saw it in a store last Christmas, so I bought it. The day I find Carmen, I'll have a present for her, ready and waiting, to welcome her back."

Amanda heard tiny footsteps rushing toward them and turned around. Hope rushed into the room, saw the stuffed toy, and ran right up to it. "Oh wow! Mommy, can I play with it?"

"No, dear, not now. It's time we went home."

Tony took the dinosaur off the shelf. "Here you go, Hope. Consider it a present. You can take it home with you."

"Oh, thank you, Tony!"

Amanda looked into Tony's eyes. "Are you sure?"

"Yes. It serves a more useful purpose making a child happy now."

Amanda watched her daughter race to the living room, hugging the blue toy to her chest. "You made her day."

"Good."

Amanda couldn't resist another glance at the practice target. Tony was a man who played by his own rules, a trained manhunter who no longer operated strictly by the law. He had kept that target as a reminder—maybe even as a motivator. She couldn't afford to let down her guard with him. She looked up at him and realized he had been watching her. His eyes were alive with desire. She glanced away. A sense of sorrow filled her as she accepted the inevitable. She would never know what it was like to stay in his arms, or to be loved by him.

"Thanks for coming by, Amanda."

"Raymond did seem eager to get that file back." She paused. "Speaking of files... Have you decided what to do about the list the kidnappers wanted?"

"Yes. I've uncovered some of the names of the investigators, but FBI informants are deep cover people. If anyone ever found out who they were, they'd be corpses, not snitches. All I can give them are possibilities gathered from rumors. It's not reliable, but it's the best I can do."

Amanda felt her chest tighten. So here was her proof that Tony was willing to risk other lives. This man would stop at nothing, using the law only when it was convenient for him.

A few minutes later, Amanda walked to the door, Hope's hand in hers. Her mind still echoed with unanswered questions. From what she could tell, Tony needed a considerable amount of money to keep his informants, but he had no job that she could see. Where and how was he getting the money to support himself and his search?

Tony helped Hope and her brontosaurus buckle up. "There. You can share a seat belt."

"Thank you," Hope answered, her arm wound tight around the toy.

The gesture pierced Amanda's heart. There was one thing she was one hundred percent certain about. When Tony found Carmen, that little girl would be showered with love.

Amanda started the engine just as another car pulled up. Tony's gaze shifted over to it. "Go. Now! It's risky for you to be seen with me here."

Another time she might have satisfied her curiosity, but Hope was with her now. It seemed as if even her minor urges were destined never to be satisfied.

Amanda quickly drove away from Tony's place. Sneaking one quick glance in the rearview mirror, she saw a tall, well-dressed man get out of the other car and walk toward Tony. She couldn't be sure, but from his clothing and height she thought it might have been the same man she'd seen with Tony in the alley.

As Amanda turned the corner, confusion clouded her thoughts. How could her heart yearn so strongly for Tony's love and his touch when she knew so little about him and when what she did know frightened her half to death? Amanda shut out the whispered longings of her heart. Wishing would not change what could not be.

Chapter Eight

Amanda sat in the living room, the open book on her lap still unread. So much had changed in her life. Tension and fear had become her constant companions. Even in her moments alone, she could never be sure what would happen next, or how safe either Hope or she would be.

The ringing of the telephone startled her out of her musings. She glanced at her watch, her heart racing. It was only nine-thirty in the evening. Maybe it was Bernice. Amanda walked to the phone, glancing at the caller ID display. It was not Bernice. The screen indicated the caller had blocked the display of their number. Picking up the phone, she took a deep breath.

Braced for the electronically altered voice, she was surprised when a recording began playing what sounded like a line from an old movie. "I'll be watching you," came the message, over and over again, from an actor who sounded vaguely familiar.

"Who is this?" she demanded.

The message continued to repeat itself in an endless loop.

Amanda hung up, shaken. Perhaps this was the kidnappers' response to her visit with Tony. Yet the indirect threat somehow seemed out of character for them. She stared at the telephone, uneasiness seeping into every pore in her body.

Amanda dialed Tony's number and was relieved when he answered immediately. "I'm glad I caught you. I just had the most peculiar phone call, and I don't know what to make of it." She gave him the details.

"It doesn't sound like the kidnappers. This seems more likely to be from the person or persons who placed the phony bomb and threw that rock through your window."

"What if the kidnappers hired someone to do this to keep me on edge? That makes a lot more sense to me than my having a second enemy."

"Unlikely. These attacks seem to have a more personal nature about them. But don't worry. In either case, I'll take care of it."

Too restless to sit still, Amanda walked to the window and glanced outside. If anyone was watching her now, they needed an infrared scope. It was pitch-black out and the street seemed deserted.

The quiet in the house began to grate on her nerves. She took a deep breath, trying to force herself to relax. Maybe a long hot bath would help. Amanda walked down the hall, stopping by the doorway to listen for Hope. Her daughter's breathing was slow and even. Taking a peek in the room, she saw Hope curled on her side, fast asleep beside the blue dinosaur. Amanda smiled, feeling a little envious.

A few minutes later, she watched the tub fill up, then stripped and lowered herself into the water. The lavender-scented bubble bath wrapped her in a warm cocoon. She closed her eyes and leaned back.

A sharp rattle jolted her into awareness, and Amanda realized she'd dozed off. She wasn't sure how much time had elapsed, but the bubbles had disappeared and the water was uncomfortably cold.

She waited for a moment, trying to figure out if she'd dreamed the odd noise, but then she heard it again. It sounded like someone was throwing pebbles at her bathroom window.

Amanda stood up carefully, revealing only her head, and opened the frosted-glass pane.

"It's me" came a muted masculine voice from somewhere close by.

"Tony?" Her robe was hanging on the door, just beyond her reach.

"I'm by your back fence. Answer the front door, will you?"

Amanda grabbed her robe and quickly covered herself as she padded barefoot to the door. Opening it, she came face-to-face with Tony wearing gas-company coveralls. "What on earth are you doing here?"

"Don't worry. The gas-company truck and my uniform should look legit enough. The van is the real thing. I borrowed it from an old contact."

Amanda let Tony in, shaking her head. "I never know what to expect from you."

"With any luck, neither do my enemies." He walked to the recorder and ejected the tape.

"The only thing recorded is that one line I repeated for you. Couldn't this have waited until morning?"

"If it's from an old movie like you said, maybe they rented it and I can track the user down. I know someone who's a film buff. I'll find out if she recognizes it. But I needed the recording now because I can only get hold of her at night."

A twinge of jealousy swept over Amanda like a dust devil coming out of nowhere. She forced it aside. "She may not be in a mood to help you if you burst in on her at this hour."

"She won't mind. She does most of her business at night."

Amanda blinked. Was he talking about a video-store owner or a prostitute? She decided not to ask.

His eyes devoured her slowly. "You're not jealous, are you?"

He was undressing her with his eyes. Suddenly, the robe that covered her seemed impossibly thin. The hunger in his eyes left her feeling weak in the knees, but she was determined to hide that from him.

Amanda glared at him haughtily. "You're delusional."

"Am I?" He chuckled softly. "Just so that everything's clear in your mind, Stacey's in charge of a crisis line. I met her when I was in the Bureau. She helped me on a case, and she's remained one of my best contacts."

"How so? I wasn't aware you worked other cases. I thought you spent all your time trying to track down your daughter."

"I have other work, but it's mostly confidential. When people go to a P.I., it's generally because they don't want to involve the police. I assure them anonymity."

She looked at him with what she considered to be admirable calm. He had told her just enough to make her even more nervous.

"Don't be afraid, Amanda. Only my enemies need to fear me."

As Amanda saw herself reflected in his eyes, fire began dancing in her blood. She felt as if she were standing before him naked and open to his hungry gaze.

"Come here, my beautiful lady," he murmured and drew her against him. "There's nothing that can happen between you and I that should cause you fear." His lips brushed the nape of her neck.

Amanda shuddered, mesmerized by the softness of his kiss and the gentleness of his embrace. Though a tiny voice within her urged her to move away, she couldn't will herself to obey. She desperately yearned to lose herself in the fiery whirlwind of pleasures he was offering her.

Tony rained moist kisses down the column of her neck, and slowly parted her robe, branding her skin with his touch. His caress was kind, yet demanding, and she couldn't help but respond to the tender assault. Drizzly, sensual feelings ribboned through her leaving her aching. She needed everything he wanted to give her. She'd been alone for so very long! Longing tore through her, enticing her to yield completely to him.

"Don't deny your own feelings. Listen to your heart. The love that's touched both of us is too rare to let slip away." He pushed the robe completely away from her shoulders.

Amanda felt it fall around her feet, but it didn't seem nearly as important as the wonderful feelings he was wrapping her in.

Entwining his fingers around her hair, he pulled her gently back, his arm still around her waist, holding her steady. "We belong together, you can feel it," he managed breathlessly and lowered his mouth to kiss the very tip of her breast.

Amanda felt his lips encircle her nipple, his tongue teasing it with its velvety softness. An exquisite heaviness centered between her legs. She felt more alive, more intoxicatingly feminine with each bit of herself she surrendered to him.

Her cares dissolved and the wonder of sensations replaced all thought. As if sensing her readiness, Tony lifted her into his arms and started to carry her to the couch.

Suddenly, she heard the ear-piercing shrillness of her smoke detector. Fear shot through her, removing the sweetness of emotions that had almost swept her away.

"What the heck?" She looked around as she urged Tony to set her down.

Then above the din, Amanda heard her daughter's terror-filled voice calling out to her.

"Mommy!"

In a heartbeat, Amanda turned, pulled on her robe and ran down the hall toward Hope's room.

Tony followed Amanda into the child's room. Seeing that Hope's fright was only a reaction to the wail of the alarm, he ran back down the hall to check the rest of the house while Amanda grabbed her daughter. The kitchen was the most likely source of a household fire, but there were no open flames or smoke anywhere when he arrived. Nevertheless, the unmistakable smell of smoke filled the area.

He lifted a small kitchen fire extinguisher from its hook, and then grabbed the plastic flashlight beside it. Ready for action, he renewed the search. Just then, Amanda appeared, carrying Hope in her arms. Hope was crying softly, holding on tightly to her mother.

"Did you find the source?" Amanda yelled. "The back rooms are clear."

As Tony glanced toward the wooden door leading to her garage, he noticed thin tendrils of smoke coming from beneath it. "Call the fire department, then go outside with Hope."

"Don't open the door. You have no idea how bad it is on the other side," she warned.

"Your car—is it parked in there?"

"No, it's in the driveway."

Tony placed his hand on the door. "It's still cool to the touch. The fire's not out of hand yet."

Once Amanda and Hope were in the other room, Tony opened the door and stepped into the garage, turning on the lights by a switch next to the door. The stench of charcoal lighter fluid filled the air, and smoke hugged the ceiling where the smoke alarm was positioned. It didn't take him long to find the fire. A bunch of rags on the concrete floor had been ignited, and the fire was pouring out thick gray smoke.

Aiming the fire extinguisher at the base of the flames, he began to spray. The contents came gushing out in a thick mist for a moment, then sputtered and trickled to a few drops. Tony grabbed several towels Amanda had placed on top of the washing machine, soaked them in water from the adjacent utility sink, and began to smother the flames. Seconds later, he heard the sirens of emergency vehicles approaching.

Ricky Biddle abruptly appeared at the kitchen door. "The fire department is almost here. Can I help?"

"No, I've got it under control," Tony said without turning around. "Just wait outside."

"Is it a gas fire?" Biddle asked, not recognizing Tony, but obviously noticing the gas company's logo on the back of the uniform.

"No, just make sure the fire department knows where the fire was," Tony ordered.

"No problem, man."

Tony stood back after he'd extinguished the last of the flames. So much for the low-profile visit he'd intended. At least his hidden transmitter had been spared. Later, on his way out, he'd stop by the recorder in the hedge and pick up the tape of any conversations Amanda had at home. It was necessary, yet spying on Amanda, particularly after what had happened between them tonight, made him feel like a snake.

He stared at the charred clump of rags, lost in thought. He was a snake, all right, but he could be a useful one. He'd concentrate all his talents and cunning on finding out who was doing this to Amanda. Then he'd stop them—permanently. He owed her that much.

AMANDA, NOW WEARING a long raincoat over her robe, stood outside as Ricky approached her. She wasn't sure he'd recognized Tony, so she decided to play it cool. There was no sense in broadcasting Tony's presence.

"I saw the gas man in the garage," Ricky said. "He says it's not a gas fire, but he sure didn't want me around. Did you smell a gas leak or something and ask them to send one of their men over?"

Amanda tried to think of a response that wouldn't blow Tony's cover. "I called them, but he couldn't find any leak."

"Then how did the fire get started?"

"I'm not sure yet. We better let the experts have a look."

Amanda watched two of the firemen talking to Tony. They'd pulled up her garage door and were sifting through the smoldering rags with metal wrecking bars.

"Is Hope going to be okay? She looks awfully scared, and tired, too." Ricky looked down at the child nestled in Amanda's arms, wrapped in one of Amanda's thick sweaters.

"I imagine she's both," Amanda conceded. Hope had stopped crying, but she still clung tightly to Amanda, her face buried in her mother's neck.

Amanda shifted her attention to an approaching fireman.

"Is this your residence?"

Amanda nodded. "Is it safe to go back in now?"

"Oh, sure. It wasn't much really, as far as fires go. But there's something you need to know. That fire was deliberately set. Someone poured charcoal lighter fluid on some rags and then set a match to them. I've called our arson investigator, and he'll be by first thing tomorrow morning. Don't clean up the garage until after he's had a chance to gather evidence."

"I need to ask you some questions, but I'd like to put my daughter to bed first. Would you give me a few moments?"

Bernice came up behind Amanda. "I rushed right over when I saw the emergency vehicles driving by. Your place smells so smoky, it'll give Hope nightmares. Let me take her to my place tonight. She can play with Winston for a while before she goes back to sleep."

"I can't just keep sending her over to your house," Amanda protested weakly.

"Sure you can! Winston loves it. He thinks Hope belongs to him. He even pouts when she's not around." Bernice gave Amanda a quick hug, then took the little girl from her arms. "Call me later."

Hope went with Bernice without protest, settling easily into the older woman's arms. Bernice had been Hope's favorite baby-sitter ever since Amanda had moved back to town, but Amanda found herself resenting how easily Hope turned to someone else for comfort. As Amanda watched Bernice taking her child, a cold emptiness filled her; then came the anger. Her daughter deserved to be safe in her own home. Whoever was doing this had not frightened her away. They had only renewed her courage and determination.

She turned to the fire chief, her gaze suddenly cold. "I want you to give me all the information you have. You said someone was trying to burn my home down?"

"No, ma'am, that's *not* what I said. A fire like this was unlikely to spread. There was nothing flammable near those rags, fortunately. In my opinion, whoever set this knew precisely what they were doing. It was meant to scare you, but not to do any structural damage to your home or hurt anyone inside."

As Tony came up, pulling his cap down low over his face, the fire chief glanced at him. "Is there a problem with the gas lines we don't know about?"

"No. I'm just a friend of the lady's," he answered, his voice gruff. "I'm not here on a call."

"Good. I hate surprises." The chief turned to look at Amanda. "We've done all we can here tonight. You'll hear from our investigator tomorrow."

As the firemen began packing up their gear, Amanda moved to one side with Tony. "We have to talk before you leave," she said quietly.

Tony stopped halfway up her driveway, then turned and went to the gas-company van. After retrieving a small brown attaché case, he returned to the house. He entered the living room and took a quick look out her front window. The street had cleared quickly and a solemn silence had descended over the area.

"What's that?" Amanda asked as he stepped to the center of the room and put down the case.

"There's someone I want to run a check on while you and I talk. I don't know if you noticed, but Biddle showed up out of nowhere. He seems to have a habit of doing that."

"So? He lives right down the lane."

"How would he have seen the smoke in the dark, Amanda, unless he'd been searching for it? He was here *before* the fire department arrived. Doesn't that strike you as odd?"

"He jogs," she answered. "Remember?"

"He wasn't wearing jogging clothes. He was in jeans."

"If you think Ricky is behind the kidnapping, you're crazy. If nothing else, he doesn't have the time. It might seem as if he doesn't do much, but that's just not true. He works his tail off. I've driven past his home late at night and early in the morning. He's always in his office. That's usually the only light on in his house."

Tony sat down next to a phone jack, then brought out a small laptop computer. "This has got an internal modem. I'm going to use your phone line for a bit."

"To do what?"

"I want to know who Biddle's been in contact with lately."

"How can you do that?" she asked, not even trying to hide her skepticism.

Tony chuckled. "I have a code that will let me access the phone company's computer using a back door, so to speak." As Tony connected, columns of information appeared on the computer screen. "What time did you say that weird phone call came in tonight?"

"It was around nine-thirty."

"Well, it wasn't Biddle who called. Or set the fire, for that matter."

Amanda looked over his shoulder. "How do you know that?"

"He was on the phone at the time. See?" He pointed to a number on the screen. "He was talking long distance for over two hours."

"I told you it was a waste of time. You didn't have to check his phone records. Doing that is probably illegal anyway."

"Of course it is," Tony admitted. "But I'm not in the Bureau anymore, where I have to get warrants and permission. I use any avenue I can."

Amanda tried to squelch her uneasiness. Tony was an impossible blend of threat and comfort, gentleness and violence. She yearned for his touch even now, though her mind fought to suppress that longing.

She practically pushed him out the door. "I'll call you tomorrow."

"If I could, I'd stay. But right now it could cause more harm than good."

Amanda nodded. For a moment, she pictured herself safe in his arms, greeting the new day fearlessly, secure in the promise of his love. Instead, she watched him leave.

Amanda walked back inside, then with one last glance toward the garage, continued to her bedroom. She'd deal with that problem tomorrow. For now, she had to get some sleep.

MORNING CAME MUCH SOONER than she'd expected. It felt as if she'd only just closed her eyes when she heard knocking at her front door. She glanced at the clock on her nightstand. It was past eight. She'd overslept.

Grabbing her jeans and a shirt from the floor and dressing as she went, she hurried toward the door. "Bernice?"

She was halfway through the living room when the phone began to ring. Amanda glanced at it, then the door, then opted to answer the phone first. "Just a second," she yelled to whoever was standing outside.

Amanda glanced at the caller ID display, recognized the day-care number, and picked up the receiver. Bernice's friendly voice greeted her a second later. "I brought Hope with me to the center this morning. You hadn't called, so I figured you were sleeping late. Hope is fine, so don't worry about anything. She's settled in the nursery playing and has all but forgotten about last night."

"Thanks, Bernice. I'll be in before long, but I've got to hang up now. I've got someone waiting at the door."

Amanda rushed to the door, wondering if it was the arson investigator. She opened it and saw a plainclothes policeman holding up his badge.

"I'm Detective Sanchez, Mrs. Vila," he said. "May I come in?"

Amanda checked the photo ID next to his badge, then glanced at his face. Satisfied, she stepped aside and waved him in. "Can I get you a cup of coffee, Detective? I was about to make some for myself."

"No, thanks, Mrs. Vila." He followed her into the kitchen and sat down at the kitchen table. "From the looks of things on your driveway, I'm guessing you had some excitement here last night."

"You could describe it that way." Amanda gave him a brief accounting. "Is that why you're here? I thought an arson investigator was supposed to come."

"He still might. I'm not working that angle. I came by to follow up on the phony bomb incident, but what happened here might be pertinent to my case. Do you have any idea at all who might be behind it?"

"No. I wish I did."

"What does your P.I., Ramos, say, or have you told him yet?"

"Yes, I have, but he has no leads." Amanda noted the distaste on the detective's face as he spoke of Tony.

"You seem like a nice lady," Sanchez said slowly, "and from what we've heard, you lead a decent, hardworking life. I hope you won't take this wrong, but I think I should warn you. Ramos is bad news. He used to be an excellent agent, but those days are long gone. He's more likely to break the law than he is to uphold it nowadays, and you have to be very careful he doesn't drag you down with him. Ramos works both sides of the fence. He's good at it, too. He can really manipulate people into doing whatever he wants. If you decide to keep on dealing with him, remember that."

Amanda felt a cold chill run up her spine. She looked away from the detective, hoping he wouldn't guess how her heart had betrayed her. Finally gathering her wits, she met his gaze. "What have the police found out that can help me? Were you able to gather any evidence from the phony bomb that could lead you to a possible suspect?"

Sanchez's expression grew hard. "The only fingerprints we found were yours, Ramos's and those of the child who found the athletic bag. There were none on the phony bomb. The alarm clock and the bag are both inexpensive brands carried at The Mart, which has six stores within a hundred miles of here. We haven't given up, though."

"When you questioned my day-care staff, did you learn anything that might help?"

"Do you think we should have?" he countered, eyebrows raised.

"Don't play games with me, Detective Sanchez. I haven't had much sleep lately. I'm dead tired and in no mood for tricks."

"No, we really *don't* have any leads yet. That's why I came here. I was hoping you might have remembered or thought of something new that would help us." Sanchez's tone was more apologetic.

"I suggest you join forces with the arson investigator. You may discover evidence that could help in both incidents."

Amanda heard another light rap at the door and excused herself to answer it.

A man in a dark blue windbreaker stood at the door. He pulled a badge from his shirt pocket. "I'm Investigator Perez from the fire department."

"Come in." Amanda led him to the kitchen and was about to introduce the two officers when they saved her the trouble.

"Hey, Sanchez." Perez greeted the detective with a handshake.

"Morning, Perez. Looks like you and I have crossed paths again. Somebody has been doing a number on Mrs. Vila, it seems."

The arson investigator turned to Amanda. "I need to take a look at your garage. My investigation could take an hour or longer. I hope that won't be a problem."

"Not at all." Amanda opened the kitchen door leading into the garage. "Please tell me if you learn anything useful, gentlemen."

"We'll keep you apprised," Perez said, then he and Sanchez left to examine the scene.

Amanda went to her study and telephoned Bernice to let her know she'd be late. "Have any personal calls come in for me?"

"The private line on your desk hasn't rung today. We did have two more parents come in to talk, still nervous about the phony bomb incident, but I took care of them. No other kids have been withdrawn."

"I really don't know what I'd do without you. I can't thank you enough. I should be handling all that," Amanda said.

"You will be soon enough," Bernice assured her.

It wasn't until close to noon that the investigators left her house and Amanda was able to go to the center. After having lunch with Hope, she walked into the reception area, where Bernice was arguing with Tony. He was dressed as a maintenance man again.

"Now what?" she demanded sharply, her attention focused directly on Tony.

Tony started to reply, but suddenly his expression softened. "You look beat. How did it go with the arson investigator?"

"I don't know. They were both really closemouthed."

"Both?"

Amanda filled Tony in while leading the way into her office. She shut the door before continuing. "The deadline for the delivery of that list the kidnappers want is almost up. Yet they haven't called. What do you think is going on?"

"They'll call." Tony rested a hip on the edge of her desk. "In the meantime, I've been doing some further investigating. You may be hearing from some disgruntled people, so be prepared."

"Like who?" Amanda said, instantly on her guard. "If you've made any trouble for me with the parents—"

"No, nothing like that. I've been following the most likely lead. Your ex-husband."

"Ron?" Amanda stared at him aghast, then suddenly began to laugh. "Boy, are you barking up the wrong tree! The only thing Ron has time for is his career. He's never behind on his child-support payments, but there's no place in his life for me or anyone else, including Hope."

"I had to check him out. When women are being harassed, it almost always turns out to be someone they know. Ex-husbands and old boyfriends are at the top of the list."

"Did you go see him?"

"Yeah. He threw me out and told his clerk to call the cops if I ever showed up again. Then he called Bernice and gave her a hard time. That's what we were arguing about when you came in."

Amanda closed her eyes, shook her head in disbelief, then opened them again. "Your capacity to create trouble never ceases to amaze me."

"You're right about him, though. He's a money-hungry jerk. Then again, I've never been too crazy about lawyers on either side of the bench. It's a holdover from my days in law enforcement."

"Ron has many faults, but he's unlikely to be responsible for what's been happening to my business or my home. He's just not that passionate about anything." The smoky fires mirrored in Tony's eyes seemed to take the words right from her lips. "But, then again, passion is never enough," she added hastily.

"Don't ever underestimate the power of fate, Amanda." Tony walked to her door. "I'll be in touch."

Amanda stared at the empty doorway long after Tony disappeared from her view. He was a hardened, self-possessed man with a battle-scarred spirit. Yet none of that seemed to matter when he looked at her with an intensity that made her feel as if she were the only woman in the world.

When Bernice appeared at her door, Amanda managed a smile. "I really appreciate your holding down the fort this morning."

Bernice sat across from Amanda's desk. "The more I'm around that man, the less I like him. I wish I could say the same was happening to you. Nothing good can come from your involvement with him, Amanda. He'll just use you. In fact, it's quite possible he's been manipulating you all along."

"What do you mean?"

"He knows you're keeping secrets, Amanda, and he wants to know what they are. You make it easy for him. Don't you see what's right there in front of you? All these accidents—the rock-throwing incident, the fire last night and even the bomb—nothing like that ever happened to you until Tony Ramos came into your life. Have you considered the possibility that he might be the one behind these incidents? You know he'll use whatever he can dream up to get you to lower your guard and start depending on and confiding in him.''

Amanda stared at Bernice. ''He wouldn't—'' She clamped her mouth shut. She knew all too well that Tony was capable of anything when it came to the search for his daughter. Imagining that he could have done all those things wasn't too far a stretch. Maybe the enemy he'd warned her about had been closer than she'd ever dreamed.

By the end of the day, the kidnappers still hadn't called, and the tension had Amanda on edge. Anything could happen at this point.

Bernice poked her head inside the office as Amanda was clearing her desk. ''Do you want Hope to stay with me again tonight?''

''Uh . . . no,'' she said hesitantly. ''I really need her with me, Bernice. We'll be all right. Thanks anyway.''

Amanda left the office quickly after that, afraid that the phone would ring and new troubles would keep her working late. The truth was that she was looking forward to a peaceful night alone with her daughter.

When Amanda entered the nursery, Hope rushed up and gave her a hug. ''Mommy, is it time to go home?''

''Sure is.'' Taking her daughter's hand, they walked to the car.

The drive home was blessedly uneventful. Although weary, just being with her daughter made Amanda feel refreshed. Tonight she'd fix spaghetti and bake some chocolate chip cookies, Hope's favorite. It would be like old times for them, before all this trouble began.

When Amanda arrived home, she was grateful to see no one was around. Maybe, just maybe, tonight would be a normal evening. As Hope went to her room to get her toys,

Amanda stepped into her bedroom. She would slip into her favorite pair of jeans and an old sweatshirt and get ready for the kind of laid-back evening she enjoyed the most.

As Amanda bent down to open the dresser drawer, she noticed an empty spot on the dresser corner. The small, framed snapshot taken of Hope and her on the shore of Cochiti Lake was missing.

She glanced all around the base of the dresser, thinking she might have knocked the picture onto the carpet. After a fruitless search, she sat on the edge of the bed, fighting to hold back tears of anger and dismay. Nothing else seemed to have been disturbed, but the photo was definitely gone. Someone had been in her bedroom—someone intent on stealing memories and a priceless piece of her life.

Chapter Nine

After making sure the windows were still securely locked, Amanda walked to the kitchen, trying to figure out where she could turn for help. The police would probably do little more than file a report. Tony was in a better position to do something, since he knew about the kidnappers, but if Bernice's theory was valid, it was possible he was behind the theft in the first place.

Unable to come up with any clear answers, Amanda decided to wait. The doors were locked, and for now at least, she knew she and Hope were safe.

It wasn't until after she put Hope to bed that she decided to call Tony, bring up what had happened, and see what his reaction would be. Just as she reached for the phone, it rang. On the display screen, Amanda saw the now-familiar phrase signifying that the caller had had the number blocked. Braced for trouble, she picked up the receiver. Hearing the electronic voice greeting her was like having someone press an ice cube to the small of her back.

"I'm ready to give you instructions for the drop. I'll only say it once. I want you to come to the Plaza del Sol Cinema at 6:00 p.m. tomorrow and watch the new science-fiction movie. Carry the envelope with the information we asked for in a shopping bag. You'll be contacted there. And one more thing."

"Yes?" Something about the sound of the woman's voice and the pause in instructions, which Amanda knew had been for dramatic effect, made her skin crawl.

"Have your daughter carry the shopping bag."

"Bring Hope? Absolutely—"

"How wonderful!" the caller said, deliberately interrupting her. "I knew we wouldn't have any trouble. You wouldn't want Ramos to lose his child forever or harm your own so very pleasant little family."

Before Amanda could respond, she heard the dial tone.

Her hands were shaking as she hung up. It wasn't a fair request. She couldn't drag her daughter into this. If the kidnappers wanted the information badly enough, they'd accept a change of plans.

She dialed Tony's number. The second she heard his voice, she blurted out the story including the part about the missing photo. "I won't take her. *No way.* It's time we made a few demands of our own."

"I'm coming over now. I have to hear that tape. Afterward, we'll work out the logistics."

"There's nothing to work out. I'll take the information to them. I'm not having my daughter in any part of this."

"Okay. Fair enough, but we need to plan this very carefully. I'm going to talk to Raymond and ask for his help. Then we'll decide on the best way to handle this."

Amanda replaced the receiver, then stared at the phone, lost in thought. Her worst nightmare had come true. The kidnappers were asking her to put her child in jeopardy in order to save another.

Thirty minutes later, Tony arrived, accompanied by Raymond. They quickly drove inside Amanda's garage and she shut the door behind them. Raymond's face was somber as he took in the remnants of the fire.

"I haven't had time to clean up in here," she admitted.

Raymond nodded. "I heard about the fire from Tony, and also about this demand for another drop. My old partner has been doing a tap dance every time I ask him what information is being passed to these people, but, for the record, if they want a kid involved, it's time to call in the cavalry. We should have a tactical team ready and give them one helluva surprise.''

"Raymond and I have already had a heated discussion over this,'' Tony said, glancing at Amanda as they walked through the kitchen and on into the living room. "The kidnappers asked for Hope to come along with you just as insurance. No way they'll harm a kid with all those witnesses around. Besides, they know I'll be there to make sure nobody gets near Hope.''

He was making sense, yet in Amanda's heart only one emotion ruled—fear. "I'm not bringing her, nor any other child.''

"They won't hurt Hope, Amanda, believe me. It's just their way of insuring that there'll be no gunfire or double cross,'' Tony said. "All you have to do is have Hope set the shopping bag down where they tell you and then walk away as quickly as possible.''

Raymond gave Amanda a level look. "Their target isn't your daughter, but it's foolish to deny that there's a risk involved.''

"We'll both be right there alongside Hope,'' Tony insisted. "We'd put a stop to any trouble in a flash.''

Amanda's thoughts raced. If she didn't comply, the kidnappers would retaliate against her. So really, the best way she had of keeping Hope safe was to do as they asked. "All right. Hope will go with me under one condition. I want you both so close you'll hear our hearts beating.''

"Done,'' Tony said quickly.

"Not so fast,'' Raymond argued. "I want to hear the tape first.''

After they'd replayed it, Amanda watched both men. Tony's eyes shone with a dangerous edge, but Raymond's expression was hooded.

"I don't like this. What did they mean about your harming your own pleasant family?" Raymond asked Amanda. "To me, that didn't sound like a threat against Hope. It sounds more like you're being blackmailed."

Somehow Amanda managed to control her voice and meet his gaze calmly. "I have no idea what they meant. Really."

Raymond said nothing for a few moments, then finally spoke. "This isn't a good time to hold back."

Amanda knew she had to think fast in order to convince both men. "The conversation is all there in the recording. I know nothing more than you, but once before, they *did* threaten me. They reminded me I could be sent to jail for delivering a file that was stolen from the FBI. I think this is their way of telling me they can blow the whistle at any time."

Raymond nodded, seemingly satisfied. "They're confident they have total control over you because of your love for your daughter. The fact that you're not willing to play completely by their rules and go without backup will give you a slight edge."

Amanda glanced at Raymond, then Tony. "Can I count on you two to work as a team?"

Raymond looked at Tony, who nodded. "We'll both be there," Raymond said at last.

"What kind of disguises will you be wearing?"

"It's better if you don't know," Tony answered. "I don't want you to look around for us, either. Trust us to be there and concentrate on following their instructions." He stood up, retrieved the tape from the machine, and placed a new one in it. "We've got a lot to do before tomorrow. We better get going. Will you be all right?"

Amanda stared at Tony. Nothing was all right. What an incredibly irritating question. "I'll manage."

Raymond picked up on her tone. "Just say the word, and both you and your daughter will be in protective custody."

"But for how long?" Tony countered. "You've got to see this through, Amanda. You know that as well as I do. You can't afford to back out now."

"I'll see it through."

Amanda escorted the men to the door. As soon as they pulled out, she locked it tight. The house was quiet. After checking on Hope, Amanda went to her bedroom. A great heaviness settled over her spirit. If she ever lost her daughter because she'd failed to protect her, nothing else would matter in her life.

Amanda lay down, staring into the darkness. She felt cut off from the one person she would have given anything to be able to lean on . . . Tony Ramos. The one man who was, in reality, probably her worst enemy.

THE FOLLOWING EVENING, Amanda took Hope to the movie theater. Hope, oblivious to the danger, was excited and barely able to sit still.

"This is great, Mommy! A play day!"

Amanda took Hope's hand firmly in hers and, keeping her close to her side, stood in line to purchase tickets. She wasn't surprised that the line was long. The new release had been highly promoted, and this was the only theater in town showing it.

Hope clutched the small shopping bag tightly, eager to help with grown-up things as she'd been asked. Amanda glanced at the young crowd. No one seemed particularly interested in her or her daughter. After waiting several minutes, she purchased the tickets and they went inside.

Seats were quickly filling up, and with the crowd pressing in on them from all sides, Amanda could barely sort out the faces surrounding her and Hope.

Amanda selected two aisle seats near the middle of the theater. From here it would be easier to escape if necessary. The crowd was noisy, but soon the lights went down and the show started.

Hope fidgeted constantly, the shopping bag by her side on the seat. Yet as the minutes dragged on, no one approached them, not even passing along the row to go for popcorn. Hope fell asleep against her arm and Amanda began to relax. Maybe the kidnappers had underestimated the size of the crowd and had decided the theater was too full to make their move.

When the film finally ended, Amanda gently nudged Hope awake. As she stood up, she saw someone waving at her. Ricky Biddle was directly across from them on the other side of the theater. She waved back, glad that the moving crowd would never allow him to cross over to them. He was the last person she needed near her now.

Hope clutched the little shopping bag as Amanda led her by the hand. They could have waited, but Amanda wanted the safety of numbers around them right now. People pressed in on them, but her grasp on Hope's hand was firm. Amanda resisted the urge to pick Hope up and carry her, knowing how her daughter disliked it. A fussy three-year-old was just about the last thing she needed to contend with at this point. They were near the exit doors when the crowd for the next showing suddenly swelled in, forcing them apart. As Hope's tiny hand slipped out of hers, Amanda bent down, frantically reaching out for her daughter among the mass of people.

"Hope!" Amanda yelled. A cold hand seemed to wrap itself around her heart, and panic surged wildly from the depths of her soul.

An instant later, a tall bearded man wearing an old fatigue jacket carried Hope back to her, setting her down beside Amanda.

"The pickup was made," he whispered.

Amanda recognized Tony's voice, but there was no time to talk to him. In the blink of an eye, he turned and disappeared into the crowd.

Hope clung to Amanda's skirt, crying. "Mommy, some man took away my bag!"

Amanda picked her daughter up into her arms, comforting her as they quickly left the theater. This was the last time. No matter how many promises anyone made, she would never bring her daughter along again on something like this. Each of her daughter's sobs pierced her heart. "Hush, Peanut. It's okay. Are you hurt?"

"No, but I was mad, Mommy!"

"It's okay, Peanut. The bag isn't important, and Mommy won't ever let anyone separate us like that again. That's a promise."

Amanda spoke with conviction. It was a message meant for whoever was listening—from Tony and Raymond to the kidnappers.

THIRTY MINUTES LATER, as Amanda entered her home, she heard the phone ringing. Once again, the caller's number had been blocked. Ready to do battle, she picked up the receiver.

"You handled things well tonight," the electronic voice said.

"Listen to me and listen well, you witch!" she whispered hoarsely into the phone. "You think I'm not a threat to you, but you're wrong. If you ever threaten my daughter again, or even come *near* her, I'll hunt you down myself. Without her, I'll have nothing to lose."

As Amanda slammed down the phone and turned around, she saw her daughter had opened the door for Tony and Raymond. Tony still wore the fatigues, but he was no longer wearing the beard. He was staring at her in surprise.

"That wasn't them, was it?"

Amanda knew who he was referring to, though out of deference to Hope, he hadn't specified. "You bet."

Raymond passed by Tony and came in wearing a shoulder-length wig in keeping with the traditional Navaho style and clothing several sizes too big. "I think you did the right thing. You've shown them that there are limits to your cooperation. They'll rethink their approach."

"Or not call back at all now that they have the papers," Tony said, his voice taut and without emotion. As Hope ran down the hall to get a doll she'd left beside the bookcase, he added, "You may have just cost me my kid."

"And protected my own," Amanda said defensively, her voice lowered. "She's *my* first priority, just like Carmen is yours."

Tony nodded slowly, his anger still obvious, but under control. "You're right. I can't fault you for what you did. But please, if they call again, no matter what time it is, let me know immediately."

Without another word, he walked out the door. Raymond stood in the entrance. "He'll work it out, Amanda. You made the right move."

Amanda watched both men drive away, then locked the door. Hope was sitting on the sofa, watching her.

"Tony was mad, wasn't he, Mommy?"

"Yes, but that's something he has to settle himself. Right now I need a promise from you, Peanut."

"Okay, Mommy."

"Never, *ever*, open this door to a stranger. Only Bernice or me. Agreed?"

"Tony's not a stranger!" the child objected.

"New rules, Peanut. I don't want an argument. Just do it."

Hope nodded. "Okay, Mommy. Now can we eat dinner? I'm hungry!"

Amanda fixed Hope a potpie dinner and a dish of applesauce. After their ice-cream dessert Hope's eyes were almost closed. It wouldn't take long for her daughter to fall asleep tonight.

Amanda bathed her daughter quickly, and tucked her into bed. Glad for a chance to sort things out in her mind, she walked to the living room. She'd just sat down on the sofa when she heard a soft tapping at the door. Recognizing Bernice's familiar knock, Amanda invited her friend inside and waved her to a seat.

"I've been worried about you, Amanda. I hope you don't mind, but I've been doing some investigating of my own."

"What kind of investigating?" Amanda asked quickly.

"I've been trying to find out more about Tony Ramos. He's the heart of all your troubles, you know."

Amanda smiled thinly, knowing there was more truth to her friend's statement than she realized. "What did you learn?"

"A few months ago, Tony dated a records clerk at the police department. He apparently talked her into compromising her work because she started passing confidential information along to him. After she got caught and fired Tony never dated her again. He cost her her job, then dropped her the second she was no longer useful to him."

"Is that what you think he's doing with me?"

"Amanda, his priority is his child, not you. You can't trust anything he says or does, no matter how badly you may want to."

"I know that, Bernice."

"Tell me you're not falling in love with him, Amanda, and I'll stop worrying."

"How could I possibly be falling in love with him? I don't know him, not really. All I know about Tony is what he chooses to tell me, and that isn't anywhere near enough."

"That's not an answer. That sounds more like an argument you're using with yourself."

"It is," she sighed. "There's an attraction, sure. But it's not love."

Bernice stood up. "You've answered my question. It's already too late for warnings."

Amanda walked her friend to the door. "I know this can't go anywhere. Tony isn't the type of man I'd want as a father for my daughter. I knew that right from the start. But the heart doesn't always listen to reason."

Bernice gave Amanda a hug. "You're a strong person, Amanda. You'll be hurt, but you'll survive and go on."

After saying good-night to Bernice and locking up, Amanda walked to her bedroom and crawled into bed. She'd never been so exhausted in her life. The pleasant coolness of the sheets and the soft weight of the summer blanket soon wiped all thoughts from her mind. Before she knew it, the world of reality receded and she began to drift into dark oblivion.

Then, out of the darkness, an image of light came toward her. A woman, shrouded in mist, appeared, standing before her. A blinding light seemed to radiate from her, making it impossible for Amanda to see her face.

"You don't have to worry. Your daughter will be yours forever." The voice sounded like wind chimes dancing in the summer breeze.

"Who are you?" Amanda heard herself speaking, yet no words came out.

"I'm a friend, nothing more. I came because you needed me. I, too, lost my daughter once. I thought I'd failed, that I'd lost everything, but I was wrong. Love found a way."

Another scene unfolded before Amanda. She saw a woman trying in vain to reach her crying infant. A veil of some kind stood between them. Though the mother was desperately trying to comfort her baby, the child seemed not to see or hear her.

Amanda felt the woman's anguish as keenly as if it were her own. Then the scene faded. "The possibilities for good are endless," the soft voice said. "For a trusting heart, sadness is never the master of joy."

Amanda woke up abruptly, the reassuring words still echoing in her mind. It was only a dream, yet it had seemed so real! She felt tears rolling down her cheeks. The anguish of the mother in her dream lingered like a cloud over her heart.

No good could ever come from having a mother separated from her child. What she'd had was some sort of crazy nightmare. No mother could ever think otherwise.

AMANDA WENT TO WORK as usual the next morning. She hadn't heard from the kidnappers since she'd hung up on them. Perhaps they'd decided to use someone else as intermediary, or maybe they were planning to let her worry for a while.

Tony dropped by her office around ten, wearing his maintenance-man disguise. He closed the door behind him before he spoke. "If you hear from the kidnappers, call my pager number. I'll get in touch with you."

His voice was low, like rumbling thunder, and the pain in his eyes was too real not to wrap itself around her heart. Up to now, she'd thought that not hearing from the kidnappers would set her free of her worries, but the possibility that Tony would walk out of her life now, filled her with despair. "If I could call them and force them to deal directly with you, I would," she said.

"I know."

Amanda swallowed the lump in the throat. She wanted to step into his arms, to somehow soothe away his pain, but she couldn't will herself to move and knew there was nothing she could do to comfort him.

"If I could only figure out what they're after." Tony looked out the window, as if searching for something. "I've been racking my brains, trying to find some connection between the Henderson file and the forgery case, but there isn't one. My gut feeling is that they're trying to hide what they're really after because it'll give me a lead to them. I don't think they've asked for what they actually want yet. If I'm right, they'll call back."

"I know I shouldn't have hung up on them. I just had to do it. Please don't hate me for that," she whispered as he started out the door.

Tony stopped in midstride, closed the door, then faced her again. "If you truly want to know what's in my heart, come over here and I'll show you."

Amanda should have stood her ground. Heaven knew she'd meant to. Yet primitive forces she couldn't resist compelled her to do as he asked, and she stepped into his arms. His touch filled her with a delicious sense of expectation.

"My Mandy, my sweet Mandy," he murmured, pulling her closer. Long, powerful fingers laced through her hair, cradling her head as his mouth dipped down to take hers. His tongue played on her lips until they parted, then penetrated the moist recesses slowly and erotically until her entire body trembled with desire.

Tony held her tightly, letting her feel the effect she had on him, telling her without words what he felt. As her intercom buzzed, he released her. "I *am* the man destined for you, Mandy, and you are the woman I intend to make mine. But first there are things we must accomplish together."

The utter conviction in his voice excited as well as frightened her. If it was only a line, it must have been a well-practiced one, because she couldn't detect any hesitation or deception in it.

She moved toward her desk, but he reached out for her again, sweeping her back into his arms. His kiss, filled with hunger, was demanding. Her knees almost buckled, but he held her firm until fires too hot to suppress raged within her.

"If you ever doubt what is happening between us, think back to this moment, and you'll know the truth in your heart," Tony uttered softly, then left the room.

Amanda reached behind her, touching the bookcase to her right for balance. She couldn't stop trembling. More so than she had ever dreamed possible, need pounded through her, making her feel empty and lonely.

As she dropped into her chair, Bernice poked her head inside. "I'll be away from my desk for a while, helping out in the nursery. I have to cover while Doris has lunch."

"All right."

Amanda leaned back, eyes closed, trying to gather her thoughts. Despite her best efforts to deny it, Tony had carved a place in her heart. The knowledge that she'd have to walk away from him when the time came, pierced her like a cold blade from a killer's hand.

The sudden ringing of the phone cut into her thoughts. Amanda picked up the receiver. Her skin prickled as the electronic voice greeted her.

"We have a new message for Ramos. Tell him to get a blank New Mexico driver's license for us. We've got a plan worked out, but he'll need your help."

"For what? Getting arrested? There's no way either of us can get something like that without stealing it."

"You can get away with it, though, if you follow my directions. An elderly guard sets the forms out on a desk behind the counter each morning, and puts them away at the end of the day. If you distract the guard and the counter workers by creating a diversion, Ramos will have enough time to get around the counter and steal a blank form. He'll have to work fast.

"Once Ramos is out of range of the security camera that covers that area, he's to drop the form into your purse. The guard behind the monitor will probably see the theft. As he goes after Ramos, you're to leave the building. Ramos will be arrested, but they won't be able to hold him without the incriminating evidence."

"What am I supposed to do with the form once I'm outside?"

"Drop it through the open window of the blue-and-white pickup that'll be parked in front of the south door."

"I can't agree to this without talking to Tony. You're asking him to risk everything without giving him the information he needs to find his daughter."

"I'll contact you again in an hour."

The line was disconnected before she could ask any more questions. Relief and fear began pounding through her. Relief because now Tony would have to remain in her life, fear because she was once again in the thick of things.

Amanda called Tony's pager number, then sat back to wait. He would return her call soon, then it would all start again—if indeed it had ever ended. Destiny. Maybe Tony had been right all along. Only, unlike him, she couldn't quite see a happy ending for them.

Chapter Ten

Tony saw Amanda's number blinking on his pager. Gut instinct told him the kidnappers had called. He hurried back toward the day care, still wearing his maintenance-man disguise. He'd had a feeling that the trail to the kidnappers might begin with the day-care center. That's why he'd staked it out for the past few days whenever he'd had a chance.

Monitoring the bugs he'd placed in her office and her home had confirmed one thing: Amanda was as innocent as he'd hoped. And Bernice hated him as much as he'd suspected. He grinned mirthlessly. She had good reason to.

He rushed to Amanda's office. She jumped to her feet and quickly ushered him inside as he appeared at her door. "They called, didn't they?" he asked.

"Yes, and with a new demand." Amanda played the tape for him.

Tony listened to it, rubbing his neck with one hand. "When they call you again, tell them that before I risk jail to get this, I want proof that they know where my Carmen is."

"All right, but I also think we should contact Raymond. We've got to cover ourselves on this."

"What do you think Raymond could do, besides bail me out?"

"I don't know, but I want someone else in our corner. If things go wrong, I want muscle there to give us backup or, at the very least, substantiate that we were coerced into this. I don't think they'll carry out their threat of exposing our role in delivering the stolen file to them, but this plan of theirs could land us both in jail. Without some way of covering ourselves, I'm not sure I have the courage to go through with this."

Tony considered it. The kidnappers would love to have him tied up with the police. Then, they could take off for good, leaving him high and dry like the last time. "I'll approach Raymond, but first I've got a few things I want to check out. This new request by the kidnappers has given me a few ideas I want to look into. There's a definite connection with this and the information they wanted on that forgery case the Bureau's handling."

"You think they're forging drivers' licenses?"

"Yes, and that could be only the tip of the iceberg. They could create whole new identities from that starting point." He walked to the door, then turned around. "At least they didn't say anything about Hope or her possible involvement in the future."

"No. I think they've backed off on that, thank goodness."

"Good. I'm relieved to hear it."

Tony walked out of the building and toward his pickup. He'd have to approach Raymond carefully. He had a plan, but it entailed bending the law, something he wasn't sure his friend would go along with. What he'd need first was a bargaining chip, something that would make things more palatable to his Bureau buddy.

AMANDA WATCHED THE CLOCK. Forty-five minutes had passed. She'd hoped Tony would return before the kidnapper's contact called. There was no telling how the caller would react when she heard that Tony had demands of his own.

Tony arrived at her office just as the phone on her desk began to ring. Amanda glanced down at it hesitantly, then up at Tony.

"Answer it. I'll grab the extension on Bernice's desk. She's not there to demand an explanation."

The electronic voice greeted her cordially, which made it all the more revolting. Amanda steeled herself to take as hard a line as necessary. Being tough had seemed easy when they'd threatened Hope, now she wasn't sure she could carry it off.

"Does Ramos understand the plan?"

"Yes, but he wants proof that you really do know where his daughter is. Otherwise, he won't do it. I won't, either."

"What kind of proof?"

Tony cut in sharply. "I'm here. Talk to me directly. No more games, slimeball."

"I'll make this fast, Ramos. We'll deliver convincing proof to the day-care-center office by two this afternoon. Be ready to move on our plan for you to steal the blank driver's license from the Department of Motor Vehicles by four forty-five today. By then, the employees there are tired, and they have a tendency to get sloppy. That's the best time to strike."

Hearing the dial tone, Tony hung up and went back into Amanda's office. "They didn't even hesitate about the proof. They're the real thing, all right. They probably know where Carmen is right now."

"They must want that form pretty bad," she commented.

"They have their own agenda. This is what they wanted in the first place. False IDs on the real forms can be worth thousands of dollars."

Amanda glanced at the photo of Hope on her desk. "I won't risk going to jail, Tony. I just can't."

"I've taken care of that. Raymond's in on this and a plan's already in motion. You'll be in no danger."

"Can I talk to him before we get started?"

"No. It's best if he's nowhere near you until after it's over. Besides, he's got his hands full at the moment."

"I want to know exactly what you've got up your sleeve."

He shook his head. "Not this time, Amanda. This involves other people's secrets. If you want, I'll sign a statement right now saying that I've coerced you into going along with a Bureau sting operation, and I'm solely responsible for your involvement. You won't go to jail, believe me."

Amanda walked to her computer, composed a short statement, then printed it out. "How's this? It's mostly what you just said."

Tony read it over. "Fine."

"Wait. I want Bernice to witness the signature."

She called Bernice into the office, and after Tony signed the paper, she handed it over to Bernice to place in the safe.

Amanda wasn't sure what Tony was up to. His story about Raymond being too busy was probably true, but she couldn't be sure Tony wasn't pulling a fast one. "You'll be back here at two to receive the proof, right?"

"I'm shooting for one-thirty, just in case they're early. In the meantime, I'll try to get Raymond to give you a call if you think it'll set your mind at ease. I'll also ask him to tail the messenger. We'll want him questioned, but not detained, in case the kidnappers are watching our every move."

"I'd appreciate that."

Amanda stayed at her desk long after Tony left. She filled out reports, then answered calls from parents and prospective clients, trying to fight her nervousness by immersing herself in her duties. Nothing seemed to work. Bernice walked in a half hour later, holding a sandwich and a cola. "Here. With all the pressure on you, I don't think you should skip lunch. You don't need to get sick."

Amanda took the food from Bernice's hands, though she wasn't hungry, and set it down on her desk. As she did, her sleeve brushed against a cup holding pencils and pens, sending them crashing to the floor.

"Oh, great. Typical of the way my day's going." Amanda bent down to retrieve them.

"I'll let some more light in here," Bernice said, opening the curtains all the way.

Amanda reached under her desk for a pencil that had rolled there and spotted something lodged under the desktop, near where the phone rested. At first glance, it appeared to be a wad of gum, but she had no idea how it would have gotten there. "Have any of the kids been in here?"

"Not to my knowledge," Bernice answered.

After reaching for a Kleenex tissue in her pocket, she pried the object loose. It was a bit too firm to be gum.

Amanda rose to her feet and placed the object on top of her desk. She stared at it, comprehension slowly dawning. Someone had been listening in on all her conversations with a tiny microphone.

Putting a finger to her lips, Amanda stepped outside her office, pulling Bernice along by the arm. Then, just for good measure, she walked out to the playground in the back, motioning for Bernice to follow. "Our conversations have been monitored," Amanda finally announced.

"The kidnappers?" Bernice sounded shocked.

"Possibly, but that doesn't seem right. They were more interested in giving orders than in listening to anything I had to say."

"But then . . . Tony—" Bernice began echoing Amanda's thoughts, her voice suddenly full of conviction.

Everyone had told her that Tony was manipulative, a user of people who'd honed that particular skill to an art. She hadn't truly believed that, but now the truth stared her plainly in the face. Tony had used the device to gather information about her, making sure he was employing all the right techniques to lower her guard. The pain of his betrayal pierced her soul.

"You have to confront him with it. You have to make sure it was his handiwork and not someone else's," Bernice said.

"I intend to do just that this afternoon. Then he and I will have to rethink a few plans. Trust between us is no longer an option." Amanda turned and headed back to her office.

From now on, she wouldn't allow anyone to manipulate her, not the kidnappers, not Raymond, not Tony. It was time for her to start calling her own shots.

FROM THE MOMENT Tony walked into her office, he knew something was wrong. His gut tightened as he looked into Amanda's eyes and saw the pain and anger there.

Unwilling to hazard any guesses as to the cause, a sure way to make things worse, he took a seat, prepared to wait her out. Then he saw the bug he'd placed beneath her desk lying on top of some files directly before him.

"Your doing, isn't it?"

Tony thought about denying it. He could always blame it on the kidnappers, but he'd always taken responsibility for his own actions, and she deserved at least that from him. His feelings for Amanda had grown deeper than he'd ever dreamed possible, and the time for lies was long past.

"I did place it in here, yes." The anguish he saw etched on her face knifed through him. "It was necessary at the time. Think back a few days, Amanda. When we first embarked on this I knew nothing about you. And my instincts told me you were holding back."

He watched her. She wasn't really listening to him. He had a feeling she was trying to remember everything she'd said inside this office during the past few days. Then her expression suddenly changed, and she glared at him, fire in her eyes. "Is there another one in my home?"

He rejected the thought of lying. He knew what was bothering her. He'd learned the threat the kidnappers had used to keep her involved and the real reason she'd allowed herself to be manipulated. He'd heard her discussing their tactics with Bernice, courtesy of the bug he'd placed in her office. He knew they had threatened to make him believe Hope was really Carmen, and that Amanda, having decided to keep Hope's adoption a secret, was especially vulnerable, though that threat was without any basis. Knowing the truth, he wouldn't have made problems for her that would have resulted in anyone taking Hope away from her. Of course, he couldn't have predicted what the kidnappers might have done had she refused to cooperate.

"There's one there, too," he admitted at last, "but I would never use anything I overheard against you."

"Where did you put it?" Her voice was the temperature of a frozen lake.

"In the kitchen, underneath the trim on a cabinet." He saw the pain flashing in her eyes.

"And now you expect me to trust your word and believe you've really contacted Raymond." Amanda shook her head. "I can't. Your word, your honor, is questionable at best."

"You can trust the way I feel, and know I wouldn't—"

She held up her hand. "Enough. In my heart, I once gave you the benefit of the doubt, but not again." Then a look of alarm crossed her face. "Wait a minute. If you placed a bug here, maybe the kidnappers did, too."

He shook his head. "Mine would have picked up interference. At least it kept you safe from them in that way." Tony looked directly at her, trying to convince her he wasn't the enemy. "Don't judge me too harshly. Remember that throughout all this, you've chosen to keep your own secrets."

"Yes, but my secrets couldn't harm you."

"Then why didn't you share them with me? I would have protected you."

"The person I need the most protection from *is* you. Were you also responsible for the phony bomb, and the rock being thrown through my window, not to mention stealing the photo of Hope from my dresser? Was it all part of your plan to control me?"

Tony stood up, anger surging inside him. "Those accusations are beneath you. Deep down, you know the answer." He walked around Amanda's desk and spun her chair around to face him. "Do you really have so little faith in me? I've protected you and your secrets. Face it, Amanda. We were both at fault. Neither of us trusted the other."

"Then maybe neither of us is worthy of love," she said, an almost numbing coldness settling over her.

"Love doesn't depend on merit to exist. It never has and it never will." Tony strode through the door and left her alone in her office.

RAYMOND KNOCKED at her door a short time later. He was dressed as a janitor and she barely recognized him. "I thought you and I needed a chance to talk. Are you okay with Tony's plan?"

"I'll be fine as long as I don't land in jail," Amanda admitted.

"There's no chance of that. Tony has uncovered evidence of a forgery ring. He's turned the information over to the Bureau and agreed to cooperate with our operation. His services are crucial to us if we're to catch this gang that's been working our area. The Bureau is on *this* case officially, and I'm heading the task force."

"How is my involvement being explained, officially, that is?"

"You were contacted by the gang because you've been dating my old partner. When you were both coerced into agreeing to the theft, my ex-partner notified the Bureau."

"I'm glad we'll be safe," Amanda confessed.

"I wouldn't call it 'safe.' Unless your performance is convincing, the kidnappers will catch on, and Tony can effectively say goodbye to his kid. That trail's been cold for too long. His chances of finding her are next to none without a good tip."

Raymond glanced at his watch. "But we're getting ahead of ourselves. Let's see what happens first, and what proof the kidnappers offer him. It's almost time for that delivery. I better leave. I've got to keep an eye out for the messenger and see if we can ID the person."

"I'm glad you'll be there."

"So am I," Raymond replied. "Remember one thing, Amanda. My old partner's not the only one with a few tricks up his sleeve. I know him very well, and I'll take care of him. That's what friends are for."

She knew that he was telling her far more than his words indicated. "I don't suppose you'd care to be more specific?"

"I've already told you more than I should have." Pushing a large carpet sweeper, Raymond left her office.

Tony arrived moments later. There was a fire in his eyes that nothing could disguise. He wanted action, she could see that plainly.

They sat across from each other and Amanda watched him. She resisted the urge to reach out and take his hand. He could make her blood simmer with desire with only one look. She was tempted to try to salvage the few things that were right between them. But there were so many conflicting emotions racing through her, she wasn't sure which to heed. "I have no more secrets from you, but you still have some of your own," she observed.

"What good would full disclosures do now? Telling you the truth has cost me enough. You refuse to believe me now, even when I do tell you the truth, that I love you and will protect you."

"I don't know what to believe anymore. I've run out of answers," she said wearily.

"You're scared, just as scared as I am." Tony walked around to her seat and pulled her to her feet. "Yet, even now, despite it all, you respond to me when I'm close to you, just as I respond to you."

She could feel the warmth of his body, but although he stood only inches away, he didn't draw her into his embrace. "Why are you doing this?" she whispered.

"To remind you that we're both just human. We can be hurt, and we have needs." As a knock sounded on her door, he moved away.

Bernice came in and glared at Tony. As she turned to Amanda, her gaze softened. "This came for you."

"Thanks, Bernice."

"I'll be right outside if you need me."

Amanda handed Tony the sealed eight-by-twelve manila envelope. He returned to his chair and extracted the contents carefully, setting them out on her desk. "Copies of a birth certificate and an adoption certificate," Tony said pensively. "If these footprints match the ones on Carmen's birth certificate, then I'll know."

"You'll know what?"

"That they forged the papers for my daughter and placed her up for adoption three years ago," he said, his voice so controlled it was flat.

"Is the adoption certificate real?"

"The documents might be genuine, but if the footprints are Carmen's, there's nothing legal or accurate about the information on them." He stood up. "I have some things to track down in a hurry. I'll be back later with a final plan for us to carry out at the Department of Motor Vehicles."

TONY MET WITH RAYMOND at a mall parking lot a short time later. He handed over the papers, then brought out Carmen's real birth certificate. "I want Joe Parker to take a look at these. He's the best in the state. If these two foot-prints are off even slightly, except for size, he'll spot it. I have to know if this is for real, and this isn't my area of expertise."

"If I ask Joe, then the Bureau *will* get officially involved in the kidnapping again. Questions will come up."

"But not right away. I know a way I can buy us some time."

"How?"

"State Senator Matt Miller owes me a favor. I finally tracked down his runaway daughter and only charged him for expenses. I even managed to keep the press off his tail and hers. I met him in alleys and parking lots, just so it would never be on the record. He'd be willing to ask the Bureau to loan him their fingerprint expert. They'd honor his request, too, if he says it's official business, even if he doesn't give them details."

Raymond nodded. "Miller's got a lot of clout. He helped us solve a federal case several months ago involving inter-state fraud. Without cooperation from his office, we couldn't have done it. It should work. And we're going to need to score a few points soon. That messenger was a dead end. Someone dropped off the package with the exact cash for an in-town delivery, like they'd used them before. No questions were asked."

"Let's get going, then. I don't want to do one more thing for these creeps until I know if they really are the ones who took Carmen or can lead me to her."

AMANDA WAITED at her office until she couldn't stand it any longer. She needed to know the plan. How was she supposed to effectively distract a guard and the workers, as well as any patrons waiting in line? She had to get a look at the layout over at the DMV building.

She picked up her purse and walked over to Bernice's desk. "I'm going out for a bit. If Tony comes by, tell him

I'm on my way to the Department of Motor Vehicles. I need to check out a few things.''

Bernice gave her a searching look. "You're not going to tell me what's going on?"

"Not yet. Believe me, it wouldn't help you to know," Amanda admitted with a weak smile.

As Amanda drove, she kept glancing in the rearview mirror. This whole situation was making her extraordinarily paranoid. She parked on the north side of the building and tried to force herself to calm down and act natural. If she appeared nervous, the guards would know she was up to something for sure, and they'd watch her like hawks.

Amanda took several deep breaths, then got out of the car. As she started across the parking lot, Tony came rushing up. He was wearing jeans and a drab-colored shirt.

"You're ahead of schedule. What's going on?" he whispered.

"I was only going to take a look inside. My distraction's got to be good, and I want to see where the camera's positioned."

"No, it's better if this is unrehearsed. Let me tell you my plan."

BY THE TIME AMANDA walked inside, her palms were sweating and her knees felt like rubber. She needed to act more casual. Learning from Tony that Raymond had only told one official what they'd be doing frightened her. She'd understood why they'd wanted to minimize the risk of a leak, but the operation had taken on a very dangerous edge. If they didn't pull it off, Tony would be placed under arrest. Though neither of them would go to jail, the next few minutes could determine whether Tony got his child back.

Amanda walked into the ladies' room, then opened the plastic bag filled with dry ice that Tony had given her. It wasn't much, but when it hit the toilet water, the room would fill up with what appeared to be smoke. All she had to do then was run out and yell "Fire."

Amanda dropped the ice into the toilet bowl, and within seconds, thick white vapor began to fill the bathroom. Amanda blocked the path of two women who started to come inside. "There's a fire in here! It's everywhere!"

The women rushed out screaming, just as photoelectric sensors triggered a smoke alarm. The high-pitched wail cut right through her ears.

Amanda hurried out, then stood with her back to the wall as people shouted and rushed toward the exit doors. In the midst of the confusion, Tony passed by and shoved the stolen form into her open purse. Quickly, Amanda joined the crowd hurrying toward the south exit.

As Amanda reached the doors, she glanced back. Tony was several feet behind her. Maybe they'd be able to make a clean getaway. She waited outside the building, and as the crowd thinned, she spotted Tony opening the door. Suddenly, two guards built like small mountains appeared and pulled him back inside, pinning Tony against a wall.

Amanda felt her heart twist as she saw Tony being manhandled. She wanted to go back, but she had her own task to complete. Walking to the blue-and-white pickup parked near the side door, she noted that the rear of the vehicle had no license plate. Amanda slipped the paper through the partially opened window and continued across the parking lot.

Chapter Eleven

Amanda returned to the center, barely managing to park her car without hitting the vehicles on either side. Thirty minutes after the theft, her hands were still shaking.

"You look awful," Bernice said, rushing to her side. "Are you okay?"

"I've been better. Have there been any calls for me?"

"No." Bernice studied her. "I'm going to get you a glass of iced tea. Why don't you go to your office and sit down?"

Once in her office, Amanda turned on her radio, expecting to hear some coverage of the incident as soon as the hourly news came on. Just as Bernice came in holding a glass of iced tea, the news came on, with the DMV story as the lead item. Tony's arrest and the diversion created by the dry ice were detailed. The police, the broadcast said, were looking for Tony's accomplice, possibly a woman.

Bernice stared at Amanda. "Tell me that wasn't you."

"If you insist. It wasn't me. Just don't hold it against me if it turns out later that I lied."

Bernice dropped down into a chair, took the iced tea, and began sipping it herself. "Well, at least Tony's in jail and out of the picture for a while. That hell is over."

Amanda thought about Bernice's words. Hell was wanting what you could never have. Right now, her worry for Tony kept her from fully concentrating on even the smallest task. "I hope that after this the kidnappers finally tell him where to find his daughter. He's put everything on the line to get her back."

Amanda glanced at the phone, dreading whatever would come next. The kidnappers probably hadn't expected Tony to be caught. Amanda was afraid that once they learned he was in jail, they'd focus on her to get what they wanted. If they reported her to the state authorities, and no one could find Hope's adoption records, she was afraid that they would start a search for Hope's birth parents. If Hope's birth father came forward, she might lose her daughter to him or even the state.

It was almost time for Amanda to leave for the day when Raymond came into her office. She felt her heart stop. "Has something gone wrong? Where's Tony?"

"He'll be out soon. I'm just here to tell you that we've verified the footprints, and except for having been taken at a later age, they match Carmen's. We tried to track down the adoptive parents listed, but the names and address were phony."

"So the FBI is now officially involved?"

"Sort of. As it turns out, Tony has made some powerful friends over the past few years. By special request, I've been loaned out to a state senator, and through him I'm working Tony's case. The Bureau doesn't know the specifics of what I'm doing, and won't for another few weeks. That was the deal that was cut."

"I'm glad to hear it. Maybe this nightmare will finally end, and the kidnappers will tell Tony where his child is."

"Tony and I will see to it that they do. That truck you placed the blank license form into could give us some productive leads. Unfortunately, we lost the driver in traffic when he went through a red light, but we have other ways of tracking him down. I'll let you know when we finish tying things up." Raymond leaned back and regarded her thoughtfully. "While I was searching the computer files, I came across something very interesting."

Something in his tone sent a chill up her spine. "What?"

"I never quite got a handle on why you were so willing to help Tony," Raymond explained slowly.

"They threatened my day-care center." Amanda's mouth was as dry as the desert sand.

Raymond shrugged. "So you said. But in the course of doing a background search on you, I tried to find Hope's birth certificate. There wasn't one filed with the state. You said Hope was born here in New Mexico, right?"

Amanda felt sick. She grasped the arms of her chair, but forced herself to meet Raymond's eyes. "Am *I* under investigation now?"

"Not officially."

"Then why don't you concentrate on what you're supposed to be doing? State employees have been known to produce bureaucratic bungles, including misplacing records. If you work at it yourself, I'm sure you'll find those records. But it's a waste of precious time. If you want to see my daughter's birth certificate, ask my lawyer, who is not my ex-husband, by the way, and handle it through him."

Raymond regarded her unblinkingly for a long time. "That's not necessary. For now."

As the federal agent stood up, Tony came into her office. He wore a cowboy hat pulled low over his face, along with a denim shirt and jeans. As he took off the hat, Amanda saw the bruise that covered the left side of his face. His eye was almost swollen shut. Amanda gasped. "What happened?"

"Oh, this?" Tony winced. "I used my eye to prevent the guard's fist from going through my head. I had to make it look good, you know."

Raymond shook his head. "You look better than the poor security guard you decked when they tried to cuff you."

"How did I know he wasn't trained in hand to hand? He should have blocked my move. I telegraphed the punch."

"The other guy, the one who finally managed to get the handcuffs on you, must have had a few moves of his own."

"Yeah, that's for sure. I think he was feeling insecure after his partner kissed the carpet."

Amanda stared at them, then threw her hands up in the air. "What is it with you two? That—" she pointed to Tony's face "—has got to hurt like hell, yet you're treating it as nothing more than a little macho game!" She shook her head and returned to her desk. "I think you both eat too much red meat," she muttered.

Raymond laughed and Tony joined him.

"Catch you later, buddy," Raymond said and headed out the door.

Tony sat down heavily. "Forgive the male posturing. It's a knee-jerk reaction. If you want to know the truth, it *does* hurt like hell." He glanced at the phone. "No news, I take it?"

"Not yet."

He stood up. "I'm going to see if I can help Raymond track down something on that pickup."

Amanda blocked his way out the door. "Take care of yourself, Tony," she implored softly. Standing mere inches from him, she was vibrantly aware of everything about him. She needed him, just as he needed her. Her gaze fell on his hard mouth, then drifted downward. Her body ached with needs only he could fulfill.

"I'll take care of both of us, Amanda." He brushed her cheek with the palm of his hand. "Trust me. I know that's a lot to ask, but I need you to believe in me."

The plea came from his soul and was mirrored in his eyes. She was shaken by its impact. "I'm not sure I'm capable of that anymore."

"You have to be willing to risk your heart. If you're not willing to do that, you'll be risking even more."

She looked down the hall as a group of youngsters was being taken single file to the playground. "It's easy for kids to trust. Once we're adults, we have more to lose, and it takes longer for wounds to heal."

"Then reach for the little girl within you. It's our only hope, my beautiful lady."

The thought of being his "lady" wove a spell around her, and her skin burned as if branded where he'd caressed her. She wanted to be his, to share in that world of gentle and fiery sensations they'd found with each other.

She stepped back into her office as he left. To accept Tony for herself was one thing, but no matter how much her heart cried out for him, she'd always have Hope to consider. Hope needed a father who was dependable and forthright. Despite everything, she still knew very little about Tony.

Amanda picked up her daughter from the nursery and began the drive home. Hope, oblivious to the actions that had such an impact on her destiny, was in wonderful spirits. She'd made a new friend and nothing seemed more important to her than that. She told Amanda everything about her exciting day.

Then, pausing only to take a breath, Hope switched the topic of conversation. "Mommy, will Tony come over tonight and play? He's nice. I want him to be my daddy."

Amanda's mouth dropped slightly. "Peanut, that's not very nice. You have a daddy."

Hope shook her head. "Daddy Ron's not home. He never comes home anymore, and he never wants to play. Tony wants to be a daddy. He likes to play. He likes you, too, Mommy. Can you ask him if he wants to come over and be my daddy?"

"It doesn't work that way, Peanut."

"Why?"

Amanda stared at the road, trying desperately to think of something a three-year-old would understand. "Well, because for him to become your Daddy, he has to be married to me and be my husband."

"But you like him, Mommy. I can tell."

Amanda wished she'd changed topics right from the start. Now it was too late. Knowing her daughter, she realized the subject wouldn't be dropped until she was satisfied with the answer. "It's a grown-up thing," Amanda said, falling back on a tried-and-true gambit.

"But he'd be a *good* daddy," Hope insisted stubbornly, then started singing a nursery rhyme about making a wish.

Amanda sighed. Sometimes her daughter was three going on thirty.

A short time later, as Amanda walked with Hope to the mailbox, Ricky Biddle came jogging by. Amanda suspected he'd been waiting in some cool shade for them to arrive. His hair was neatly combed, and despite the heat, he didn't seem to have worked up much of a sweat.

"I saw you at the movie theater the other day. Did you like the movie?"

"It was exciting," she answered, hoping Ricky wouldn't expect her to comment on specifics. If her life had depended on it, she wouldn't have been able to describe one single scene.

"I heard on the radio that Tony Ramos was arrested. I'm really glad you're rid of him, Amanda."

Amanda gave him a sharp look. "You shouldn't judge people you don't really know, Ricky," she said firmly. "Rumors are notoriously inaccurate and a lousy way to tell what someone's really like." As she said it, she realized how much she'd been guilty of the same thing. She'd passed judgment on Tony before they'd really known each other, all based on innuendo and rumor.

"Let's not get into an argument," he said plaintively. "I came to ask you over for a quiet dinner for two."

Amanda stared at him, surprised he'd speak that way in front of Hope. "Ricky, we're friends, that's all. I'd like to keep it at that."

"Then why have you been sending me all those signals, giving me all those interested looks?" he demanded, suddenly angry.

"What on earth are you talking about? I've treated you like a neighbor, that's all. We hardly ever talk. We both go our own way," she said, trying to soften the impact of her words.

"I'm not good enough for you to date, is that it? Ramos, that rude bully, is okay, but I'm not? There's gratitude!"

"Gratitude for what?"

"I've always been there when you needed someone. Not that you noticed, or that I care. I'm not anyone's doormat."

As he ran off, Amanda stared after Ricky in surprise. Of all the reactions she'd expected from him, that hadn't been one of them.

"I don't like Ricky," Hope said.

"We both agree on that, Peanut."

Hope tugged at her mother's hand. "Come on, Mommy. I'm hungry!"

Amanda smiled at Hope as they walked inside the house. "Are you ever *not* hungry?"

Hope ran to her room to get her toys, oblivious to Amanda's last comment.

Amanda walked directly to the kitchen. There was one bit of business she intended to take care of before anything else. Searching underneath her kitchen cabinets, she found the bug Tony had placed there.

Amanda stared at the tiny object for a long moment, then dropped it into the garbage disposal and flipped on the switch. There was an awful crunch, then the whine of whirling blades. So much for that. Turning on the faucet, she watched the stream of water flow into the drain. Then she began preparing dinner.

TWO HOURS LATER, as Hope played before her on the living room rug, Amanda felt a sense of peace. She glanced at the chair across from hers and imagined Tony there. How wonderful if they could have been a real family!

Breaking the thought, she stared at the caller ID by the phone, forcing herself to face reality. With all the problems facing her, here she was daydreaming about playing house. With her daughter, it was cute. With herself, it merited psychotherapy.

Hearing the phone ring, Amanda's heart leapt to her throat. She glanced at the display and noted the call was being made from a pay phone.

Just then, Hope, eager for something else to do, glanced up at her. "Mommy, can I play dress up? I'll be careful, promise!"

Amanda nodded. As her daughter left the room, Amanda quickly picked up the telephone.

The electronic voice that greeted her was not cordial this time. "Ramos is trying to find out who we are. You have to divert him. Start interfering with his investigation."

"Why should I do that? He's done everything you asked. You're the ones who aren't holding up your end of the bargain."

"I've got a news flash for you, Amanda. Hope isn't legally yours. We didn't erase the records. They were never there."

"You're crazy. I was married to an attorney. He filed those papers."

"No, he didn't. He was afraid of getting arrested and disbarred. The adoption papers your sister-in-law signed contained the signature of Hope's birth father. But his signature was forged, because he was never told about the baby or the adoption. Think back. You'll know I'm right. We can make sure that Hope's birth father will show up and invalidate the adoption. Then your daughter will be taken away from you so fast you'll never know what hit you."

Amanda's stomach knotted and her flesh became covered with goose bumps. She'd never looked that closely at the adoption papers, trusting Ron to take care of the legalities. Searching her memory, she tried to remember everything she could. She recalled that Hope's birth father had moved, but she'd assumed Ron's sister had located him long enough to get the signature. If that wasn't the case, and the kidnappers could prove it, the entire adoption might be invalidated.

"I'll do what you ask," Amanda said weakly.

"Good girl," the electronic voice praised, then the line was disconnected.

Amanda now understood more than ever why the kidnappers had chosen to deal with her. She was the ideal contact since they had the perfect leverage.

As she erased the taped message, Amanda realized just how deep into trouble she was getting. She couldn't expect Tony to trust her if she lied to him. Yet the last thing she wanted was for anyone else to suspect Hope's adoption hadn't been legal.

Amanda stared at the phone. Although she had no wish to confront Ron, she had to know the truth. There were so many questions she needed him to answer. Had he forged that signature himself or taken it to someone else? Were some of the other papers forged, too? She remembered how thrilled she'd been when he'd brought Hope home only days after telling her about the child. She'd seen it as a blessing at the time. Now, except for the love she shared with Hope, it all seemed to have become a nightmare.

Amanda picked up the phone to call Ron, then set it down again quickly. She was terrified of finding out that Hope wasn't legally hers, that it had all been a sham. If that were the case, and she confronted Ron, he'd be sure to try to cover his tracks. With everything else going on, and with her life under such close scrutiny by whoever was behind the threats, it was very possible things would break wide open. Once others knew, it would only be a matter of time before Hope would be taken from her, and there'd be nothing she could do about it.

Amanda sat up when she heard the doorbell ring. Nervously, she peeked out the window. It was Tony in his repairman's disguise again. As soon as she opened the door, he walked inside. "What's been going on?"

Panic swelled within her, but she struggled to keep her thoughts clear. She knew exactly what she had to say and the words came out automatically. "Tony, things are getting out of hand. I need to trust you, but I'm not sure I can. The truth is I know very little about you. Do you realize I don't even know how you make a living? A few cases here and there surely isn't enough to account for the large sums it takes to pay off informants. Yet you always seem to have enough."

Tony sat down in one of her chairs and looked across the room, staring at the books on a shelf. Finally he spoke. "Most of the money I've been using comes from a sizable trust left to Lynn by her father. That fund should have gone to Carmen, but I've been using it to stay afloat while I searched for her. I've hated doing that, believe me, but I had no choice. All the money and time I've had has been used searching for my child."

Amanda nodded. "I can understand that, more than you know." She picked up a photo of Hope from her coffee table. "All I ever wanted was a family. I never knew my dad, and my mother died when I was ten. I was raised in foster homes. I remember saving up and buying a pretty ceramic cottage. In my mind, I pictured all the rooms and what the furnishings were like. I knew some day I'd have a home where I'd be needed and wanted, a place filled with children.

"But my dreams have never really come true. Ron couldn't father a child, and he only adopted, I think, in order to cover that fact. Ron never wanted Hope, or the real me. He wanted a woman he could show off at parties, one who would look good in a photo on his desk. When all was said and done, I had to accept that my daughter would also grow up without a father. But I found my own strengths and gave Hope a home and surrounded her with love. She, at least, was mine. Then after I got that crazy phone call with a message for you, it turned everything upside down." Amanda shook her head. "Nothing could ever have prepared me for that call. I don't know...maybe dreams aren't meant to come true."

Tony came up and placed his hand on her shoulder. "No one can take Hope away from you. She's your child. What's the problem?"

Amanda realized the time for full disclosure had come. Halfway measures were no longer good enough. When everything was at stake, everything had to be given away. She took a deep breath and proceeded to tell him about the latest threat made to her. She even admitted erasing the tape. "If you go after your child, I'll lose mine," she said, moving away from him.

Tony considered what she'd told him for a long moment. "If they know the adoption wasn't legal, they'll use that whenever it suits them. You have to concentrate on the real threat facing you, Amanda, and I'm not it. If we work together, we may both end up with our kids."

Amanda met his gaze. The honesty and courage shining there wrapped itself around her, filling her and pushing away her fear. A genuine alliance with a man thought of as dangerous by his enemies didn't seem so bad all of a sudden. And even more importantly, for the first time, she didn't feel so utterly alone.

"I don't know how to protect Hope," she admitted.

"First of all, you've got to get her out of town, some-place where no one would know where to find her."

"Out of town? Are you crazy? My daughter belongs with me!"

"Even if that's not the safest place for her?"

Amanda's shoulders slumped. "There's only one person I'd trust with Hope. Bernice."

"Too obvious."

"That's the best I can do."

"Then call Bernice," he said. "Ask her to come over. Maybe she has a suggestion."

Amanda made a quick phone call and ten minutes later Bernice arrived. She gave Tony a hostile glance, then looked at Amanda with concern. "What's going on?"

Amanda gave her the highlights quickly. "So Tony seems to think that Hope would be better off someplace else for now."

Bernice nodded slowly. "Unlikely as it may seem, I agree. But I know of only one place where she'd be as safe as she is with you or me."

"Where?"

"My sister Miriam's. You and I took Hope there once and she loved it. She spent all her time watching the horses and cows."

"I remember. The farm's about an hour from here, east of Galisteo. It's in a very remote area, if I recall correctly."

"You do. It's a hard place to find, even when you've been there before."

Amanda nodded. "Even with a map, we ended up lost in the middle of nowhere—twice!"

"It sounds perfect," Tony said, then turned to Bernice. "Do you think your sister would be willing to put Hope up for a few days?"

"She'd love it. Miriam has no more kids at home, and that kind of place just cries out for children." Bernice gave Amanda a hug. "I know this is very hard for you, but Hope will be safe there. I'll even leave Winston with her as added insurance. That dog won't leave her side and nobody will be able to get near her unless Winston knows them."

A wave of anguish engulfed Amanda. What she'd feared most was losing Hope, and now, in order to keep her safe, she had to send her baby away. Her heart was slowly breaking into a million pieces.

"All right," Amanda said at last. "I'll tell her I've got to go away on business for a few days and we've arranged for a special treat for her."

Bernice put her arm around Amanda's shoulders. "I realize how hard this is for you. I don't think you've been away from Hope for more than a night since she was born. But you're doing the right thing. She'll be safe at Miriam's."

"Yes, but it does hurt. She should be safest with me." Amanda's voice was barely a whisper. Dread chilled her soul as she thought ahead to the nights when the house would echo with silence.

"It will all be over soon, Amanda. I promise. This *will* end," Tony said, conviction in his tone.

"Shall I arrange for this tonight?" Bernice asked.

"Yes," Tony answered. "We'll smuggle Hope out of town immediately."

Amanda took a long, deep breath. "I can sneak Hope out and drive her to the ranch as soon as Bernice checks with her sister. It won't take me long to pack up Hope's things."

"It's a good plan. We'll make sure it works," Tony said. "I'll follow along well behind you, Amanda, but I'll be there to make sure nobody tails you. Give me about an hour, though, to get some different wheels. In case I need it, I want something with a more powerful engine than my pickup."

Amanda nodded her agreement. So much had separated them in the past, but this time they were in perfect accord. Both were parents, fighting for their children. Amanda saw the understanding that flickered in his eyes, and her heart reached out to his.

Bernice cleared her throat. "I'll call Miriam now. She'll be happy to take care of Hope, believe me." She headed for the kitchen.

Tony joined Amanda by the window. Placing one hand on her shoulder, he slowly turned her around. "With all that's going on, I may not be a good role model for any child at this point in my life, Amanda, but I do care about you, and I care about Hope. You can trust in that completely. I know the streets, and I know criminals, maybe far too well for your tastes. But right now, that knowledge is exactly what you need in your corner."

She suppressed a shiver. Tony could be ruthless, but to fight the kidnappers, she'd need him there beside her. Since the day when Ron had placed that tiny little girl in her arms, Amanda had stopped defining herself as one person. Hope had claimed a place in her heart so thoroughly that she couldn't even imagine how she'd ever gotten by without her. A few times she'd entertained the thought of adopting a second child, but Amanda wasn't sure she could ever love a second child as much as she loved Hope.

Yet now she was being asked to send her little girl away because she was no longer capable of keeping her safe. Her heart breaking, she prepared to do what she had to for the safety of her child.

AMANDA DROVE CAREFULLY as she headed out of town with her daughter. Once she hit an empty stretch of highway, she noticed a blue sedan in the distance behind her. Tony would guard them well.

As they traveled down the highway, Hope was full of questions. Hiding the truth from her child would be the hardest task of all.

"Mommy, I want to go with you! Why can't I go?"

"Peanut, I'll be away a very short time, and I'll call you often, I promise. Besides, you're going to love being at Miriam's."

"Can I help feed the ponies?"

Amanda swallowed back her tears, determined not to break down in front of her daughter. "I'm sure you can. And you know what? Winston will be coming out to stay with you, too."

"Yay!"

Amanda sang nursery rhymes along with Hope, helping pass the time. They arrived an hour later. Despite everything, to Amanda it seemed as if the time had sped by much too quickly.

Amanda took Hope to Miriam, who sat waiting for them on the porch swing. Hope suddenly spotted the horses in the corral and dashed to the end of the porch for a better view.

"Mommy, look! Big ponies!"

Miriam laughed. "We don't have the ponies anymore, Hope, but we do have some mares. You'll like old Betsy, I'll bet. She's the chestnut horse with the white socks. She'll happily carry you around the arena as often as you want."

Amanda glanced at Miriam. "Are you sure it's safe?"

"Betsy carries my grandkids. She's steady as a rock. Of course, I'll be leading her around. It's not as if I'm turning the mare over to a three-year-old," she said with a laugh. "Don't worry, Amanda. Hope will be well taken care of."

Hope watched as a mare nuzzled her foal. "Mommy, look at the baby horse!"

Amanda nodded, not trusting herself to speak. "Make sure nothing happens to my little girl," she said, looking over at Miriam.

"I will." Miriam lowered her voice. "Bernice didn't tell me much, except that you're in some kind of trouble. I'll make very sure Hope is safe. Nothing will harm her here. Don't worry."

Amanda gave Hope one last hug and kiss and watched as her daughter walked with Miriam to the corral. Hope's attention was riveted on the colt. Knowing her daughter would be all right, Amanda left and reached the highway a half hour later. Glancing around, she searched for Tony, but he was nowhere to be found. Then, as she rounded a curve, she spotted his sedan parked on the hillside opposite the road. He'd chosen well. From there, he could see for miles.

Secure in the knowledge she hadn't been followed, Amanda returned to the city. As they approached a rest stop by the road, Tony closed the gap between them. The highway was deserted as the shadows of evening covered the area. Tony came up from behind her vehicle and pointed to his left. Amanda pulled in next to a cluster of picnic tables, and Tony followed her in.

"We have to talk," he said, sitting down beside her. "I need to get Hope's adoption papers from you, Mandy. Maybe I can track down some leads with them. Most forgers leave telltale signs that can be traced back to their previous work. Could be anything from the brand of paper to inks and typefaces."

Amanda hesitated. "I can give you any information you need."

"I won't turn you in. Surely you know that by now, Mandy. My concern is getting Carmen back, not taking Hope away from you."

Amanda nodded slowly. "All right. I'll let you see them, but it's too late today. I'll have to stop by my safe-deposit box. I don't keep those papers in my home."

"To the best of your knowledge, was Ron ever involved in anything illegal?"

"I truly don't know. Ron *never* talked to me about business."

Tony looked at his watch. "I've got an appointment with a contact tomorrow. She's learned of a counterfeiters' ring that's operating in this area, providing documents and IDs to anyone who can meet their price. If you can get the adoption papers while I'm talking to my informant, we can meet afterward and I'll take them to be checked out by experts."

"I'll let you see the papers, study them, and do whatever you need, but I'm not turning them over to you. Raymond is now involved in this case. If there *is* something wrong with the adoption papers, he probably wouldn't hesitate to set things in motion that could cost me my daughter. I can't risk that."

"I don't have to turn the papers over to him."

"Then you won't mind that they stay in my possession. It's non-negotiable, Tony."

"All right."

"You *will* need me along when you question people about the counterfeiters, though. I'm acquainted with those adoption papers. If what makes Hope's papers forgeries entails more than a phony signature, something more along the lines of a certain type of seal, for example, that means this was more than a one-shot deal with Ron. If he's involved in a major way, then there's a chance I may have overheard something I didn't consider important at the time, or I might have seen something that could help you."

Tony nodded. "Sounds reasonable. You're in, then. I'll follow you back to your place. Try to get some sleep. I'm going to take care of a few details, like dropping by Raymond's to see if he's learned anything new, then hit the sack myself. I'll be by in the morning to pick you up. We'll ride together."

THE NEXT MORNING Tony drove across town with Amanda. "This meeting is going to be out in the open," he said. "It's the only way I could get K.T. to meet me. K.T. is into a variety of scams and always keeps an ear open to what's happening in this town. She's one of my best informants."

"There's nothing on this road except an old cemetery," Amanda said, looking around.

"I know. She said that it was the perfect place. It would remind us both what people did to informants."

Amanda suppressed a shudder. "How will she react to my presence?"

"She knows who you are. That bomb scare at the day-care center got a lot of attention. I don't think she'll clam up on me."

They parked just off the cemetery grounds, then walked in through an old wooden gate in the long, low adobe wall. Amanda noticed a small crowd of mourners leaving a graveside service. "What's she look like?"

Tony gestured to his left. "She's right over there." He called Amanda's attention to a young woman with long, dark hair and sunglasses. Her long black skirt and conservative blouse made her blend in easily with the mourners.

The woman took a step back as they approached, then glanced behind them. "What are you trying to pull, Ramos?" K.T. asked, her voice taut.

"You know who this is. She's helping me."

"Yes, I know who she is," the woman admitted. She gave Amanda a probing, speculative gaze. "From what I hear, you've also got everything on the line."

"What have you heard?" Amanda asked.

"Rumors mostly, that claim you were one of their first clients." She shrugged. "But this was just gossip, nothing more."

"Get to the point, K.T. We're pretty much out in the open here," Tony growled, his gaze darting around. "Have you got something worth the price or not?" He reached into his pocket and brought out a roll of bills.

"Oh, I think you'll definitely like this." K.T. reached into the pocket of her skirt and brought out a sheet of carefully folded paper.

Tony scanned it. "It's a birth certificate and a social-security number for a Jeremy Robertson. So what?"

"Ask your former partner in the Bureau. He'll know who Jeremy Robertson is. He arrested the guy last week."

"For what?"

"I'm not doing all your work for you, Ramos." K.T. smiled. "Do you know Jack Lumet?"

"I've heard of him."

"He's started a new business. It's in a room behind Pedro's Pool Hall. Go tell him you're looking for Hugo—that's the code—and he'll open the door."

"What's happening there?"

"I've earned my money. Go do a little work for yourself." She took the bills from Tony's hand. "It's time for me to disappear for a while. I'll be leaving town. It's been nice doing business with you." She started to walk off, then glanced back. "Don't try to follow me."

"Wouldn't think of it," Tony replied.

Amanda started to walk back to the car, but Tony touched her shoulder, holding her back. "Not yet. Let K.T. get away first. Otherwise, she'll get nervous. Last time she got nervous, she put a bullet in my front tire. Both cars were moving at the time. It was a polite warning. She always hits what she's aiming for."

"She seemed so nonviolent," Amanda said, surprised, "not the type to be a deadly shot."

"On the streets, no one is quite what they appear to be," Tony said softly.

Chapter Twelve

Tony drove away from the cemetery quickly. "I'm going to drop you off at your day-care center. You probably have work to do. Then I'll go check this out."

She shook her head slowly. "No. I think it's best if I stay away from the center for now. I think it's too dangerous for me to be around the kids. There's no telling what the kidnappers are going to do next at this stage," she said sadly. First she'd been separated from her daughter, now from the work she loved. She felt trapped in an endless nightmare. "Bernice is fully qualified to take care of the business for me until I'm able to put in regular hours again."

"Then why don't you get the adoption papers from the safety deposit box? You agreed to show them to me."

"No. Not now. I'm seeing this thing through. I'm going with you. You're not cutting me out now."

"Well, you certainly can't come with me, not on something like this. I have no idea what I'm going to be walking into. Worrying about you isn't going to help me at all."

"Then don't. I can take care of myself."

He groaned. "All right. I don't want to waste time arguing. K.T. sometimes pulls a fast one. I don't want her to warn Jack that we're coming."

Tony drove to the pool hall K.T. had told him about. Motorcycles lined the parking area closest to the building, and the rest of the lot was occupied by oversize pickups. Two heavily tattooed men with bulging muscles stood by the front door, drinking beer from long-necked bottles.

"Pedro's boys. Will you reconsider coming in with me now?"

"And stay out here by myself? Not on your life."

As they reached the entrance, one of the men suddenly blocked Tony's way. "You're not welcome in here anymore, Ramos. Get back in your car and take off while you still have all your body parts."

"Cut the formalities, Frankie. I haven't got time. I'm looking for Hugo."

"Tough."

The man threw a right-hand jab, but Tony slipped inside the blow, landing a heavy fist on the man's jaw, slamming him against the door with a thud. Suddenly, the second man blocked Tony's way, his fists up. Now that Amanda saw him close up, she realized the goon was a full head taller than Tony and twice as wide. Tony didn't stand a chance.

"Gentlemen, enough posturing!" she enunciated in her best teacher's voice. "I'm here on business. Mr. Ramos is simply escorting me."

The big guy took a step back and looked down at her in surprise. "You have bad taste in men, lady. Next time, try to pick one who doesn't have quite so many enemies."

Tony managed a smile for Amanda, then returned his attention to the two men. "You boys are still in the way."

"Don't push it, Ramos," Frankie said, folding his burly arms across his chest.

Amanda stared at Frankie, who seemed to have recovered instantly from Tony's punch. He looked as if he spent his days bench-pressing trucks. "We're here to do business," she said briskly. "We're not looking for trouble. If you'll kindly introduce us to Hugo, I would appreciate it."

"Let them pass," a voice just inside the slightly open door ordered. Something about his tone indicated that this was the person who made the final decisions around here.

As they were led through a maze of sweaty men and pool tables to the back room, Amanda's hands went cold and her heart began racing. She was proud of herself for getting them this far. Tony's fists would have only resulted in bruises and broken bones, possibly including his own.

"Your 'friend' will be in shortly," the man said, opening a door for them.

As Tony and Amanda entered a dimly lit storage room lined with cases of beer, the door was promptly shut behind them. Amanda looked at Tony questioningly.

Before Tony could say anything, a young man in his midtwenties strolled in. "Hello, Jack," Tony said.

"The name's *Hugo*. What can I do for you?"

"I need some information." Tony brought out the paper K.T. had given him and placed it atop a case of beer. "Is this your work?"

"What's in it for me?"

"I got you out of a jam once. It's payback time," Tony answered.

The man nodded and looked at the document resting on the carton. "This isn't my work, but I wish it was."

"Let's see a sample of what you can do."

"The score's even now. Nothing's free from this point on."

When Tony stepped forward menacingly, they suddenly heard a shout, then the crunch of wood. A flurry of shouts and thuds continued, then a gunshot blast echoed just outside the door.

Tony pulled Amanda toward him and dived to the floor with her. Pushing her next to the wall, he shielded her with his body. "Stay down."

"FBI," they heard a familiar voice yell.

"We're in a raid?" Amanda asked, horrified. "I can't afford to get arrested!"

A second later, Raymond burst into the room. He glanced at Tony and Amanda in surprise as they rose from the floor. "What the—"

As two more agents rushed into the room, Raymond hustled Tony and Amanda out into the pool hall. "We'll square this later," he told Tony in a harsh whisper. "You're lucky as hell that I'm in charge and that the senator is in your corner." He escorted Tony and Amanda past the line of officers and the men facedown on the floor. When they got to the parking lot, Raymond turned to Tony. "I want a full statement later, clear? But just tell me right now. Is this linked to the kidnappers' forged documents?"

"My source led me here, but no, Jack isn't the guy we're looking for." Tony fished out the birth certificate for Jeremy Robertson. "This is what I got from my source."

"Interesting. Robertson's a known associate of Henderson, the armored-car robber. We arrested Robertson last week, but he had an ironclad alibi. He wasn't in league with Henderson. The two had a falling-out a year ago. Robertson claims that he never dealt with Hugo, and that he knows nothing about Henderson."

"I think he told you the truth. Jack said these papers weren't done by him. Obviously my source knew of only one counterfeiter in the area making phony documents and attributed a lot more to him than he was capable of producing. So there's somebody else out there taking up the slack. And they're better than Jack."

"What's next?" Raymond asked. "Do you have another lead you can follow?"

"I may. I'll be in touch."

Once they were underway, Amanda leaned back against the seat and tried to stop shaking. "I've never been in a place like that in my life, much less been caught in a raid. With any luck, I'll never have to go through that again."

Tony raised an eyebrow. "You stayed cool. That's the important thing. You've got guts, Mandy. You stood up to those thugs and never blinked an eye."

"I just used my common sense. Brawn wasn't getting us anywhere."

"Sometimes it's needed."

"Maybe it is, but so far I'm the one who experienced less trauma." She nodded toward his skinned knuckles.

Tony rolled his eyes but chose not to answer. After several minutes, he finally spoke. "I've got another idea I want to pursue, but I've got to act now. You've seen how fast things can go wrong. Do you still want in?"

"You bet. Where are we going?"

"We're going to pay Bobby Serna a visit. He and I haven't met, but I know what he looks like. Bobby's served time for passing bad checks and has worked for Jack in the past. It's possible he's involved in this scam, too. But first I've got to make a quick stop to change my appearance a bit. I'm going to play the role of a high-stakes gambler on the run from creditors—the back room kind. A mustache and a Western-cut jacket should do it."

Amanda glanced down at her long skirt and cotton top. "Am I okay in this?"

"Sure. It makes you look sexy, and what better outfit for a man's mistress?"

She choked. "A man's *whaaat?*"

"That's *your* role. Don't you like it?"

"Not particularly."

"How about if you pose as my wife? That, I think, would suit you far better." He smiled gently, as if he were keeping a secret from her.

A fierce longing assailed her. "It'll do," Amanda managed to reply.

Tony stopped at a gas station. "I'll be right out." He took a small suitcase from the trunk of his borrowed sedan, then went into the rest room. When he came out, he looked entirely different.

Amanda stared at him. He looked good in a mustache, and the brown jacket with the silver-and-turquoise bolo tie made him look wonderfully male, yet elegant. "I approve," she said with the ghost of a smile as he slipped behind the steering wheel.

He raised an eyebrow. "Don't get too attached to the look. I want you to be prepared. I may have to get down and dirty."

"Where are we going?"

"The racetrack. Don't worry, I never resort to violence unless it's the only way."

"But you like the physical action," Amanda observed. "That's why you're in the business you're in."

"I enjoy the challenge, that's true. Once I find Carmen, though, that'll change. I'll have to put in more office time than fieldwork. I intend to make my agency the best in the Southwest. It won't all happen at once, of course, and it'll take hard work, but it will happen."

She believed him. If there was one thing she knew about Tony, it was that he never gave up.

Once they arrived at the racetrack, Tony parked and led her toward the crowd of racing fans gathered by the rail. "Serna is short and in excellent physical shape. He's got salt-and-pepper hair and black eyes. He's a fancy dresser and tends to wear Stetsons."

Amanda's gaze passed over several men in hats and came to rest on a man standing near the gates, watching the horses. He was wearing an expensive-looking light gray jacket and dark pants. The brim of his black hat covered his face, making it impossible to get a clear look at his features. "Like him?"

"That's our man, all right. Let's go have a chat with him, but let me handle this, okay? If we push him too fast, he'll spook on us and we'll get zip." Tony strolled up casually and took a spot at the rail next to Serna. "Number three looks good," Tony said casually. "Know his best time on this track?"

"Check the racing form. I prefer the long shots, so I'm going with Sonny Boy. He's got a few good races in him yet. Maybe this will be his day."

"My luck's better when I stay with sure things. The more the risk, the less they seem to pay off for me."

"Lady Luck's unpredictable. That's what makes her so much fun."

Tony turned his back to the track and leaned back, staring at the stands. "If you're who I think you are, we have a mutual friend."

"Who?"

"Hugo."

"Yeah?"

"Unfortunately, just as I drove by to enlist his...shall we say, services, he had members of a government agency drop by unexpectedly. I think his shop's going to be unavailable for a while." Tony deliberately avoided being too specific. If nothing incriminating was said between them, Serna would be more likely to give him the information he needed.

Serna's eyes grew wide. "When did you say this happened?"

"Less than a half hour ago. The guests are probably still there."

Serna glanced at his watch. "Thanks for the tip. It looks like a good time for me to go see how the horses are running out of state."

"I did you a good turn. How about doing one for me? Hugo's unfortunate situation left me in a jam. He had some papers for me and my wife. Fortunately for us, no photos were included."

"You need another source?" Serna turned and gave Amanda an appreciative look.

Tony nodded. "One who's good and can work fast. We need to be somebody else right away."

"Hugo was the best for the money. There is another provider, but he comes at a very high price. And you can't deal directly. Everyone is screened."

"I'll manage."

Serna nodded. "Okay. Call Ron Vila. He's a lawyer. Cagey guy. Does the screening, I suppose. Tell him Bobby sent you. He won't deal with anyone who doesn't come recommended."

Hearing her ex-husband's name, Amanda felt her heart leap to her throat. For endless seconds, the ground seemed to tilt and shift out of focus.

As Serna walked away, Tony put his arm around her waist for support. "You don't look so good. Are you okay?"

"I'm fine. It just took me by surprise. I never thought Ron would be capable of involving his law practice with something so blatantly illegal. I knew he would take shortcuts when it was to his advantage, but nothing like this. The person who's playing this game bears no resemblance to the man I married."

"I know that the longer you walk the line between what's legal and what's not, the easier it gets to cross over."

Amanda looked at Tony, tempted to ask him if he was speaking from personal experience, but she didn't dare. She wasn't sure if she could take an honest answer, at least not now.

"To answer the question in your eyes," he said, "I still respect the law. It was my job to uphold it for too many years to lose that. But in order to find Carmen, I've had to spend my time cultivating a network of informants and being, at least outwardly, one of them. I'm an honest man, Mandy."

"But I know you spent time in jail before I met you," she countered, unable to stop the words. The truth would demand courage from both of them, but its time had come.

"The creep I went after was in the business of picking up runaways. The police had suspected him for years, but couldn't touch him for lack of evidence. By the time he released the girls he abducted, they were usually too frightened to testify. Then he made the mistake of picking up the daughter of a friend of mine." He shrugged. "I convinced him right away to tell me where she was. That convincing carried a price, and I paid it."

"Was that the only time you were in jail?"

Tony didn't answer directly. "I'm not telling you that everything I've ever done was right. But when I've broken the law, it hasn't been so I could make a buck."

Amanda looked over at Tony as he started the car. "What now? Ron will certainly not talk to you, no matter what your disguise is. If he's involved in this, at even the lowest level, you can bet he knows precisely who you are."

"Yes, and that's why I'm going to need your help. You have to get me into your ex-husband's office. If that's not possible, then you're going to have to go over there and take a good look around."

"Ron wouldn't trust me now! If I do go see him, he'll make sure I'm not left on my own for more than half a second. That assistant of his, Katrina, is just as bad."

"You have to find a way to plant a bug in his office. Trip over something, drop your purse, do whatever it takes, but you've got to leave one where they won't find it. It's the only chance we've got now."

Amanda took a long, deep breath. "I'll do my best." She hesitated a moment. "Do you have a listening device in your little bag of tricks—the one where you got your gambler's outfit?" Seeing him nod, she added, "Then let's go over to Ron's office now. I want to do this as soon as possible. If I think about it too much, I may just blow it by telling him off."

"You *cannot* do that. Listen to me. It's crucial that he doesn't know you're really on to him. If he suspects, we could lose our opportunity."

"I know." Her shoulders slumped. "I'll tell him I must speak to him about discrepancies I found in Hope's adoption papers, and that I won't take no for an answer."

"That sounds all right. I'll wait for you in the parking area behind the building. He'll never know I'm there."

"Let's do it."

As AMANDA WALKED INSIDE Ron's plush, wood-paneled outer office, Katrina Clark stood up and blocked her way.

"You can't just come in here without an appointment, Amanda." The tall blonde stared at her with venom in her eyes. "What are you doing here anyway? You're not his client."

"And I never will be. But I am Ron's ex-wife and the mother of his child. Either tell him I'm here, or I'll do it myself."

"He's a busy man. You're not going to be able to see him now."

Amanda met Katrina's gaze squarely. "Get out of my way. I'm not here to cause trouble. I just need answers to a few questions. If you push me, however, I'll create a scene that will have every person in this office building rushing to your door."

Katrina cursed, then sat back down in her chair. "I'll see if he has a moment."

Ignoring Katrina, Amanda opened the adjoining door and went inside. Ron was comfortably seated in a leather chair, talking on the phone. As she walked in, he glared at her and abruptly finished his conversation. Clad in an expensive gray suit, Ron had almost achieved the look of old money. Now she knew how he'd earned it.

"You're always busy, Ron. But so am I. I just have a few questions I want you to answer about Hope." She took a seat across from his desk, the tiny listening device in her cupped palm.

"Then it can wait. Make an appointment and come back later."

"No, Ron, it *can't* wait, and I'm not moving." She stood up suddenly and gripped the desk. Her hand below the edge, she quickly stuck the bug to the wooden underside. "I'm tired of having you always put me off. Hope is important to me, and I need you to answer one question. How could Hope's birth father have signed those papers if he wasn't even in the state?"

Ron shrugged and leaned back in his chair. "Okay, so we did a bit of creative writing. You wanted the kid, didn't you?"

"I still do, Ron," she said softly.

"Then take my advice and keep your mouth shut. You got your baby and that's what matters. Has someone been questioning you about this?"

"No," she replied, keeping her expression neutral. "It was just a discrepancy I noticed while unpacking my private papers."

"Then unnotice it, unless you want Hope's sleazy father to find out and have her put in a foster home until the courts decide who gets her."

"How can you be so cold-blooded about this?" Amanda stood up so fast her chair nearly toppled over.

"She was never *my* kid. The adoption was something I arranged to make you happy. I *did* love you once, Amanda."

She felt the tears stinging her eyes. They were on two separate wavelengths. He would never understand her. "With you, it's always the same. Things are more important than people." She waved a hand over his desk, accidentally knocking over a photo. Amanda glanced at it. "Look what you keep on your desk. The snapshot of some cabin in the forest, not a person." She shook her head. "I feel sorry for you. If things are all you value, things are all you'll ever have.'' She turned and left his office, passing Katrina without a glance.

As Amanda stepped out of the building, she looked around for Tony's car. He was speaking to someone who looked like a street person on the other side of the parking lot. Then she saw Tony slip the man some bills and walk away.

Amanda was waiting for Tony when he returned to the car. "What was that all about?" she asked.

"Wally's going to stay within range of the bug and monitor the tape for me."

"Are you sure he can be trusted?"

Tony nodded. "He was a cop once. He dropped out after he was in a shooting incident. The exchange of gunfire claimed the life of an innocent bystander. It wasn't his fault, but he never got over it. He sleeps in a little apartment behind his brother's house, but he spends most of his days on the streets. He still works with law enforcement from time to time as an informant for some bucks, and he's always been there for me, particularly whenever I'm pursuing a lead on Carmen. He knows me, and he knew my family."

It seemed like Tony's friends were all people who lived on the fringes of society, yet now she understood him well enough to know where he stood and trust his judgment. Tony had his own code of honor. He gave back what was given to him. He was as protective of his friends as he was lethal to his enemies. "I hope the listening device pays off. Ron is always so careful. I can't see him ever letting his guard down."

"That's why *you* had to do it. Your presence would disconcert him. He'd lose some self-control and have feelings like anger, or jealousy, or both, without even being aware of it." Tony shrugged. "By the way, where did you plant the bug?"

Amanda explained what she'd done. "I don't think he ever suspected."

"If my gut instinct is right, he does periodic sweeps of his office anyway. He'll find it sooner or later, but hopefully it'll be later."

They were pulling out of the parking lot when Wally, the man Tony had spoken to, came around the corner of a building and waved quickly at them.

"You may have stirred up more than you know, Mandy," Tony said. "I think we're about to get a lead."

Chapter Thirteen

Tony drove into the alley across the street. As he came to a stop, Wally approached them. "I've got something already. Your subject called a guy named Lonnie and talked about some kind of license form that turned dark when it was put in a copier. They're useless now, and Vila used some very interesting adjectives to describe you."

"Lonnie?" Tony mulled over the name. "The name doesn't ring a bell."

"New talent," Wally said. "Lonnie Sierra. He's into counterfeiting, but he's just a laborer, so to speak. Lonnie's definitely not the brains of any operation."

Tony shook his head. "Any idea where I can find him?"

"He works for the state government. It's a clerical job, but it lets him access the paperwork and forms that become birth certificates and such. He walks off with blank originals and turns them over to his boss, who's in the business of providing new identities. Of course, they also blackmail some of their clients, so the money keeps flowing—one way."

"Thanks, Wally." Tony brought out his roll of bills, but Wally shook his head and stepped back from the car window.

"Just find your daughter, man. It's about time she came home."

"You got that right." As they got underway, Tony picked up his cellular phone. "We're close, Amanda. I can feel it. I'm going to call Raymond. We're going to need his help on this. There's no way around it." He paused for a moment. "We're also about to find out if I was right about a leak in the Bureau. This is not the way I would have preferred to deal with this, but we're under the gun here. We have no other options."

"We have to find one. You can't call Raymond. If we get him involved, he's going to find out that there are discrepancies in Hope's adoption records. I'll lose my child."

"No, you won't lose Hope. The papers may have to be drawn up again, but her birth mother did give her up for adoption. There's no one to contest custody."

"Except for the birth father."

"*If* he's still around," Tony countered. "And if he even knows about Hope. They've been threatening to get him to turn up and make trouble, but he hasn't been in the picture in what, three years? Even if he finds out about a daughter, it's not likely he'd try to establish a claim after all that time."

"You're probably right, but this whole thing makes me uneasy."

"You're borrowing trouble, and your fears are being used against you. Your child is safe, and I'm getting close to finding mine." He took a deep breath, then let it out again. "You can't have it both ways, Amanda. You've told me you don't approve of my vigilante tactics, but now you want to circumvent the law and withhold evidence." He paused for several moments. "There's another side to this, too. If Ron finds out you're trying to prove he's protecting the kidnappers, he may blow the whistle on Hope's paperwork and try to weasel out of it somehow. The problem is, he'd claim you knew about the forged signature, and you'd be put on the defensive trying to prove you didn't. It could get dicey then. That's why we need to bring Raymond in on this. Your best chance is to put all the crooks in jail at the same time."

"All right," Amanda agreed. "Let's finish it."

Tony dialed Raymond's number at the Bureau. After a brief wait, he heard his ex-partner's familiar voice. Tony filled him in quickly on what he and Amanda had uncovered. "If Sierra's involved, we have to smoke him out. Unfortunately, what I've given you isn't enough for a search warrant, because the bug was illegal."

"I wish you'd played this by the book."

"No time for that, even if I'd been able to get a warrant. But I've got an idea. Why not pull a bluff? Send a couple of your boys over there and roust Sierra. Then keep one guy near to see what he does after your boys leave."

"I still couldn't legally confiscate the papers."

"But you'd still confront the supplier and put the ring out of business for a while. And if you squeeze Sierra enough, he may cut a deal."

"I'll give it a try."

Tony placed the receiver down. "I don't know how you want to play this, Mandy, but I'm going to find out where Sierra lives and go over there. I want to see this thing going down."

"Then I'm coming with you."

"Somehow that's what I thought you'd say."

FORTY-FIVE MINUTES LATER Tony parked uphill from a simple adobe residence located in an isolated canyon. Sierra's number and address had been listed, so finding him had posed no problem. He waited, binoculars in hand, for the Bureau team to finish setting up Lonnie Sierra.

Minutes dragged by as the agents remained inside. After almost an hour had passed, the pair of agents stepped outside, got into their car, and drove off. Once around a curve, the car slowed down and the passengers jumped out. One of them was Raymond.

"Now we wait to see what Sierra does," Tony said.

Fifteen minutes went by. They could see Raymond watching Sierra's house from behind a stand of piñon trees.

Before long, Amanda heard Tony mutter something under his breath. "What's up?" she asked.

"Sierra is on the move. He's taking boxes out to his car. They've got him now."

Tony and Amanda watched from their position as the FBI car returned and the agents moved in. Sierra bolted for his truck in a flash, firing off a shot with a handgun in the direction of the approaching car.

"Good," Tony said. "He's given them probable cause now."

Moments later, Tony's cellular began to ring. Tony picked it up. "Yeah, I've been watching the show. I'm uphill from you," Tony said, then chuckled. "No way I was going to stay away. What's the surprise? You know me well enough to expect it."

"I've anticipated you, buddy boy. Like you said, I know you too well. I saw you and Amanda up there half an hour ago." Raymond sounded amused.

Tony cleared his throat. "What do you mean?" he asked cautiously. "Exactly when did you anticipate me?"

"You know exactly what I mean. It's like the photos of that doctored file I let you sneak out of my office. The camera you hid in my jacket pocket was small, but not *that* small. What you got was government approved. I figured that it was the least I could do to keep your butt out of jail."

"You mean you knew all along I'd have to do a number on you?"

"Knew and preempted you. You're not in deep with the Bureau, not like you thought anyway. What you 'stole' from my office had been prepared especially for you. Things have been much more official than you realized, all the way down the line. You want to come down?"

"To throttle you, sure," Tony growled.

Raymond laughed. "You can always *try*. I could use a light workout."

Tony filled Amanda in as they drove down to meet Raymond. To his surprise, Amanda started laughing. "I fail to see the humor," he growled.

"I hope you always remember this, Tony. You don't always have to deal under the table to get what you want or need. You underestimated the value of friendship from the very beginning."

His voice dropped to a deep murmur. "Maybe. But I never underestimated you, or the power of the feelings that have grown between us." He reached for her hand and brought it up to his lips.

The kiss sent a thrill through her, but before she could respond, Raymond rushed over to meet them, and for once, he was smiling.

"On top of the boxes the suspect was hauling out, I found an interesting list of names," he told them. "Seems like the forgery ring has a number of 'friends' who have been bribed or blackmailed to look the other way. That's how they've obtained original documents without getting caught. We also found several blackened copies of drivers' license forms. Guess they just discovered the paper you gave them doesn't perform well when exposed to the heat of a copier." Raymond grinned.

"So the people who know about Carmen will be contacting me again."

"With luck, yes. We're going to try our best to keep this arrest under wraps, but there's no telling how long it'll be before word gets out."

"Did you find any leads to the others in the ring?" Tony asked.

Raymond handed him Sierra's list of people associated with the forgery ring. "Anyone here whose name stands out for you?"

He nodded. "Jeremy Purcell. You know him, too. He's the guy who configured the age-progression software the local police and the Bureau field office here use. He's been helping me generate the sketches of Carmen for my flyers."

"He's not legit, not as of two weeks ago. I just learned he's in the base lockup in Albuquerque. He tried to break into a government computer, the Department of Defense's, no less, and they backtracked to his home. The DOD guys want him raked over the coals. They're out for blood."

"I'm going to have to have a chat with him," Tony said.

"He's not a very talkative fellow."

"If he's being paid, I want to know by whom. If it's blackmail, I want to know why. I have a bad feeling about this."

It wasn't until they were in the car that Tony noticed how quiet Amanda had become. "What's wrong?"

"Don't you see what's happening? We never find answers, just more questions."

"We found one answer. Though it's very bad news, I'm glad to find out now. I might have been hitting my head against a wall for years."

"You mean because of the age-progression software?"

He nodded. "There's no telling when this guy went bad. I may have been handing out an age-progression image of Carmen that has been tampered with."

"That doesn't seem likely. Other children have been found using those images generated by the same software, right?"

Tony nodded slowly. "I may be borrowing trouble, but I've got to check it out." Tony dialed Raymond's pager. "Before I try to talk to Purcell, I'd like to have you check out that age-progression software," he told Raymond.

"Good idea. Then we'll know exactly where we stand. I'll meet you over at the Bureau office," Raymond said. "Because of your cooperation in the sting at the DMV, it's okay for you to come openly."

"Good. Let's just hope like hell I'm wrong."

Tony gripped the steering wheel so tightly his hands began to ache. The possibility that he'd wasted months or even years circulating an image that didn't resemble his daughter filled him with rage. The kidnappers had managed to outwit him at every corner. But that was about to stop. He was about to become their worst nightmare.

AMANDA STOOD BEHIND Tony as the technician at the Bureau ran two test photos. Both came up reading negative for faults.

"I guess I worried for no reason," Tony said.

The three men relaxed visibly. Raymond managed a smile. "We were all concerned. The implications could have affected a lot of parents and a huge number of cases still pending."

Amanda glanced at Tony, hating herself for the thought she was about to bring up. She could see no other way of pointing it out, either, except by being painfully direct. "Gentlemen, I really don't know much about this type of software, but is it possible to alter only a portion of the program, or trigger a false image by entering a key word? For instance, I noticed that you enter the name of the missing child at the beginning of the process, before the image is generated."

Tony looked at her, nodding. His eyes grew dark and he, obviously, understood where her conjectures were leading.

Amanda continued. "Suppose the name, Carmen Ramos, initiated an altered image, while all the other names entered created what they were supposed to do. It would allow your test images to come out right—and the altered one to remain undetected."

Tony looked at the technician. "Is that possible?"

The technician, a small blond-haired man with thick glasses, sat up abruptly. "It *is* possible for an expert programmer to alter software to do almost anything with the appropriate command. Since our software requires a name entry, what you've suggested is entirely possible." The technician turned around as one of the administrative assistants came into the room. "Patricia, do you still have your daughter's baby picture?"

"Sure. It's on my desk, along with the one that was taken of her this year. Samantha's in the first grade now, you know." She smiled proudly.

"We really need to borrow both those photos, if you don't mind."

"Will I get them back?"

The technician nodded. "We only need them for a few minutes. How about it?"

Patricia returned with them a few moments later. Amanda and Tony noticed that Samantha had beautiful blond hair and green eyes, just like her mother. "Damage them and it's your life," she said with only a trace of a smile.

"They won't be damaged. Promise."

The technician typed in Samantha's name and age, then fed the baby picture into the computer's scanner. The composite that appeared on the screen moments later looked remarkably similar to the first-grader's photo.

"Okay," Raymond announced. "Now repeat the process exactly as before, except enter the child's name as Carmen Ramos instead."

The technician nodded and began to type.

"Let's hope I'm wrong about this," Amanda whispered.

Raymond nodded, but Tony seemed not to hear. His gaze was fixed on the computer screen.

A few minutes later, a new image slowly came into focus. A dark-haired, brown-eyed girl appeared on the screen, and to Amanda, she looked just like the last image Tony had posted at the day-care center.

"They undermined my search from the start." Tony's voice mirrored the savage and lethal anger boiling up inside him.

"It's not all bad news, buddy," Raymond said. "Think about it. If they went through all this trouble to keep area residents from identifying your daughter, I'd say there's a very good chance Carmen is still around Santa Fe somewhere."

Tony considered Raymond's conclusion. "It's a thought."

The technician glanced up at them. "If you have another photo, a clear one we haven't used before with this software, I can run it through under a different name. We'll have the genuine image then."

"I do have one, but not on me."

"Okay. In that case, give me a day to run a file-by-file check on the program. Maybe I can find where it's been altered and correct it. I'd rather not run anything else through it until I'm sure to what extent it's been tampered with."

Tony left the Bureau offices with Amanda, clearly discouraged. "I'm beginning to think that the people who've been pulling our strings don't really know where Carmen is, at least not currently. They were even ready to make me believe, by using forged documents, that Hope was really my daughter, just to keep me spinning in circles while I did their dirty work. In the light of this new discovery, I'm beginning to think that they lost track of my child a long time ago—if she ever survived the accident."

"You're exhausted and in no shape to think anymore. You need some rest, Tony. How long has it been since you had a full eight hours?"

"About three years," he admitted slowly.

"We both need some sleep. I'm past thinking rationally at this point myself." The thought of returning to her empty house sent a chill through her. "Problem is, as tired as I feel, I don't want to go home," she admitted. "Not with Hope still away."

"I know what you're feeling. Even the thought of being home when the house is totally empty makes your insides knot up. I went through that, only it was a lot worse after Lynn and Carmen were . . . gone.''

''I don't think I could have survived what you did.''

''You would have. You're very strong. But the pain stays, no matter what you do from then on. It puts a shadow over everything in your life after that.''

''Time didn't ease your pain, because the matter was never resolved. You knew Lynn was gone, but Carmen's fate was and still is a big question mark.''

''What's eating me is that I still have to consider the possibility that my child is gone forever. All these years I've purposely blocked that from my mind. I just couldn't deal with it.''

Amanda reached for his hand and covered it with hers. ''Don't give up yet. It's too soon.''

''Or way too late,'' he finished, turning onto her street. Tony pulled into her driveway and parked. ''I'll walk you to the door, then you go get some rest.''

''I don't want to be alone again tonight,'' Amanda whispered, her voice raw.

His gaze locked with hers. ''Neither do I,'' he said, his voice a husky murmur in the confines of the car.

''Then stay.''

''Yes.''

Tony's body shook as he walked to the front door with her. He needed to touch her, to lose himself in her warmth and softness, to feel her naked and vulnerable beneath him. Fires danced through him as vivid images formed in his mind.

As Amanda unlocked the door, his eyes strayed to her silky hair and the way it drifted against the curve of her neck. He thought of brushing it aside and raining kisses on the soft flesh, then lower, down her body, until she writhed wildly in his arms.

The fire in him grew hotter. When she closed the door behind them and turned, he saw the same vulnerability and need mirrored in her eyes. Her nipples had tightened into hardness, and the light bra she wore under her cotton top did nothing to hide them.

Sensing the passion within him, Amanda wound her arms around him, nestling her head on his shoulder. He shuddered, desperate now for the warmth inside her.

When he felt her lips nuzzling his neck, a charge of electricity surged through him. He tilted her chin upward and bent down to take her mouth. His lips pressed against hers, his mouth widening to take more, needing her sweetness. Her soft sighs drove him crazy. He wanted more; closeness wasn't enough. He had to possess her.

Amanda wriggled against him, pressing the lower part of her body against his stiffened manhood. The movements drove him mad. "We won't make it to the bedroom at this rate," he said in a raw whisper.

She continued to rub against him. "I need . . . so much."

Tony lifted her skirt and felt the soft skin beneath her panties. Sinking to his knees before her, he guided her undergarments downward, exposing her to him. "Lean on my shoulders," he said, his voice a jagged groan in the night.

He brought her to his lips and kissed her deeply, savoring her sweetness as she cried out his name. Passion ruled him, and he knew he would possess her tonight. She was his, body and soul.

When Tony sensed that Amanda could take no more, he lifted her easily into his arms, carrying her to the bedroom. He placed her gently on her bed, the banked fires in him gathering force. He wouldn't take her quickly. This was the time to show her his love, to make her feel cherished and desired. Every time she lay down in her soft bed from this moment on, he wanted her to remember this night—the fires and the ecstasy.

He unbuttoned her cotton top, then unfastened the front hook of her bra. Her clothing lay spread around her like flower petals unfurled. He lifted her skirt, allowing its fullness to drape to the side, while revealing all the intimate places that still glistened with his love.

Amanda looked exquisitely vulnerable and beautiful. The thought formed and vanished as he surrendered to one driving force, the desire to be one with her.

He stripped off his own clothing and settled himself gently over her. Tony felt her readiness as her hips moved upward, seeking him. The tip of his shaft touched her opening, yet he forced himself not to enter her.

"Say it, Mandy. Tell me you love me."

The words frightened her. She didn't want to say them out loud. "I need you, Tony, with all my heart."

"No, Mandy. Tell me you love me. You feel it, I know. It's there in your heart. Say it." An urgency he couldn't contain impelled him to sink a little deeper into her body, though he still did not penetrate her fully. "Tell me," he repeated. She tried to arch against him to draw him farther in, but he slipped one hand to her hips and held her steady. "Are you mine, Mandy?" He shuddered with the effort his restraint was taking, but made no move to complete their union.

"I love you, Tony. I'm yours." She arched her body again as he drove down. "Just as you are mine," she murmured.

He felt a shock of pleasure jolt through him as her body pressed hotly to his. His nerves were on fire, the flames centering in his groin.

Her body was open to him, and he plunged into its warm depths over and over again. Clasped tightly inside the velvet walls, he was consumed by raw and desperate pleasures.

A flood of release lifted them high, then relief allowed their spirits to flutter gently downward. In that shining aftermath, there was only one truth. They loved each other, and no matter what life held for them, nothing would ever erase what they'd shared.

He held her long after her breathing had evened and her body relaxed with the peace that came with sleep. He didn't want to sleep. He wanted to enjoy the warmth of her body against his. Yet exhaustion took its toll, and soon he drifted into the yawning darkness that reached out to him.

FROM THE DARKNESS that encompassed her, Amanda heard a familiar voice calling. She turned around to see the woman who'd visited her before.

"Your heart has shown you the truth. Now follow the path carved out for you. Your happiness lies there."

"All I'll find through my love for Tony is a broken heart. He's used to making his own rules, to getting whatever he wants at any cost. I need a man who'll want more children, who'll teach them about honesty and love through example, not just words."

"The answers you need lie just ahead. Don't give in to despair."

The vision vanished, though Amanda tried to call out to the woman to wait.

"Wake up, Mandy!"

Startled, Amanda's eyes flew open. She saw Tony's face and relaxed back into his arms. "These dreams . . ."

"Nightmares?"

"No, not exactly. I keep having these dreams about a woman telling me that everything is okay. But I don't understand any of them."

"Dreams can be confusing. The subconscious mind sometimes jumbles everything together," Tony murmured soothingly, holding her close.

"The strange part is that the woman who speaks to me seems just as real as you or me!"

"Hush." He brushed her forehead with a kiss. "No more dreams. This is our time." He touched her lips with his own.

Amanda shut her eyes. If the present was all they were destined to share, then she'd treasure each precious second. She snuggled deeper into his arms. Tony was solid and so very real. She gave herself over to the love he offered and felt his body harden. The fever of wanting returned and, gathering strength from life, they found each other again.

Hours later, the ringing of the phone awakened them with a jolt. Amanda reached for it, instantly alert when she heard Raymond's voice. She handed the receiver to Tony.

"Something break on the case?" Tony asked quickly.

"We analyzed phone records and something curious turned up. Sierra never called Ron Vila's office, but half a dozen calls this past month went from Sierra to Katrina Clark's private number. Do you know who the woman is?"

"Ron Vila's paralegal and secretary."

"Correct. We're doing a background check on her now. I'll let you know what we turn up."

Tony hung up and gave Amanda the details as he dressed. "How long has Katrina been working for your ex-husband?"

"Since before he and I were married. That's part of the reason why she's always hated me, I think. She had her own designs on him, and I got in the way. I always thought Katrina was much more his type. Now maybe it turns out I was right."

"I'm going to check with Wally. Let's see what that bug of yours turned up."

"Am I reading you right? Do you think Katrina's that heavily involved?"

"You tell me. How much influence does she have over your ex-husband?"

"I've never really known that. I've never been able to read anything from her but resentment, especially since I came back to Santa Fe and Ron also decided to return here with her and open an office in town."

Amanda dressed quickly, following Tony. As she hurried out the bedroom door, she glanced back. Many things had been said between them in the heat of passion, things that might never be said again. An overwhelming sadness filled her as she realized the pain of relinquishing a love never meant to be.

"You ready?" Tony asked, interrupting her musings.

Amanda nodded and hurried after him to the front door. They were just about to step outside when the phone rang. She ran to pick it up and froze as she heard the electronically altered voice.

"We're ready to turn over the information on the Ramos kid. Can you pick it up?" the voice asked.

Amanda motioned Tony to the extension. "Where and when?"

"It will be waiting just outside the Rancho del Sol when you arrive if you leave right now. Do you know the dude ranch I'm talking about?"

"Sure. It's south of Santa Fe, off State Route 14." Amanda saw Tony pick up the extension carefully.

"Right. Look for a packet on the large boulder that marks the turnoff to the ranch."

Hearing the dial tone, Amanda replaced the receiver and repeated the portion of conversation Tony hadn't heard. "It looks like they're going to keep their word after all."

"I doubt it. They could have mailed us the stuff. This has all the earmarks of an ambush, but I've got to play it out. This time, though, I don't want you with me. It's going to be extremely dangerous."

"We could call Raymond."

"He'll want to take over, get a tactical team together and cover all the bases. I don't want to wait that long."

"Well, you're not pushing me out of the way. There's been danger all along. I'm going, even if I have to follow you in my own car. I want whoever threatened my little girl thrown in jail just as badly as you want whoever took Carmen." She picked up her purse from the sofa. "Let's go."

They drove south out of the city. In the early morning hours, most people were heading toward Santa Fe, not out of it, and they had almost no traffic to contend with.

Tony made the turnoff the freeway onto the almost deserted state road, heading to the landmark the kidnappers had mentioned. They spotted the large boulder near the intersection of the pavement and a long gravel road. A thin piñon forest began less than a hundred yards away.

"There!" Amanda pointed. "But I don't see anything that looks like a package on it."

"Maybe it's on the other side." He slowed the vehicle down, glancing around. "Stay in the car. With all the brush and piñons for cover, this is a great place for a sniper. Get behind the wheel, keep the engine running, and wait for me."

Amanda's gaze drifted slowly over the tree-dotted foothills to the east, to the small mountain range beyond. It was a beautiful summer morning, the air still cool, and the sun shining from a clear sky. Everything was quiet and peaceful. Maybe they'd finally reached the end of the line. She prayed for Tony, hoping he'd find the news he'd been searching for for so long. As she glanced over at him, she saw Tony edging closer to the boulder in a crouch, his hand on the butt of the pistol at his waist.

She looked around, unable to see any cause for alarm. Then, the loud crack of a rifle shattered the serenity surrounding them.

Chapter Fourteen

Tony dived to the ground, rolling behind the boulder as another bullet ricocheted harmlessly off the limestone. He couldn't see the sniper, but from the trajectory of the bullets, he had a good idea of where he was.

Amanda stepped on the gas and pulled up next to him, shielding Tony from the gunman's view with the car. As she reached over and threw the passenger door open, he jumped inside instantly. "Go!" he shouted.

Amanda floored the accelerator. The wheels spun on the gravel, spewing clouds of dust and stones behind them as they sped back onto the highway. "Did you find the information?"

"There wasn't anything there. It was a setup. But it's a good sign. This means we're getting close, and they're running scared."

"Can't Raymond arrest Ron and Katrina with what he's got now?"

"No way. There's not any physical evidence leading to them. Besides, if Raymond makes a move on Katrina, Ron and the others before I get whatever information they have on Carmen, I'll never find my daughter. I have no other leads. And they do know *something*. They had the bracelet."

Amanda drove quickly home, hoping the kidnappers would try to contact her again. They found Raymond waiting for them in his car as they pulled up.

"What are you doing here? Has something happened?" Amanda asked, looking around quickly.

"I came by to talk to your neighbor, Ricky Biddle, but he wasn't there," Raymond said, walking inside the house with them. "I never stopped digging into his background, you know. Well, I finally uncovered something. About eighteen months ago, Biddle was accused of stalking an old girlfriend of his. The charges were dropped. That's why I didn't find out sooner. But this made the guy interesting to me, so I took a hard look at everything he's told you." He glanced at Tony and rubbed the back of his neck. "His alibi for the time of the fire in Amanda's garage is bogus."

"He wasn't really on the phone?" Tony asked.

"No. He was transferring a computer file via modem, and that whole operation can be made totally automatic. He could have been anywhere at the time."

"You said you just came from his place?" Seeing Raymond nod, Amanda continued. "Are you sure he heard your knock?" Amanda asked. "He's usually there this time of day."

"The house was silent, except for a barking dog in the back. The curtains were drawn and there were no lights on. I can only go by that if he doesn't answer the door. I don't have enough for a search warrant. Not yet anyway."

"I'll pay him a visit later on today," Tony said. "Maybe he'll decide to talk to me."

"Go by the book, Tony. Don't muddy the water, or it'll get thrown out of court."

"Wait a second," Amanda interrupted. "Do you guys think Ricky is the kidnapper, or that he's involved with them in any way?"

"One or the other," Raymond answered calmly. "We know Jeremy Purcell altered the program, but he may have had help. Biddle's a good candidate for that. He's paid to write computer programs, and let's face it, the guy always shows up when there's trouble.''

Amanda shook her head. ''I've always thought of Ricky as obnoxious but harmless. I never dreamed he'd turn out to be so twisted. I'll tell you one thing. I'm never again taking people at face value. Those days are *over!*''

AFTER RAYMOND LEFT, Amanda walked over to the phone. ''I can't stand it anymore. I'm going to call Hope.''

''Don't use your home phone. Use my cellular. If they're trying to find Hope in order to get more leverage, they may be accessing the numbers you dial. Considering the computer hackers we've linked to the kidnappers, that's not such a reach. At least with the cellular, you'll cut down on the chances of their tracking her down. They wouldn't be expecting me to call your daughter.''

Amanda walked outside to his car and dialed Miriam's number. After talking to Miriam and learning that Hope was outside brushing the horses with Dean, Miriam's husband, Amanda relaxed. Her daughter hadn't been touched by the confusion surrounding them here.

As Amanda started back, she saw Tony come to meet her at the door. ''Let's get going, Mandy.''

''Where?''

''You and I are going to pay Mr. Biddle an impromptu visit.''

They walked up the gravel road and arrived at Ricky's a few minutes later.

Amanda glanced at the driveway. ''If Ricky was home, his motorcycle would have been parked by the door, under the porch. That's where he keeps it.''

''Good. Then we can take a look around at our leisure. You never know what we'll find.''

''You mean peek through windows?''

''Sure. If he's not here, it can't hurt.''

Amanda hurried after Tony as he walked toward the rear of the house. "Wait, Tony! Remember, he's got a dog inside."

"What kind?"

"A rottweiler."

Tony stopped in midstride. "That changes things."

"But the dog's inside the house, not out."

"No problem, then. Just be quiet when you approach a window. With any luck, he won't hear us." Amanda behind him, Tony crept up to a side window and looked in. The living room was covered with stacks of computer printouts and file folders. Even the sofa lacked enough space to sit down. "This guy doesn't have a lot of outside interests, does he?"

"Tony, be reasonable. We're not going to learn anything out here. Let's just go back to my place and wait until he returns."

"In a minute. Don't be so impatient."

Amanda looked over her shoulder. This was making her nervous. The idea of skulking around anyone's home, peeking in windows, invading their privacy, was repulsive to her. "If he's as smart as you give him credit for, he's not going to leave evidence lying out in the open where anyone can see it."

"You never know," Tony whispered, and kept walking toward the back of the house, staying close to the outside wall. The curtains were drawn on the first set of windows they passed, but a crack between the curtains had been left in the next. Tony leaned forward, cupping his hands on the pane to see in. "Amanda, go back to the car and wait for me there."

"You don't actually believe I'm going to leave you here now, do you?" She moved in beside him and glanced inside. "I—" She staggered back, going pale all of a sudden. "I don't believe it."

Tony steadied her, gave her hand a hard squeeze, then went back to the window. He studied the interior, anger making his muscles grow taut. Photos of Amanda, obviously taken without her knowledge, were plastered all over the walls.

"Should we call Raymond?" she managed to say at last.

"Taking photos isn't against the law. What *we're* doing is."

"But these . . ." She shook her head. "I walk with Hope to my mailbox every day. I never saw anyone hanging about."

"He used a big telephoto lens for most of these."

"He snapped a photo of me in my bathrobe through my window. To do that he had to have been in my backyard."

"None of them shows you undressed at least. It could have been worse."

"This is bad enough," Amanda said, her voice shaky. She felt dirty somehow. Her private moments, like playing with Hope in the baby pool in the backyard, were there on the walls of some man's home. She shuddered. "I had no idea . . ."

Tony gave her a sympathetic look. "There's a framed photo on his nightstand. That wasn't taken with a telephoto. It's a snapshot of you and Hope at a lake."

Amanda turned back to the window and looked inside. "That was taken from my bedroom. It was the one I kept on my dresser, the one I told you had been stolen."

"Certainly that's evidence that he broke the law. But it's not enough by itself."

"What are you talking about? He took it from *my* bedroom!"

"He could claim he found it out by the road after the incident with the fire, for example, and that he hadn't quite gotten around to returning it to you."

"Ricky probably would say something like that. He's smooth. I'll give him that. But now I'm convinced he really did set that fire. Maybe he was jealous, I don't know. I mean, he's obviously a full-fledged creep."

Tony moved to the next window. "At least he only keeps one of you in his study, but believe me, you don't want to see it."

Amanda moved forward. She caught a glimpse of herself in a wet T-shirt, braless, playing under the sprinkler with her daughter. Her breasts showed clearly, accentuated by the water and thin material. "That son of—" Suddenly, a dark beast slammed against the pane, rattling the entire window frame. Amanda recoiled from the glass. "That's his dog! I wondered where he was."

The dog barked furiously, sending a spray of spittle onto the glass. Then, to their surprise, the animal suddenly ran out of the room.

"Why did he turn and run like that?" Amanda asked, puzzled. "If Ricky had driven up, we would have heard his cycle."

Tony considered the mystery for a second. "Tell me there's no doggie door."

"No, there isn't. Ricky doesn't like them." Amanda heard a creaking sound and looked around for its source. A massive snout was forcing up the sash of a partially open window. "Oh, great. I never expected a doggie window!"

Tony grabbed her hand thinking quickly. If they headed toward the front of the house, the dog, already halfway out, would, no doubt, get them as they went by. With Tony pulling her by the arm, they ran toward the old cottonwood farther along the side of the house. "Climb!"

"I can't climb trees! I haven't done this—" She heard a thump as the animal leaped to the ground, eager for the chase. Without hesitation, she jumped to the first branch and scrambled up.

Tony was right behind her. He'd just hoisted himself onto the branch beneath Amanda, when the dog pounced, his jaws snapping inches from Tony's leg. "Forget it, boy. I'm not a hot lunch."

The dog sat down at the base of the tree, eyeing them. Its throaty growl made Amanda's hair stand on end. "We can't go back down there. He'll rip us apart."

After carefully assessing the situation, Tony said, "We've got one chance. We crawl over this branch, past the trunk, to the branch on the other side that's just above the garage. Then it'll just be a matter of getting onto the garage roof, walking across, and jumping down into the empty lot on the other side of the wall."

Amanda glanced nervously at the dog, then at the branch. She'd always hated heights, and this wasn't improving her phobia. "We could stay here until Ricky gets home. After he puts the dog away, I'll take care of Ricky. You could look the other way while I punch him right on the nose."

"As much as I would enjoy seeing that, I think I better warn you. Ricky may *not* call the dog off. He may call the cops instead, and have us arrested."

Amanda closed her eyes, trying to suppress the rage building inside her. "The man is such a creep."

"Agreed. But that knowledge won't help us in our current situation."

"All right," she said with a sigh. "We'll do it your way." She began crawling up toward the branch. At least the tree was easier to hold on to near the trunk. The skin on her palms and thighs, however, was being scraped off by the rough bark. "Remind me never to climb a tree with a skirt on." Amanda stopped once she got to the trunk. "Hang on for a second. I need a breather."

Tony gave her bare legs a teasing glance. "So do I," he drawled.

"Don't get cute. I'm in no mood."

"Yes, ma'am." As he looked away, he got a glimpse through the window of Ricky's garage. "You didn't tell me Ricky also had a car."

"I didn't know he did." Amanda leaned down, angling for a peek. "It's an off-white sedan, like the car that tailed us that time."

"There's no license plate on it now. Interesting. Still, it's not anything we can use in court," Tony answered.

Mumbling sourly to herself, Amanda continued across to the other branch. Her legs felt as if they were on fire. Finally they reached the top of the garage and stepped onto the roof below.

Walking across the flat roof to the other side, Tony climbed down and then reached up to help Amanda. "Climb over the side and let yourself go. I won't let you fall."

"Are you kidding? If I let go, I *will* fall. Gravity does that to you."

"Okay, get technical." Tony exhaled softly. "You'll fall, but I'll be right here to catch you."

Amanda studied the edge of the roof. It really wasn't that far to the bottom—a little under ten feet, if she judged it right. If she climbed over, her feet would be more than halfway down before she even let go. "Step aside. I'll do this on my own."

A second later, she released her hold on the roof ledge. As she dropped, Tony reached out and caught her in his arms.

"Put me down! I didn't need help," she protested.

Amanda dusted herself off while the dog barked furiously on the other side of the wall. Then he leaped up, his claws scraping near the top.

"Let's get out of here before he finds a way to get over that wall," Tony said. Silence descended as Tony drove back to Amanda's. It wasn't until he pulled into her driveway that he finally spoke. "Time's running out, Mandy. The kidnappers are going to bolt like they did before. I have to find a way to force Ron to tell me what he knows, or I'll never find Carmen."

"What do you have in mind?"

"When Ron brought Hope to you, were there any personal effects that came with the baby?"

"Just a blanket."

"Did you keep it?"

"Sure. It was pretty. It was all hand embroidered. Hope uses it for her dolls nowadays." She led the way to Hope's room, walked over to the toy shelf and pulled it out. "Here it is."

Tony took it in his hands and stared at it for a long time.

"I don't see how you could use this against Ron," Amanda said, puzzled by his behavior.

"I have an idea, but I need to talk to Raymond first. I want him to use some of his informants." Tony placed the blanket back on the shelf. "I'll see you again in a few hours."

"I'll go with you," she said, accompanying him to the door.

He shook his head. "No. Not this time. You'll have to trust me on this. I'll explain later, but right now I've got to get going."

Amanda watched Tony leave, uneasiness spreading through her. She returned to Hope's room and brought out the blanket again. He'd stared at it with such an odd expression on his face. Yet if the blanket itself had been important, surely he would have taken it with him. The only assumption she could make was that it had somehow triggered an idea for him.

Amanda sat on Hope's bed, staring at the empty room. She missed her little girl. The childless house was filled with a silence so thick it seemed to have substance. She lay back on the pillows that still smelled of Hope's baby shampoo.

All she felt right now was emptiness. How had things gone so wrong? Amanda closed her eyes, and her body began to drift peacefully. The quiet enveloped her in a soothing cocoon. Then an image began to form slowly, like a photo being developed before her eyes.

"You," Amanda said, recognizing her nightly visitor. For the first time, the image was clear and she could make out the details of the woman's face. Her green eyes danced and her auburn hair cascaded softly around her shoulders.

"I came to say goodbye," the woman said. "Tony will need you more than ever soon, just as you'll need him. You're on the brink of your greatest dream or your most haunting nightmare. In the end, the choice will be yours. Just remember, some things come only once in a lifetime."

"Wait! Who are you?"

The image seemed to flicker then coalesce once again. "I was drawn to you, Amanda, because as mothers we share a common bond of love." The image faded, but the stone that hung from a chain around the spirit's neck continued to glow. The opal flashed with fire and bathed Amanda in gentle flames filled with warmth and love. Then, in the blink of an eye, that vision was gone, too.

Amanda woke up slowly. The woman had seemed so real, not just a figment of her imagination. She accepted that reality now, with a certainty that came from the depths of her soul.

Just then the phone rang. Amanda walked almost unconsciously to the living room and picked it up.

"Amanda, it's time we talked." Ron's voice was clear and unmistakable. "And *don't* try to record this. Believe me, you're going to want this conversation to stay private."

"I'm not recording," Amanda said, sure now that he had found the bug she'd placed in his office. "What do you want?" Fear for her child and herself suddenly grew in intensity, touching a primitive level nothing had ever reached before.

"Hope *wasn't* my sister's child. The papers I gave you are *all* forgeries. If Tony Ramos finds out, you'll lose the girl for sure, Amanda. Hope *is* his child. I rescued Carmen from the wreck. I'd been drinking, and Ramos's wife was already dead, so there was nothing else I could have done. I couldn't risk calling the police, but if I'd left the baby there, she would have died. We couldn't have children together, and I knew how badly you wanted to be a mother. So Katrina kept the child while I forged the papers. When enough time had passed to make my story believable, I brought her home to you."

Amanda's head was spinning. She grasped the arm of the sofa, afraid she'd fall, then lowered herself onto it. "You're lying. You couldn't have done something like that."

"You kept whining about not having kids. I gave you a child, and you never even had to lose your figure. You should be grateful."

"Grateful?" Her heart felt as if it had been caught in a vise. "How can you live with yourself knowing what you've done?"

"The question is, are you going to play on our side now? You've got to sidetrack Ramos, Amanda. He's getting too close. And if we go down, you'll lose your kid, I promise. One blood test is all it would take to prove that Hope is really Tony's baby girl."

Hope was *hers*. Amanda loved that child with every fiber of her existence. "I don't know what I'm going to do. But whatever it is, it won't be with *you*."

"You need my silence, Amanda, and it's for sale. I want an answer."

"I have no answer to give you!" she nearly shouted into the phone. "It's your fault I've been living a lie all these years, and you've put an innocent man through hell. How could you have done something like this?"

"To survive, and to earn a living for us, if you remember. But my actions aren't the question now. Will you keep Ramos off our trail?"

"I need a chance to think this out."

"There's no time, Amanda. I'll have to take your delaying tactic as a no. So be it. You've made your choice. Now you'll have to live with it."

The next sound she heard was the dial tone. Amanda began to tremble. Her world was coming apart at the seams. Her ex-husband, the man she'd once loved and trusted, had betrayed her and the little girl she'd grown to love as her own.

Amanda thought of Tony and what he'd come to mean to her. Anguish as black as night filled her. They shared a child . . . and their love for her would tear them apart.

Chapter Fifteen

Tony met Raymond in the parking lot beneath the Bureau offices. "I need another favor from you. I want to run Carmen's picture through the age progression. Right now, if possible."

"Sure. Did you bring a new photo of Carmen with you?"

Tony reached for his wallet and took out the one he had retrieved from his desk at home. "It's not big, but it's a clear portrait."

"We've worked with worse." Raymond led him through the rear doors to the technician's office. "What's the rush all of a sudden?"

Tony told Raymond about the blanket Amanda had shown him. "It looks like the one Lynn bought for Carmen at a crafts fair. I remember when she brought it home. She'd just found out she was pregnant and was so excited she'd started shopping right away."

"It's not conclusive," Raymond said. "There could have been dozens of others sold that looked just like it, if it was a popular pattern. Can you positively identify that blanket as the same one?"

"No, I can't. But Hope is almost exactly the age Carmen would have been." Tony hesitated. "The only problem with this theory is that I know this is what the kidnappers threatened Amanda with at the start of all this. They told her they'd make her life miserable by making me believe Hope and Carmen were the same child. They didn't pretend it was actually true. It was more in line with putting one over on me, then letting me stir things up.''

''Maybe they didn't want Amanda or you to suspect it really was true. Or maybe it isn't. At this point, there's only one way to know for sure. You and Hope have to have blood tests.''

''I can't approach Amanda with this, not yet. I want to have more evidence first. That's why I want this age progression done.''

Raymond handed the photo to the technician, and they waited as the program was initiated. Impatience tore at Tony's restraint. The possibility that Hope was his Carmen, that he'd finally found his daughter, seemed almost too good to be true.

Minutes ticked by, turning into eternities, as the program finalized the image. Finally Raymond tore the sheet from the printer. ''It *could* be Hope. There are many similarities, but it's not an exact match by any means.''

Tony studied it. His instinct, that tool he'd learned to rely on throughout his life, now failed him completely. He couldn't be sure, not from this. As he studied the image, he could see Hope's smile and her eyes, but he couldn't be sure his perceptions weren't tainted by wishful thinking. Maybe this was what the kidnappers had hoped for all along, and why they'd been so certain they could convince him.

''I'm still not sure,'' he said at last. ''And I won't approach Amanda until I am. It wouldn't be fair to her, or Hope. That little girl has already been through the breakup of one family. She doesn't need news like this and a visit to the doctor's.''

''I think we have to find out more about Biddle, too. If he knows something, we need to get it out of him,'' Raymond said.

Tony told Raymond about what he and Amanda had learned. "The guy's a scumbag, that's for sure. He's involved, but there's no telling to what extent."

"Let's go to the source, then, and find out."

Raymond drove Tony over to Ricky Biddle's home. Tony checked the porch for the motorcycle, but it still wasn't there. Something seemed different about the place, however. Tony glanced around. "Hang back. Something's not right."

"Like what?"

Tony remained silent, trying to pinpoint the uneasiness he felt. "The curtains in the front room. Those were drawn, but now they're open. And remember the dog. He would have heard the car. With open curtains, you'd think he would have been at least watching, probably barking."

Raymond reached back and rested his hand on the butt of his weapon. "We'll take it nice and easy."

They approached the front door from the side, making sure neither of them became easy targets. Tony stood off to the right as Raymond knocked. There was no answer, nor did they hear any sign of the dog.

Tony crept up to the front window and glanced in. "Doesn't look like anyone's home. I'm going to take a look around the back."

"We'll both go. But try to remember we don't have a search warrant."

"No problem." Tony led the way to the bedroom, intending to peer through the slit in the curtains like before. Only this time he found the curtains wide open. The photos were not on the wall, and the framed snapshot of Amanda and Hope was missing from the nightstand. Wordlessly, Tony moved to the other side to get a look at the study. "The guy's cleared out. The photos are gone. So are several boxes of papers that were there before, as well as a whole lot of computer equipment."

"In that case, I'm going to have the police put out an APB," Raymond said.

As they were making their way to the car, they heard a loud crash, like wood splintering, at the front of the house. Tony and Raymond began to run and reached the driveway just in time to see a white sedan racing toward them, shattered pieces of the garage door still flying off the hood.

Raymond jumped to one side and rolled into the bushes, the car narrowly missing him. Tony crouched, pistol in hand, and fired off two shots.

The left rear tire seemed to explode, and the car veered sharply to that side, crashing into a cottonwood tree. The frightened rottweiler jumped out the shattered rear window and was halfway down the block by the time Raymond and Tony reached the car.

Biddle was scrambling out the passenger door when Tony grabbed him. Raymond quickly cuffed the shaken man.

"I was only going to go after my dog. My brother will look after him, but I wanted to make sure he was okay."

"He was well enough to run. No more games. We know you're in this up to your neck," Raymond snapped.

"I would never hurt Amanda. I love her!"

"What's your connection to her ex-husband, Ron Vila?" Raymond demanded.

"Who? I don't know what you're talking about."

"Kidnapping is a *federal* offense," Raymond warned.

"Who's been kidnapped? Amanda?"

Raymond gave Tony a look, then hustled Biddle to the Bureau car. "You'd make it a lot easier on yourself if you come clean. We know you've been terrorizing Amanda Vila for some time."

"I only tried to let her know how much she needed to be protected. I wanted her to come to me for help. I would have taken care of her."

"Did you set the fire?" Raymond asked.

"Yeah, but it didn't hurt anyone. I was careful."

"And the phony bomb at the day-care center?" Tony barked.

"Three sticks and a clock aren't a bomb. I would never have hurt her! All I wanted was for her to need me, and maybe love me, too."

As Raymond placed Biddle in the rear seat of the Bureau car, Tony's pager went off. Using Raymond's cellular phone, he dialed Amanda's number. Her frightened voice chilled him to the bone.

"It's Hope. She's gone," she blurted, her voice unsteady. "Somebody's kidnapped her."

RAYMOND DROVE TONY down the road to Amanda's home while he used the radio to notify the police about his prisoner and call animal control. "Do you think they're going to use the girl to get more concessions from you?" Raymond asked finally.

"No. They'll probably repeat their M.O. and vanish, just like they did three years ago. They'll use the fact they have her to stall for time, and then split. But this time they won't succeed in taking her away from me."

"You're now convinced that Hope is really Carmen?"

"Not one hundred percent convinced, but I think the fact that they took her tends to support that."

As they pulled up in front of Amanda's house, Raymond remained in his seat. "I don't think we should have the cops come *here* to take custody of my suspect. I'll meet them a mile down the highway."

"Good idea. I'll call you just as soon as I've got the whole story."

As Raymond drove off, Tony rushed to the front door. Amanda was waiting, her face pale with terror. "They've taken her. They've taken my little girl."

"Who took her?"

"I'm not sure. Miriam called me. Someone lured Winston into a closet and locked him in there, then took Hope out the back door. She'd been lying down for a nap. Miriam had just gone out to the barn to call her husband to the phone. The only thing she knows for sure is that Winston got in one good bite, because there were pieces of bloody trouser cloth still stuck to his teeth.''

"We've got to catch them before they leave the area," Tony said.

"Nobody's going to take my daughter anywhere," Amanda said, rage filling her. "I want to go to Ron's office. He's involved in this, and I'm going to make sure he rots in jail for the rest of his life."

"First things first." Tony picked up Amanda's phone, dialed Raymond's car-phone number, and gave him the details. "Pick up Ron Vila."

"I'll do that. I'll also put out an APB on Katrina Clark and Hope. I'll place the airport and bus stations on alert. They won't get out of the area."

Amanda grabbed her purse and started to head out the door. "I'm going over to Ron's. I have to talk to him alone."

"What's going on, Mandy?" Tony grasped her shoulders and forced her to face him. "There's more to this than you're telling me."

The phone only rang once, but Amanda broke free of Tony and dived toward it. "Yes?"

"I don't have time to play games, Amanda. Listen carefully."

"Ron! Did you—"

"Shut up. I've got Hope. You thought you could hide her at your friend's sister's house. You forgot, I know all about Bernice. Tracing all her in-state calls was just too easy. But don't worry, the little brat is fine for now."

"Why are you getting her involved in this? Let her go. You don't want her, you never did." She saw Tony pick up the extension in the kitchen.

"You're right. I don't want her. And just as soon as I'm out of the country, I'll tell you where to find her. But if I'm arrested, Hope is as good as dead. She can't survive alone where she's at, not for long. Back off, Amanda, or you'll kill her. Hope's the only family you've got left. Don't blow it for yourself."

"Vila, if anything happens to that child, I'll find you no matter where you go," Tony snapped. "Tell us where she is, *now!*"

They heard a click, then the dial tone.

Tony looked at Amanda. "You know that we can't play it their way. If they have time to get away, we'll never learn where Hope is being kept."

"Ron won't kill her. He doesn't have it in him. He's no murderer."

"Maybe not, but what about the others he's allied himself with? Are you certain about them?"

Amanda swallowed back her tears. "What do you want from me, Tony?"

"You know Ron better than anyone else. Where would he hide if he knew the police and the Bureau were after him?"

"I don't know!"

"*Think!* Does he have a hideaway place or a friend he would stay with?"

"Katrina and Ron have known each other for a long time. Maybe he's with her."

Raymond walked in through the open door, picking up the last of Amanda's words. "You can count on that. I sent some men over to their office. Their papers have been put through the shredder and they've cleared out. We do have one lead, though. There was an impression left on one of the pads with the name of a small charter airline. We're tracking it down."

The cellular phone at his waist began to ring. Raymond answered it, then issued a few terse instructions before turning back to Amanda and Tony.

"A woman fitting Katrina Clark's description is waiting for a charter flight at a small airstrip between Santa Fe and Taos. She's alone and the ID she's using doesn't match the name we have on the APB. But, if it is her, that's to be expected."

"I'm going over there. I'll be able to identify her for sure," Amanda said.

"Good idea. Sierra implicated both Ron and Katrina a short time ago. They've been creating phony identities for criminals for years. Their latest client, Jonathan Henderson, was paying enough for them to retire."

"He'd certainly have the funds after that armored-car heist," Tony said.

Amanda tried to concentrate on what Tony and Raymond were discussing, but her only concern was for Hope. "Do you think Katrina knows where Hope is?"

"Yes. But she may not tell us. If she's that loyal to your ex husband, she may decide to take the fall by herself and give him time to make his getaway."

Amanda's mind reeled with visions of her daughter, scared and alone someplace. "Give me some time with Katrina. I guarantee that witch will tell me everything she knows." Her voice was suddenly very cold.

"Let's get going, folks," Raymond said. "Tony, you follow me in your car. I hope to be needing my back seat for prisoners."

Tony's finger's were clenched tightly around the steering wheel as they got underway.

Amanda opened her mouth as if to speak, then shut it again.

"What's on your mind?" Tony asked.

"We're caught in an all-or-nothing situation," Amanda said in a taut whisper. "There's something you have a right to know."

"Go on," he said, his voice filled with emotions too raw to conceal.

Amanda swallowed back her fears, forcing herself to go on. "I received another call from Ron earlier. I erased it, because I was afraid of what you would do." Amanda's voice shook. She paused for a moment, gathering her courage, then continued. "I found out that Hope is not legally mine. It wasn't just a matter of forged papers, either. Everything was a sham. Hope is a kidnap victim."

Tony never once took his eyes off the road. "What are you saying?" he croaked.

"My daughter, Hope, is Carmen."

Tony pulled to a stop in the parking lot of the small, private airstrip. "I've searched so long and so hard. I never figured it would end like this."

"And now?" Amanda was afraid to speak above a whisper.

"You're afraid I'll take Hope away from you," he observed.

"Will you?"

"I need my daughter," he said slowly.

"I need her, too. I may not be her birth mother, but I am the only mother she's ever known. And I love her with all my heart."

"I know," he said softly. "But..." Tony took a deep breath, then let it out. "We'll have to deal with this later. Right now, we should both be concentrating on one thing only—getting Hope back safely."

"You're right." Despair, black and suffocating, slammed into her. As Amanda walked through the doors of the small building, creating a brief distraction, Katrina broke free from the police officer holding her and grabbed the revolver from his holster.

Holding everyone at bay, Katrina stepped back, angling her way to the entrance. "Hate to disappoint you, people, but I'm not going to jail."

Amanda moved toward her. "I don't care where *you* go, but I want my daughter back."

Katrina glowered at her. "Tough. If you were drowning, I'd toss you a shark. You've ruined everything." She pointed the gun at Amanda, gripping the weapon with both hands. "If you know any prayers, say them fast."

Suddenly, there was a loud pop, and Katrina was slammed against the wall. She crumpled slowly to the ground without a sound.

"No!" As Amanda ran to Katrina's side, she saw a state policeman in an adjacent hallway rising to his feet. Smoke was still curling up from his pistol. Amanda knelt beside Katrina's still body. A mass of blood had appeared in the center of her chest. "You've got to tell me!" She shook the lifeless body as if trying to will it back to life.

"She can't tell us anything now," Tony said, pulling Amanda up gently.

Raymond crouched next to Katrina and felt for a pulse at her neck. "It's over."

Amanda let out a tiny, anguished cry. "It's *not* over!" She turned to face Tony. "You've got as much to lose as I have! Do something! Where's my daughter?"

Tony grasped her tenderly by the shoulders. "Listen to me. You're the only one who can help us now. Think, Amanda. Where would Ron have taken her?"

"I don't know!"

"Slow down, man," Raymond warned. He took Katrina's purse from the counter and dumped out the contents. "There's a credit card receipt in here dated yesterday. It's from Jessie's County Store. Mean anything to you?" he asked Amanda.

"No, I've never heard of it."

"I have." The officer who had shot Katrina spoke up. "I own a cabin a few miles from there. It's near Jemez Springs."

Amanda stared pensively across the room, an idea forming in her mind. "I remember Ron bragging once, after our divorce, that he'd bought a cabin in the mountains. He was fixing it up.''

"Where's the property?''

"I don't know. I've never been there. All I know is that he mentioned a spring and a creek nearby.''

"I'll have the state police check the real-estate records. We have the county records, so let's see what comes up. In the meantime, maybe we can find something else in the suspect's car that'll help us narrow it down even more,'' Raymond said quickly. "Let's go take a look.''

Amanda hurried outside, following Raymond's lead. When they reached Katrina's car, Raymond opened the front door and reached into the glove compartment. It contained only the owner's manual, the registration and a flashlight.

The state police officer came up to them. "We have a location. Ron Vila bought a real fixer-upper at the edge of the National Forest,'' the officer said. "Shall I get a team together and go check it out?''

"No!'' Amanda protested, looking at Raymond. "You can't walk in there without jeopardizing my daughter!''

"She's right,'' Tony added. "I have a better idea. I'll go up by myself, the last part on foot. One man is hard to spot. If Hope's being kept there alone, I'll get her out. If not, I can create a mild diversion, anything that will make whoever's keeping Hope in there come outside to take a look.''

"We have to check out the location first.'' Raymond picked up the mike from his car. "I'm going to contact the Forest Service. Maybe they know the layout of the terrain around here.''

As Raymond spoke, Tony made his way back to the car. Amanda noticed what he was doing and followed him. "You're *not* going there alone.''

"I have to. Two people will be a lot easier to spot than one.''

Raymond approached as they argued. "If it comes to that, I suggest you both go. A frightened child is more likely to go to her mother than to someone she barely knows."

Tony's eyes narrowed with pain. "I won't jeopardize Hope's life. I'm just going to see if she's there."

"If she is there, and you try to sneak her out, you'll need me," Amanda argued.

"You're both getting ahead of yourselves. First, we'll have the rangers check out the place. Maybe it's visible from one of the watchtowers by telescope. That could save time and effort."

"You do what you have to. I'm heading up there now," Tony said flatly.

"No one's going to go near that cabin until we know what we're up against." Raymond crossed his arms over his chest.

Amanda glanced at Tony. In her heart, she knew that he'd never place Hope in jeopardy, but at the moment, she was more worried about what Ron might do. "News of Katrina won't be on the radio, will it?"

Raymond shook his head. "I've already taken care of that. I can't suppress the story forever, but we'll have a few hours delay."

Tony slipped into the driver's seat of his car. "The least we can do is stop wasting time and start heading over that way."

Raymond nodded. "Agreed. But stay cool. If I have to, I'll place you in custody, clear?"

Tony started the engine as Amanda joined him inside the car. She remained silent, watching the trees along the side of the forest road. If there was one time she wished she could have looked into the future, this was it.

"She'll be okay," Tony said flatly, reaching for her hand and holding it securely in his.

"Everyone keeps telling me that," Amanda answered wearily.

"Who's everyone?"

"The people most involved." Amanda gave him a wan smile. "The woman I keep meeting when I'm asleep constantly assures me of it, too."

"I'm talking reality, not dreams." Tony shook his head.

"They're more than dreams. I can't explain it, but that woman *is* real."

"Did you recognize her?"

"No. She said she'd come to me as one mother to another. She'd lost her child once. I saw it in the vision. She was reaching for her baby, but a misty barrier kept them apart. It was so sad. Then the image cleared, and I saw the woman as she is now. There was light all around her. As she started to fade, it seemed as if the stone on her necklace, like an opal, glowed with a fire all its own."

Tony glanced at Amanda, a startled look on his face. "What did the woman look like?"

"She had soft-looking auburn hair and shimmering green eyes."

Tony slowed down slightly and, releasing her hand, reached into his back pocket. He flipped open his wallet and pulled out a photo of a woman holding a baby. "Does she look familiar?"

Amanda stared at the photo, as if transfixed. Although the snapshot was small and showed signs of wear and tear, she immediately recognized the woman and the necklace. "Yes. Is she your wife?"

"The photo is of Lynn and Carmen."

Amanda nodded slowly. "Of course. I understand now. Lynn never stopped watching over Carmen. No grave could conquer the love she felt for her child."

Chapter Sixteen

Raymond signaled Tony to pull over to the side as they neared the turnoff that led to the cabin. Raymond parked on the shoulder of the road and walked over to meet them. "I just got word from the Forest Service. They can't see that cabin from the watchtower, but one of the rangers hiked over to a hill near it and took a look through his binoculars. He spotted a blue Jeep parked a short distance downhill from the front door.

"Ron drives a blue Jeep. Did anyone see Hope?" Amanda asked anxiously.

Raymond shook his head. "The ranger didn't stick around, but he's willing to take one of our guys up there. He said that someone with a high powered rifle should be able to take Ron out if he came outside. I've sent our best man up, but it'll be a while before he's in position."

Raymond leaned back against the car, a pensive look on his face. "We have another problem right now. We need to draw the suspect out of the cabin, while someone gets a look inside and checks for Hope. It looks like our man doesn't have any accomplices with him, but we can't be sure of that. So if the little girl cries out, things might get tricky."

Amanda stared up at the road. "If the Jeep is parked on a slope, I have an idea," Amanda said.

"From what the ranger said about the terrain, I think it's a safe bet," Raymond said.

"I had my car roll downhill one time when my emergency brake wasn't quite set and the vehicle slipped out of gear. Something like that would certainly cause Ron to leave the cabin. He would have to run after it and stop his vehicle before it got damaged. He wouldn't give Hope a second thought under those circumstances. Things have always meant more to him than people."

Raymond smiled. "Excellent idea. Now we just have to figure out a way to get a man close to his vehicle, unseen."

"Have two of our guys pick up some fishing equipment and walk by near enough to the cabin for Vila to hear them," Tony suggested. "Have them be joking back and forth, carrying a six-pack of beer. Something like that is perfectly normal out here. While they've got his attention, I'll sneak up on that Jeep and start it rolling. After our guys have Vila in custody farther downhill, I'll slip inside the cabin."

"No. We'll do it together," Amanda said flatly. "If there's another kidnapper inside, someone will have to protect Hope and keep her quiet while you take care of the threat."

Raymond considered it. "I don't know about all this. You two are civilians."

"But I know the child," Tony said, "and I've had training no civilian ever had. More importantly, the longer we wait, the more we risk that the news of Katrina Clark's death will be leaked to the press. Once Vila hears that, there's no telling what he'll do. We have to move now."

"Let's do it," Raymond agreed after a brief pause.

TONY CREPT TOWARD the cabin, careful to stay behind trees or brush as much as possible. After all these years, he'd finally found his daughter. But she was someone else's little girl now, and the bond that existed between Amanda and Hope was as real as any claim he had on Carmen.

He shook his head, forcing himself to concentrate on the matter at hand. There would be time for decisions later. Right now, the priority was to get Ron Vila out of that cabin.

As he neared the Jeep, he glanced around carefully and settled low behind a thick bush. One false move now, and he'd blow the entire thing. When he heard Raymond's men passing on the opposite side of the cabin, clowning around and laughing, Tony ran toward the Jeep in a crouch, reaching it in seconds. He had a slim-jim, a handy tool used by cops to unlock vehicles, but it wasn't necessary. Ron hadn't bothered to lock his Jeep, certain it would be safe out here. Tony smiled with satisfaction. After all these years, he'd finally nail this jerk.

Tony slipped the Jeep out of gear and released the emergency brake. The vehicle lurched, and he gave it a shove to keep it rolling. Just to make sure Vila heard it, he slapped the side of the Jeep with his palm loudly, then quickly dived behind cover.

Tony watched Vila emerge. He paused outside the cabin for a second, looking around curiously. Then, seeing his Jeep bouncing downhill, he cursed loudly and sprinted after it. Tony ran up and ducked inside the cabin, gun drawn. He glanced around, but the cabin was still. No sound coming from anywhere.

Tony moved toward a closed door in the back, kicked it open, and entered in a crouch. The room was empty. He turned around to continue his search and saw Amanda at the window, trying to force up the sash.

"You were supposed to wait," he whispered harshly. "I would have called you on the radio in another minute or two."

"So sue me," she said, crawling inside. "Where's Hope?"

"She's not in this room."

Suddenly, they heard a hollow scraping noise against the wall. Tony turned around, pistol ready, but Amanda grabbed his arm. "No!"

Hope crawled out from under the bed and launched herself into Amanda's arms, sobbing. "Mommy, I don't want to stay here. Take me with you."

"Shh, Peanut. Who else is here?"

"Just Daddy. He hates me, Mommy!"

"Your daddy doesn't hate you, Peanut. Believe me." She glanced at Tony as she said it.

He lowered his weapon and placed a hand on his daughter's shoulder. "Nobody hates you, sweetheart. If only you knew just how much you are loved."

Hope buried herself deeper into Amanda's arms, recoiling from his touch. Sorrow knifed at his gut. He'd entertained dreams of taking Hope with him, but what had just happened proved to him without a doubt how foolish the idea had been. His Carmen was lost forever. Hope belonged to Amanda.

Tony watched them both for a few moments. Maybe this was the best thing that could have happened. A little girl needed a mother, and no one could ever love his daughter more than Amanda did.

He walked out of the cabin, leaving them alone, and met Raymond outside. Ron Vila had been handcuffed and stood to one side, another agent beside him.

"Everything okay here?" Raymond asked.

Tony nodded, then walked over and stood face-to-face with the man who'd taken his daughter three long years ago. The pain of irrecoverable loss burned through him. He reached out and grabbed Ron by the collar, pulling him out of the agent's grasp. "I could kill you for what you've stolen from me."

At that moment, Hope and Amanda stepped out of the cabin. Hope saw Tony and ran up to him. She tugged at his pant leg, pulling him away from Ron.

"No, Tony. He's mean. He'll hurt you!"

Tony released Ron instantly, then bent down and touched his daughter's face in a light caress. "He won't hurt anyone ever again, sweetheart."

"Come home with Mommy and me. I want to go home!"

He saw a tear roll down Amanda's face and something stung at his own eyes, but he told himself it was just glare from the sun. "I'll take you back home right now, sweetheart. You and your mommy you will be safe there from now on."

HOURS LATER, TONY SAT with Amanda and Hope in the child's bedroom. The little girl had finally fallen asleep, nestled between them.

He could hardly bring himself to leave, but he knew the time had come. With each minute he stayed, it only became harder. Tony stood up slowly, then bent down to kiss his child goodbye.

"You're not taking her, are you?" Amanda asked gently.

"No. She's yours. I failed her once and forfeited my claim on her." He gazed down at Hope, love shining in his eyes. "You know, I spent years dreaming of the day when I'd finally find my daughter. But I never thought I'd walk out of her life without even telling her who I was."

"Tony, she has a right to know you're her father."

"So she can say goodbye to me?" He shook his head. "It's time for me to step out of both your lives. I love you, Amanda, but I don't know if you would ever believe that my feelings for you are separate from my wish that we all become a family. Without that leap of faith, that trust that perhaps I don't merit, I can't stay. I don't want you to live every day wondering if I'll change my mind and take Hope away." Tony started to leave, but then turned back to pull Amanda into his arms one last time. "Goodbye, my love," he whispered, then took her mouth in a hungry, soul-searing kiss.

Amanda staggered as he released her, her knees nearly buckling. Before she could catch her breath, he was out the door. She went after him, but as she reached the porch, Hope suddenly ran past her.

"Tony, don't go!" Hope launched herself into his arms as he turned.

Tony held his daughter tightly. "I thought you were asleep," he said, his voice thick.

"Don't you love us anymore?"

"Yes, but I can't—" Unable to tell his daughter he wouldn't return, he looked at Amanda for help.

Amanda smiled gently. "Hope needs you and so do I. We'd both like for you to stay. Permanently."

Tony held Amanda's gaze, and for one breathless moment, he could barely speak. He glanced down at his daughter. "Looks like I'm already home. Come on. I'll tuck you into bed."

"Me, too?" Amanda teased.

Tony smiled at Amanda, loving promises shining like fire in his eyes. Scooping his daughter up in one arm, and wrapping the other around his future wife, he brought them all back home.

OFFICIAL RULES

FLYAWAY VACATION SWEEPSTAKES 3449

NO PURCHASE OR OBLIGATION NECESSARY

Three Harlequin Reader Service 1995 shipments will contain respectively, coupons for entry into three different prize drawings, one for a trip for two to San Francisco, another for a trip for two to Las Vegas and the third for a trip for two to Orlando, Florida. To enter any drawing using an Entry Coupon, simply complete and mail according to directions.

There is no obligation to continue using the Reader Service to enter and be eligible for any prize drawing. You may also enter any drawing by hand printing the words "Flyaway Vacation," your name and address on a 3"x5" card and the destination of the prize you wish that entry to be considered for (i.e., San Francisco trip, Las Vegas trip or Orlando trip). Send your 3"x5" entries via first-class mail (limit: one entry per envelope) to: Flyaway Vacation Sweepstakes 3449, c/o Prize Destination you wish that entry to be considered for, P.O. Box 1315, Buffalo, NY 14269-1315, USA or P.O. Box 610, Fort Erie, Ontario L2A 5X3, Canada.

To be eligible for the San Francisco trip, entries must be received by 5/30/95; for the Las Vegas trip, 7/30/95; and for the Orlando trip, 9/30/95.

Winners will be determined in random drawings conducted under the supervision of D.L. Blair, Inc., an independent judging organization whose decisions are final, from among all eligible entries received for that drawing. San Francisco trip prize includes round-trip airfare for two, 4-day/3-night weekend accommodations at a first-class hotel, and $500 in cash (trip must be taken between 7/30/95—7/30/96, approximate prize value—$3,500); Las Vegas trip includes round-trip airfare for two, 4-day/3-night weekend accommodations at a first-class hotel, and $500 in cash (trip must be taken between 9/30/95—9/30/96, approximate prize value—$3,500); Orlando trip includes round-trip airfare for two, 4-day/3-night weekend accommodations at a first-class hotel, and $500 in cash (trip must be taken between 11/30/95—11/30/96, approximate prize value—$3,500). All travelers must sign and return a Release of Liability prior to travel. Hotel accommodations and flights are subject to accommodation and schedule availability. Sweepstakes open to residents of the U.S. (except Puerto Rico) and Canada, 18 years of age or older. Employees and immediate family members of Harlequin Enterprises, Ltd., D.L. Blair, Inc., their affiliates, subsidiaries and all other agencies, entities and persons connected with the use, marketing or conduct of this sweepstakes are not eligible. Odds of winning a prize are dependent upon the number of eligible entries received for that drawing. Prize drawing and winner notification for each drawing will occur no later than 15 days after deadline for entry eligibility for that drawing. Limit: one prize to an individual, family or organization. All applicable laws and regulations apply. Sweepstakes offer void wherever prohibited by law. Any litigation within the province of Quebec respecting the conduct and awarding of the prizes in this sweepstakes must be submitted to the Regies des loteries et Courses du Quebec. In order to win a prize, residents of Canada will be required to correctly answer a time-limited arithmetical skill-testing question. Value of prizes are in U.S. currency.

Winners will be obligated to sign and return an Affidavit of Eligibility within 30 days of notification. In the event of noncompliance within this time period, prize may not be awarded. If any prize or prize notification is returned as undeliverable, that prize will not be awarded. By acceptance of a prize, winner consents to use of his/her name, photograph or other likeness for purposes of advertising, trade and promotion on behalf of Harlequin Enterprises, Ltd., without further compensation, unless prohibited by law.

For the names of prizewinners (available after 12/31/95), send a self-addressed, stamped envelope to: Flyaway Vacation Sweepstakes 3449 Winners, P.O. Box 4200, Blair, NE 68009.

RVC KAL